LUCKY PENNY

LUCKY PENNY

Melinda)
Blessings
Pat Daum

Patricia Daum

Lucky Penny is a work of fiction. All incidents and dialogue are products of the author's imagination and are not to be construed as real. Any resemblance to persons living or dead is entirely coincidental.

Dedicated to:

Ann Penney Poliquin

FOREWORD

Faith Bradford grew up in a small town in New York State, a child of innocence and privilege. In 1965, during her senior year in high school, she discovered she was pregnant.

Her parents were heart-broken by the news. This was not the future they had imagined for their youngest daughter. However, instead of subjecting her to shame and sending her away to a home for unwed mothers, they enveloped her in a cocoon of love and understanding and devised an ingenious plan to keep her pregnancy a secret. As they made arrangements for a private adoption, their message to her was always, "This baby is a blessing."

Once Faith was secure in the knowledge that her newborn daughter had been placed in a loving home, she locked the memory in a tiny corner of her heart and went on with her life.

Life went on for Penny Whitmer, too. The precious baby girl was adopted in 1966 and raised by a loving family in southern Florida. She was a happy, active child who was secure in the knowledge that she was adopted and had a family that dearly wanted her. She had never felt like there was something missing in her life.

Her blue-collar family had given her a strong foundation and work-ethic. The motivated young woman worked her way through college and law school, eventually becoming a successful attorney.

Learning about her birth parents had never been on her radar, until after she had a child and approached her 40th birthday. After going in for her annual check-up and once again leaving the family medical history section blank, she thought she should try to get more information – for herself and her daughter.
With trepidation, she contacted Children's Home Society in Florida to begin the search for her birth parents' medical histories.

The search would unlock a devastating tragedy and a 40-year-old family secret that would change the lives of Penny and Faith forever.

PART ONE

CHAPTER ONE

Oakfield, New York
August 1965

"It's firecracker hot!" Adam Collins exclaimed as he and his best buddy, Wayne Woods, sat on a wooden bench in the stifling heat and gulped down an ice-cold bottle of Dr. Pepper.

The rusted Coca-Cola thermometer hanging outside the barn door registered 95 degrees, an unusually hot day in western New York State.

The two teenagers were working for Adam's dad during the summer before their senior year and had put in a full day's work. The morning had been spent putting the finishing touches on one of his dad's custom-made 16' Crowncraft camping trailers. The final prep and clean-up on the vehicle was done, everything inside and out was "clean as a whistle."

It had taken a lot of elbow grease and dozens of shop towels to polish the birch paneling and matching cabinets. The duo had washed the camper-size ice box and matching pink stove and could see their reflections in the aluminum back splash. They wiped down the pink vinyl seats in the dinette and sleeping areas, then on hands and knees scrubbed the tiny toilet compartment and mopped and waxed the black-and-white checked vinyl floor. With a final flourish, they hung the pink-and-white striped valances above the windows and covered the bunks with matching coverlets.

Once the inside was finished, they began to scrub the outside. Adam scampered up a rickety ladder to wash the roof and playfully squirted Wayne with the garden hose. His buddy didn't complain on this hot day. "Gosh, that felt good!" he exclaimed.

They proceeded to wash, rinse and hand dry every inch of the camper exterior with a chamois cloth. When they were finished, the white aluminum was spotless and the bright pink trim gleamed in the summer sunshine. The camper was ready for Dad's final inspection and the customer who would be taking delivery later in the day.

This one was sure to be an eye-catcher.

Crowncraft Truck Caps was a small manufacturing company located on the edge of a 20-acre farm just outside Oakfield, New York, about three miles northwest of Batavia. At the front of the long, narrow tract was a handsome red barn that had been converted into a shop where the Crowncraft custom trailers, campers and truck caps were made.

Andrew Collins, Adam's dad, had spent his entire life in the Oakfield area. His parents, Luke and Grace, were "salt of the earth" folks who had provided a loving home for him and his three siblings. Andrew was raised on the 20-acre farm and developed a strong work ethic at an early age, helping his mother gather eggs and carrying kindling for her cook-stove. By the time Andrew was in grammar school, he and his siblings could be found working in the garden, hoeing weeds and picking fresh corn, beans and tomatoes for the family's supper table.

As he grew stronger, his winter chores included carrying a bucket of coal into the house and stoking the fire each morning in the pot-bellied stove. Once the fire was going, he wolfed down a hearty breakfast prepared by his mother; then he and his siblings bundled up and walked a half mile to Five Corners, a one-room school house. The Collins kids were lucky, some of their school mates walked two miles.

On days when it was bitter cold or the snow was deep, Luke would pile all the kids in the front seat of his pick-up truck and drive them to school on his way to work.

Five Corners was a well-constructed one-room school house that had been built in 1927 and by the time Andrew entered first grade, the school was modernized with electricity, water and heat. In the spacious room, the children sat at old-fashioned wooden desks with attached seats. The desks were lined up in tidy rows with the youngest of the two dozen students sitting in the row nearest the teacher's desk. The sun rays shining through the towering windows flooded the school room with natural light. Students would often be caught daydreaming as they watched the squirrels playing in the ancient oak tree whose branches hovered over the school house.

The Collins family lived on the farm until Andrew finished the eighth grade. At that time, the school system didn't provide transportation to high school for the country kids, so the family rented out the farm house and barns and moved into nearby Oakfield, where the children could further their education.

Andrew was a motivated student and he became the first in his family to graduate from high school. Mr. Ken Retallic, his shop teacher, recognized that Andrew had a talent for mechanics and detail work. Following graduation, he helped him secure a tool-and-die apprenticeship at the Doehler Die Casting Company in nearby Batavia. Andrew was grateful for the opportunity. He lived at home, drove his dad's old Ford pick-up truck to work and his steady income helped to support the family.

Weekends were spent working along-side his father, Luke Collins. Luke was the local repairman and a gifted mechanic who could fix anything – from toasters, to lawn mowers, cars, trucks, tractors, combines and even snow plows. He owned and operated Luke's Fixit Shop, working out of a garage in Oakfield, in the alley off Main Street, behind Eddie's Bar. Much like the proverbial mailman, neither rain, nor sleet nor freezing temperatures, not even a blizzard, would keep Luke from his work.

Andrew continued to work for Doehler until the attack on Pearl Harbor, December 7, 1941. With patriotism at an all-time high and all his buddies shipping out, he enlisted in the Army Air Corps in February 1942. It was a great fit for him and his mechanical talents. He was sent to a specialized technical training center in St. Petersburg, Florida, where he completed his basic training and also learned to service and maintain aircraft and aircraft equipment. After training, he was assigned to the Avon Park Army Airfield in central Florida where he spent the remainder of the war servicing and rebuilding engines on hundreds of planes, including the B-17 Flying Fortress and B-26 Marauders.

By October of 1945 the war was over, Andrew was honorably discharged and he returned home to Oakfield and a job at Doehler. The company was grateful to have the experienced tool-and-die man return. While he had been in the service, the company had expanded to four divisions and had a new name, Doehler-Jarvis Inc. The end of the war resulted in a bonanza of peace-time orders and steady work for Andrew and the other returning veterans.

Andrew was thankful for the work and overtime hours because he was seriously thinking about becoming a family man. He had always had a sweet tooth, and he had become a frequent customer at the Rexall Drugs soda fountain. It was only a dozen steps around the corner from his father's shop, and he was smitten with the dimpled darling behind the counter.

"You make the most delicious chocolate ice cream sodas I have ever tasted," he said.

"I bet you say that to all the girls," she said with a giggle.

Debbie Crandall was just shy of five feet tall, plump, with curly blonde hair and hazel eyes. She was the younger sister of his best friend, Tom Crandall, and Andrew had known her since childhood. When he and Tom were teenagers, Debbie had been this annoying little pest who had always wanted to tag-along. However, while he had been away, she had grown up and become this beautiful young woman.

Andrew didn't waste any time in proposing. A few months later they were married in the chapel of the Oakfield United Methodist Church and honeymooned in nearby Niagara Falls. In 1947, ten months after their wedding, they welcomed their first child, Carol. Adam followed in 1948.

In 1958 opportunity knocked. Debbie's brother Tom had started making truck caps part-time in his garage and was so busy he recruited Andrew to help him in the evenings. The two men realized there was a growing need for truck caps and discussed starting a company. To be profitable they would need a larger space. Where would they get the financing? They had some savings, but with their growing families they weren't in a position to move forward.

Then, as fate would have it, Luke Collins passed away and left the 20-acre farm to Andrew. It was a sad time for the Collins family, but Andrew and Tom set aside their grief, prepared a simple business plan and headed to the bank for a loan. They would build the truck caps in the large barn where Luke Collins had serviced farm machinery and use the property as collateral. Another childhood friend was recruited to join their new venture and on a-wing-and-a-prayer, Crowncraft Truck Caps was born.

In the early years, the three men worked long hours producing standard truck caps. They kept a small inventory on hand and frequently posted "Truck Caps for Sale" ads in the local papers.

Before long, local tradesmen began requesting custom caps. An electrician needed a different set-up than a plumber, roofer or finish carpenter. And some folks just wanted a truck-mounted camper to use when hunting and fishing. The long hours and hard work began to pay off. As the company became more successful, Andrew hired more employees, retrofitted the barn and added additional equipment.

With family vacations and camping grounds popping up all over the area, a friend suggested that Crowncraft try building camping trailers that could be towed behind a car or a small truck. Always ready to try something new, the young company added the 16-foot campers to its line in 1961. The campers were all custom made, and before long satisfied customers began referring their friends. Demand was strong, and customers sometimes waited three months for the finished product.

Andrew Collins had a handful of devoted employees, and due to the quality of his work Crowncraft developed a loyal following. While most of their orders were from residents in western New York state who loved camping in the Finger Lakes region, he had customers throughout the United States, including Arizona, Florida, Georgia and North Carolina.

The farm property also offered some additional financial benefits. Behind the shop, a gravel lane led from the spacious parking area to a smaller red barn where the family kept four riding horses. A weathered wood-burned sign nailed above the barn door read "Welcome to Bell Oak Stables." Beyond the stables – perched on a knoll at the end of the lane – was the once proud farm house where Andrew had spent his childhood. The house was in disrepair, but was currently being rented by Russ Miller, one of the Crowncraft employees, and his family.

By the mid-1960's Adam and Wayne worked regularly in the shop and earned extra money by caring for the horses, watering and feeding them and mucking the stalls. When families from the nearby towns came for an afternoon of horseback riding on the property, the friendly boys would grab a bridle, saddle the horses and help the riders mount and dismount. Although they didn't give lessons, the teens were very patient with the little kids, lifting them up on the saddle and leading the horses around the enclosed pasture. The tips they received became gas money.

Patricia Daum

Over the summer of 1965, the two 17-year-olds had matured into young men. They had developed strong muscles from working in the shop and made a great team. Adam, the spitting image of his dad, was a slender six-footer with a mop of sandy hair. He had an outgoing personality, a smile for everyone and a perpetual twinkle in his deep blue eyes. Wayne was a hair taller than Adam but outweighed him by 40 pounds and was sturdy as a bear. He had a shy personality, but with his dark hair, dark eyes and rugged good looks he had no problem attracting the girls.

Adam and Wayne had been friends since grade school and did everything together. Through elementary school and junior high, they had been in Cub Scouts, Boy Scouts, Little League and Pop Warner baseball and Pee Wee football. While they always had fun, they were not outstanding athletes. By the time they entered high school, they gave up on sports and began spending more time helping out at Bell Oak Stables and doing odd-jobs for Adam's dad.

They quickly learned that the stable was a great magnet for girls who loved horses. When the boys turned 16 and got their drivers licenses, they began dating some of the regulars who came to the stable to ride. On this particular Friday they rushed to finish the stable chores so they could meet up with two of the pretty "townies" from Batavia.

As they finished spreading fresh straw in the last stall and filled the water trough, one last time, they heaved a sigh of relief – they were done for the day. They looked a mess. Their hair and shirts were soaked with perspiration, sweat was dripping down their red faces, and a dusting of hay and straw coated their hair and blue jeans.

The boys planned on driving home to Oakfield for quick showers and clean clothes but couldn't resist turning on the garden hose and dousing their heads and necks in cold water. "Oooh, that feels good!" Wayne groaned.

With hair dripping wet, they stopped in the shop office to say good-bye to Adam's dad. Andrew Collins shook his head at the sight of them and tossed a clean shop towel in their direction. "You might want to dry off before you get in that nice car," he said with a grin.

Leading them out toward the pink-and-white camper, Andrew said, "Before you leave, let's put the finishing touch on this beauty." They ceremoniously attached the chrome Crowncraft logo, with the tiny crown above the capital "C," and stepped back to admire the finished product.

"Boys, you did a fine job on this camper today," Andrew said. A big smile crossed his face as he handed each boy a crisp new $10 bill.

"Drive safely and have fun tonight," he said.
Wow, this was unexpected!

"Thanks, Dad, see you later," Adam said, as he gave his dad a hearty hug.

The two friends climbed into Adam's 1959 Chevy Impala sports sedan. As they drove away, they spotted Russ Miller and his little girls, the family renting the farmhouse, and waved good-bye.

Patricia Daum

***

Adam loved this car. His father, the master "wheeler and dealer" had traded a new truck cap for the car a few months before Adam's 16th birthday. The sports sedan was mechanically sound, but it had needed major body work to repair a large dent on the passenger side where the car had been side-swiped. Father and son spent hours working together to refurbish the vehicle.

With his dad's mechanical ability, the shop's paint specialist working his magic, and a lot of elbow grease from Adam, the sports sedan looked new. It was an impressive car with a sculpted hood and fancy radiator grill. It featured an unusual flat-top design with an expansive windshield, a wide wrap-around rear window and huge tailfins. Andrew, always the perfectionist, had special ordered the original paint colors, a stunning Gothic Gold and Satin Beige.

Adam's father had presented him with the car keys on his 16th birthday and for the past year he had been proud to drive the superb sports sedan up and down Main Street on Friday nights. None of his friends had a car like this! He relished the admiring glances and hoots and hollers from everyone as he drove by.

In addition to looking good, the car had muscle. It was powered with a rebuilt 280 horsepower 348 cubic-inch engine with Turboglide and a three-speed auto transmission. Earlier in the week Adam had read in an old Mechanix Illustrated magazine that the car showed a 0-60 mph of 13.1 seconds. The boys were ready to try it out.

As they left the parking area on Lewiston Road, they turned on Maltby Road, revved up the engine and took off. The two-lane road was flat and straight as far as the eye could see. They sped along the road with all the windows rolled down, the air rushing in bringing welcome relief on this muggy afternoon. The radio blasted music from their favorite Billboard Top 100 station. They sang along to the Rolling Stones, "I Can't Get No Satisfaction," the Beatles, "Help" and "Eight Days a Week."

The blazing sun lit up the blue summer sky, and every now and then a puffy cloud crossed the sun's path and offered a minute of shade. Speeding through the countryside they passed acres and acres of golden tasseled corn fields and newly plowed ground. The rural landscape was interrupted by an occasional farm house and barn. The Holstein cows at Meadowbrook Dairy raised their heads as the boys sped by.

Up ahead in the distance they spotted a familiar car, a royal blue and white 1957 Chevy. It was their friend Ron Barrett who was always bragging that he had the fastest car. "Let's see if we can catch up and pass him," Wayne challenged.

"We'll show him who has the fastest car," Adam laughed as he floored the accelerator.

His car raced toward Ron's reaching speeds of 80-90 mph. Soon they caught up and as Adam made the move to pass his friend, he realized he was going too fast. He braked hard, lost control and the car rolled over and over and over again, finally coming to a stop in a cornfield.

In an instant their lives were changed forever.

Horrified at what had just happened, Ron pulled off to the side of the road, stopped his car and rushed across the field to help his friends.

"Are you OK? Are you OK?" he screamed.

He heard one weak reply.

"I think I'm alright."

It was Wayne. Miraculously, during all the revolutions, he had been tossed into the back seat and had climbed out of the upside-down car. When Ron reached him, Wayne was stumbling around in a daze and a large goose egg was appearing on his forehead.

"Where is Adam?" Wayne asked.

"Adam, Adam, are you OK?" they shouted.

There was no response.

Scanning the area frantically, they found him 40 feet away crumpled amid the corn stalks. Adam had been hurled from the vehicle and was a bloody mess. He was unconscious and barely breathing as Wayne and Ron carried him to the side of the road. Minutes later, as his friends stood by helplessly, Adam took his last breath.

A passing car screeched to a halt – the driver terrified by what he saw. A large golden car flipped on its roof. Two young men, huddled over another shape on the ground.

One of the guys stood up, his hands clutching his head. Looking around wildly, he noticed the driver and cried out, "Please! Please stop at the next farm house   and   call   the   police!   Our   friend   is   dead!"

CHAPTER TWO

Oakfield, New York
August 1965

It had been a good day for Andrew Collins. Shortly after the boys left, Don and Lorene Phillips arrived to pick up the camping trailer they had ordered. While Andrew wasn't fond of the customer's color selection, Mrs. Phillips was "tickled pink" and Mr. Phillips was pleased that his bride of 50 years was happy.

Mrs. Phillips kept raving about the pink vinyl seat covers and the pink-and-white valances and coverlets. Andrew couldn't wait to get home to share the good news with his wife and treat her to dinner at the new restaurant in Batavia. Debbie had spent hours searching for material in just the right shade of pink and had sewn the valances and matching coverlets. She would be thrilled that Mrs. Phillips was happy with the finished product.

The couple had recently retired and looked forward to trying out the camper in the local campgrounds before they headed to Florida to spend the winter. Their four grandchildren were joining them for the weekend and they planned to put the camper to the test. Could it truly sleep six people?

While his wife was inspecting the interior of the camper, the men began shooting the breeze and discovered they had something in common. They had both been airplane mechanics in Florida during WWII. While Andrew had been in the Army Air Corps stationed at Avon Park, Mr. Phillips worked as a civilian at the Opa Locka airport near Miami.

"Please call me Don," he said. "After the war, I kicked around with a few of the airlines and ended up retiring from Delta in Atlanta. Lorene and I sold our home in Georgia and bought a little place up here near Syracuse to be close to our kids and grandkids. But the winters up here are too cold for us, so I guess you can call us snowbirds."

Andrew nodded knowingly, "Avon Park and Opa Locka were pretty nice during the winter, so your plans are good. But do you remember those summers? Oh my God, it was hot and humid with no breeze! You could hardly catch your breath," Andrew said.

"Yes, I remember," Don said. "But I also remember being thankful that we were in Florida, not getting shot at by the Germans or Japanese!"

Returning to the present, Don said, "you know, it's a small world. We are heading toward Avon Park this winter. We made reservations at a new campground in Sebring, supposed to be close to one of the lakes."

The two men hitched the camper to Don's Buick station wagon, and with a final handshake and wave good-bye, Don and Lorene Phillips drove away to begin their retirement adventure.

As Andrew was getting ready to drive home and share the good news with Debbie, a New York State patrol car pulled into the driveway. Andrew had been a member of the Oakfield Volunteer Fire Department for a number of years and knew many of the troopers. Sometimes they would stop by for a chat or to get a cold drink out of the pop machine.

But he didn't recognize the trooper with the dark sunglasses who approached him now.

"Wonder what this is about?" he thought.

"Mr. Collins?" the deputy asked.

"Yes," he replied.

The officer cleared his throat and struggled to say, "There has been a terrible auto accident on Maltby Road. I am sorry to inform you that your son Adam has been killed."

The words struck Andrew like a lightning bolt.

"No, No, that can't be true!" Andrew cried as he leaned against the trooper's car for support. "Adam and Wayne were just here! They worked hard today. I gave each of them a new $10 bill and told them to have a good time tonight. Adam can't be gone!"

Andrew gasped and clutched his chest, trying to comprehend the impossible.

"How did this happen?" he asked. "What about Wayne?"

The deputy gave him the awful details and then asked, "Do you live nearby? Would you like me to drive you home?"

"No, no," replied the stunned father. "I think I can drive. Just give me time to collect myself. I live nearby in Oakfield, but please follow me. You will need to help me tell my wife."

While the officer was delivering the devastating news to Andrew, Russ and his wife Gloria ran down the lane from the farmhouse.

"What's happening? Is everything OK?" they asked, fearing the answer.

Andrew shook his head, unable to speak. The officer shared the sad news.

"Oh, my goodness, how awful!" Gloria said, as the tears began to fall. "Adam is such a great kid! He is dating my sister, Faith. They were going out tonight!"

Her anguish rose, and she cried. "How am I going to tell my baby sister that Adam   is   dead?"

13

CHAPTER THREE

Batavia, New York
August 1965

Over in Batavia, Faith Bradford and her best friend, Sherri, were waiting for their dates to pick them up.

"I wonder what's keeping Adam and Wayne?" Faith asked.

"They probably had to work late," Sherri said.

The boys from Oakfield were always lots of fun and the two couples had planned on spending a typical Friday night. They would cruise Main Street Batavia in Adam's cool car and then meet other friends at the Red Hot. The drive-in restaurant was a gathering spot for the local teens and was a place to "see" and "be seen."

Earlier in the day the two girls had walked downtown on a shopping spree. Now as the sun began to set, the girls passed the time by admiring each other's new outfits. Faith had purchased pastel madras plaid Bermuda shorts and a pink polo top, while Sherri had selected white pedal pushers and a sleeveless blue linen shirt.

"Wonder what the guys will think of these outfits?" Sherri asked, fluttering her eye lashes and swinging her shoulders in a flirty manner.

The girls were sitting under the green-and-white striped umbrella on the patio at Faith's house sipping a glass of ice-cold lemonade when Faith's mother, Rachel, came out to join them. She had just arrived home from the country club.

"How was your golf game today?" Faith asked, knowing that her mother was aiming for the women's club championship.

Rachel seemed distracted. "Fine, fine," she said. But she appeared troubled, as she stood near the girls and gripped the back of a patio chair for support.

"Faith," she said, turning to her daughter. "Your sister just called with some dreadful news."

Rachel touched the gold cross on her necklace and chose her words carefully, "Adam and Wayne won't be coming tonight. There has been a horrible car accident on Maltby Road. Wayne is OK, but Adam died at the scene."

"No!" both girls shouted in unison. "This can't be true. What happened?" they cried as they rushed to Rachel.

"I don't know," Rachel said as she clutched the sobbing girls in a group hug. "But we will try to find out."

"Mom, this is so sad." Faith wailed. "My life will never be the same!"

Faith had no way of knowing just how prophetic her words would be.

CHAPTER FOUR

Oakfield, New York
August 1965

The next morning the headlines in the local papers read "Oakfield Boy Fatally Injured" and "High Speed Cited in Fatal Crash."

There were more details about the crash, and to the horror of friends and family one of the articles had a photo of the accident scene showing the upside-down car and Adam's body lying beside the road.

Three days later, the Oakfield United Methodist Church was packed with mourners on a steamy August afternoon. Everyone in this small, close-knit community was at the funeral to pay their respects to the Collins family and to share the family's grief in the loss of their son.

Dark clouds had been threatening all morning. As the service began, the heavens rumbled and the rain came with a vengeance, beating against the stained-glass windows of the stately old church. The air was stifling inside the church, and the fragrance from the dozens of floral wreaths and funeral baskets was suffocating.

Church ladies in their Sunday best fanned themselves with the funeral program while their husbands loosened their ties. Men and women alike were reaching for hankies.

Adam's simple pine casket had been placed at the front of the church and the sight of this young man taken in the prime of his life was heartbreaking.

Rev. Joel Tobias, the youth pastor of the church, was officiating at his first funeral. As he stood at the podium offering words of comfort and God's promise of eternal life, he struggled to contain his emotions. He was a recent graduate of the seminary and had formed a strong bond with Adam and his friends, who were active in the church's youth group.

At the end of the service, Andrew was stoic as he stood at the head of his son's casket. He greeted each person as the steady stream of mourners filed by. There were childhood friends and neighbors, members of his Odd Fellows

Lodge, the Genesee County Prayer Breakfast Committee, the Oakfield-Alabama Lions Club and the Oakfield Fire Department. It was a comfort to him and Debbie to know that so many people cared.

Debbie was overcome with emotion as she sat in the front pew with Adam's sister, Carol, and shared hugs and tears with many of her friends. The couple prayed that their faith would help them through this horrible ordeal.

Andrew had attended many a funeral, but never for someone's child. He kept thinking, "You are not supposed to outlive your children." He had such high hopes for Adam and had imagined that someday they would be working together at "Crowncraft and Son."

It pained him to see Adam's friends and classmates who were trying to grasp this tragic loss. Andrew couldn't speak when Wayne walked up. Wayne, who was like a second son, grabbed the older man in a bear hug, and they both struggled to gulp down sobs. The teen was bruised and battered from the accident and had a large bandage on his head, but he also suffered inwardly, unable to understand how he had lived and his best friend had died.

Wayne was followed by two teenage girls. Andrew recognized Sherri and Faith from their care-free days of riding at Bell Oak Stables. The last time he saw Faith was when she had been Adam's prom date in the spring and the smiling couple had stopped by the Collins' home for the customary photos.

That evening the tall, pretty girl with rosy cheeks was wearing a green formal that complemented her strawberry blonde hair. His handsome son had been decked out in a rented tux with a white dinner jacket. What a cute couple!

On this day, Faith looked very different. The heartbroken girl was wearing a black dress that she had hurriedly purchased from Alexanders department store. Her rosy cheeks and big smile were gone. Her skin was pale and blotchy; her eyes, red and puffy.

Faith walked along the receiving line and blinked back tears as she hugged Adam's sister and his parents. As she looked hesitantly into the open casket, she thought that Adam looked like a waxen figure, not the vibrant boy that she knew. His hands were crossed over his chest and she noticed her class ring on his pinkie finger. As she leaned over the casket, she kissed him on his forehead. She recoiled – he was so cold!

Later, back at home, Faith gathered Adam's class ring, their prom photo, the newspaper clippings about his accident and the funeral card and placed them in an empty box of candy that Adam had given her for Valentine's Day. She gently caressed the pink satin of the heart-shaped box as she tucked the memories away in the bottom drawer of her vanity.

After Adam's funeral she never returned to Bell Oak Stables. The memories were too strong.

PART TWO

CHAPTER FIVE

Batavia, New York
September 1965

As her senior year began, Faith tried to put the sadness behind her and the memories of Adam began to fade. They had attended different high schools, so she didn't find herself looking for him between classes. She kept herself busy and life moved on.

As a member of the Batavia High School color guard she practiced after school each day with the band, learning new routines that they would perform for all the home football games. She and Sherri were excited the day they received their new uniforms and rushed home to try them on.

Within minutes they were in Faith's bedroom admiring the new look – short, pleated royal blue skirts, white satin blouses and royal blue sashes embroidered with the Blue Devil logo. The white patent go-go boots and sparkly blue head bands provided the finishing touch.

"I think these look great!" Sherri said as she straightened her sash. "And don't you just love these boots?"

"I think they are so cool. Let's see what my parents think," Faith said as they marched down the stairs.

"I love your new uniforms," Faith's mother raved as the girls twirled around and modeled their outfits.

"Wow, you girls look fantastic!" Faith's father said. "We have to get a picture. Let's step outside in front of the old maple tree. The red leaves are brilliant this year and will be a great backdrop."

During football season the girls performed with the award-winning Blue Devils Band during half time and received cheers from the crowd as they strutted on and off the field. They also marched in festivals in the nearby towns including the annual Oakfield Labor Day parade, the Genesee County Fall Festival and the Mumford Apple Festival.

In addition to color guard performances, Faith posed for her senior picture, began thinking about college and attended Y-Teen activities with Sherri and her friends. She didn't have a new boyfriend, but a cute band member invited her to the Homecoming Dance.

Her teenage life was returning to normal, but shortly before Christmas Faith began to notice subtle changes in her body. She was gaining weight and her skirts were becoming snug at the waist.

"What's going on?" she thought. She tried to remember when her last period had been. "Oh my God! It was July!"

Her periods had always been irregular, and with everything that had happened, she hadn't given it a thought.

Now the thought hit her like a sledgehammer: "Could I be pregnant?"

***

Faith had first met Adam Collins when she and Sherri were 13 years old. During the summer months the girls would ride their bikes from their upscale neighborhood in Batavia to Bell Oak Stables and would spend the afternoons there riding the trails and just hanging out. While they enjoyed horseback riding, they also had fun flirting with Adam and Wayne, the Oakfield boys.

Each summer the girls would rekindle their friendships with the cute boys and by the time they were 15, they were holding hands and stealing kisses. Once the boys turned 16 and Adam got the super cool car, they had the freedom to meet at places other than the stables.

On the weekends, the two couples would double date, go to a movie at the Batavia theater, drive up and down Main Street, and stop at Red Hots Drive-In. Eventually, they would find a secluded place to park and make-out.

In the spring, Adam asked Faith to attend his junior prom and she accepted. She was excited about attending her first formal dance and she didn't have to go far to find a dress. Nestled in the corner of the guest bedroom closet was an assortment of beautiful formals that her two older sisters had left behind. She chose a beautiful long dress with an emerald green velvet top, and a white silk organza skirt that Gloria had worn years earlier. It was a perfect fit for Faith.

She bought a pair of white satin pumps, and her mom loaned her a pair of white elbow-length gloves and a satin evening purse to complete the outfit.

The day of the prom, Faith spent a couple of hours at the local beauty shop having her hair swirled into a perfect French twist, with an extra dose of hair spray to keep every hair in place. With a final touch of pink lipstick, she looked radiant.

A few minutes before Adam was scheduled to arrive, she walked into the library. As her father looked up from his desk, he was stunned. His baby girl had been transformed into a beautiful young woman.

"So, what do you think, Daddy?" she asked as she held her skirt and spun around.

"Faith, I think you look beautiful and so grown up," he said. "I have the camera ready for some pictures. Let's take a couple before Adam arrives."

Her date had also been busy getting ready for the special night. Adam had ordered a tux with black pants, white jacket and a green cummerbund to match Faith's dress. While she was getting her hair done, he had spent the afternoon cleaning and waxing his car to perfection. Then, his final stop was Allyson's Florist in Oakfield to pick up Faith's corsage and a matching boutonniere.

Adam was brimming with excitement as he pulled the shiny sports Impala up to Faith's house. When she opened the front door, he couldn't help but exclaim, "Wow, Faith, you look great!"

Adam handed her a beribboned box with a corsage of green-tipped white carnations to match her dress. Her mother stepped in to tie the corsage on Faith's wrist and neatly pin the boutonniere on Adam's jacket. Her dad snapped a dozen photos of the cute couple, before Faith finally said, "Daddy that's enough!" And then it was off to Adam's family home for another round of photos with the Collins family.

"Bon Voyage" was the theme of the prom which was held in the Oakfield High School gym. The junior class had done an amazing job of decorating for the event and Adam's father had even been recruited to construct a sturdy facade that resembled a ship. The high school art students finished the project with a flourish and the SS Hornet (the school's mascot) was a big hit.

A local DJ played songs from the Billboard 100 and couples danced to the popular songs from their favorite artists, including the Beatles, the Supremes and the Four Seasons. Faith and Adam weren't shy, they gyrated to the Twist and Mashed Potato and during the slow dances they held each other tight, her head resting on his shoulder.

As they were cuddled up in the front seat of his car after the dance, they both agreed it had been a wonderful and memorable evening. Then, Adam kissed Faith and said, "Would you like to go steady and wear my class ring?"

"That would be nice," Faith said wrapping her arms around Adam's neck. "Does that mean we won't be dating anyone else?"

"Yes," he said savoring the special moment with a lingering kiss.

As spring rolled into summer Adam began showing up at Faith's house more often. On Friday evenings they were double dating with Wayne and Sherri, going to the movies and cruising Main Street. On Sundays, while her parents were at the country club playing golf, the two teens would spend the afternoon snuggled together on the front seat, driving through the countryside and stopping in remote areas for some heavy necking and petting.

One memorable Sunday afternoon in July, teenage hormones kicked into high gear and they became intimate for the first time. Adam's family was out of town and in the heat of the moment, they found themselves heading up to his sister's bedroom. They didn't use protection but were careful not to go "all the way."

Two weeks later, Adam was killed in the auto accident.

CHAPTER SIX

Batavia, New York
December 1965

Christmas was always a festive time at the Bradford house. Each room of the spacious home was decorated with fresh evergreens, red velvet bows and poinsettias. A huge tree laden with multi- colored lights and treasured family ornaments dominated the living room. A vintage nativity set took center stage on the mantle, while a serene Virgin Mary statue could be seen in the entry.

Faith's parents enjoyed sharing the holiday spirit. It was a time for entertaining and there was a constant stream of guests throughout December, as Rachel hosted her book club, bridge group and golf friends. Their guests caught the holiday spirit as soon as they arrived at the traditional two-story home. Clear twinkle lights lit up the shrubbery along the front walk and evergreen wreaths hung from each window.

Katherine, the live-in housekeeper and cook, loved to bake and the house was brimming with the delicious aroma of cinnamon and ginger.

Each year, the extended family would gather on Christmas Eve for a traditional dinner, and then Christmas Day was set aside for the immediate family.

Christmas 1965 was slightly different. The Bradford's two eldest daughters had moved away. Laura was living in Japan and Gloria and her family had moved from the Bell Oak farmhouse to Medina, New York, which was 30 miles away. Instead of everyone coming to the Bradfords' home, Faith and her parents traveled to Gloria's for Christmas Day.

Robert Bradford's black Cadillac Fleetwood Brougham had a huge trunk that usually held shoe samples and sales manuals. Today, it was filled with a toy store full of packages – dolls, strollers, games, books, two tricycles, a bicycle and a red wagon. There was also a new outfit for each child, plus warm hats and mittens. There was so much stuff, that Faith shared the spacious back seat with the overflow. "This is just like being on Santa's sleigh!" she exclaimed.

There was always a white Christmas in northwestern New York State and this year was no exception. As the Bradfords pulled out of their driveway Christmas morning, they marveled at the beautiful landscape. A light snow had fallen the night before and the tree branches and rooftops glistened in the early sunlight. As they backed out of the driveway, they rolled down the car windows and waved to their neighbor, Mr. Law, who was grooming his backyard ice rink. "Merry Christmas!" they shouted.

After driving through the silent snow-covered countryside, they pulled into the lane leading to Gloria's new home. The white farm house sat in the middle of ten acres along with a four-stall red barn and fenced pasture. Candles in the front windows gave a welcoming glow and a simple evergreen wreath hung at the front door.

"Oh, my goodness, look at the cute snowmen!" Faith said. "The tall one has a Santa hat and the smaller ones are supposed to be reindeer; they have branches for antlers."

"They are adorable," said her mother. "I bet your sister and the kids had fun making them."

With seven little children under the age of nine, Christmas Day was full of chaos and fun. The kids could hardly contain their excitement when their grandparents arrived and they jumped up and down when the adults began carrying in packages. The grandparents stacked the presents around the tree that the children had decorated with strings of popcorn, red-and-green paper garlands and paper ornaments. A warm fire was burning in the fire place and red felt stockings adorned with each child's name hung from the fireplace mantel.

Before they were allowed to open the presents, Gloria insisted the children follow a Bradford family tradition – everyone lined up from smallest to tallest and marched around the cozy farm house singing "Happy Birthday Jesus," with Grandpa Bradford capturing the treasured moment on film. Then, the rowdy cherubs descended into the living room where there was an explosion of wrapping paper, ribbon and boxes. The little ones screamed with delight as they opened their presents and ran to show their parents and grandparents what they had received.

Patricia Daum

The grandparents and Faith had fun playing with the little ones and their new toys, but after enjoying a delicious dinner it was time for the children's nap and time for the grandparents to head home.

"I'm exhausted!" Robert said as they pulled out of the lane. "With those little girls climbing all over me, I felt like a jungle gym," he sighed.

"You know you loved every moment. It reminded me of when our girls were   young,"   Rachel   said.

CHAPTER SEVEN

Batavia, New York
December 1965

During the holidays Faith was able to hide her "tiny secret" under winter sweaters. She didn't want to spoil the festivities, and her family enjoyed their traditional Christmas with no one suspecting what the new year would bring.

It took all her courage, but the day after Christmas Faith went into her parent's bedroom and confided her suspicions to her mother. At first, Rachel couldn't believe it. Her naïve daughter must be mistaken. Thinking back, Rachel could only recall Faith going on a couple of dates since high school began in the fall.

Examining Faith's swollen tummy, she asked, "When did this happen? Who is the father?"

"It was back in July," Faith said, surprising her mother.

"Oh my God," thought Rachel. "She is already five months along." But a bigger surprise was yet to come.

"Mom, Adam Collins is the father," Faith confided as the tears started to flow.

Rachel inhaled sharply, hearing the dead boy's name. She listened to her daughter struggling to speak through her sobs. "We only did it once and I didn't even think we went all the way. It never entered my mind that I could get pregnant."

As the two sat on the edge of the bed, Faith felt her mother's arms wrap around her shoulders and she leaned into her comforting embrace. "This can't be happening to me. What am I going to do?" she cried.

Rachel rocked her daughter gently and then looked directly into her hazel eyes. "Faith, we need to tell your dad, but first, I'm going to call your Aunt Theresa. She is always good in difficult situations and she will help us decide what's best for you."

"Have you told anyone about this?" she asked.

"No," Faith said.

"Good, let's keep this a secret for right now," Rachel replied. "Please don't tell a soul, not even your best friend, Sherri. It will make it easier for you and everyone involved."

As Rachel stood to gather herself for the next step she said, "Why don't you finish putting away the Christmas gift boxes, while I call Theresa."

"We will tell your dad after dinner."

Faith felt calm again. She knew her mother and aunt would come up with a solution. And she certainly was not going to share this secret with anyone. She didn't want anyone whispering behind her back or shunning her. She had heard stories about those "bad girls" who had been sent to homes for unwed mothers, given up their babies and then returned to school. They were never treated the same.

The Bradfords had already gone down this road. Four years earlier when her older sister Gloria turned 17, she began dating Cosmo Bianchi, a sexy Italian guy from the other side of town. Her parents were distressed with the relationship and prayed it was just a phase. However, right before high school graduation, Gloria announced that she was pregnant. She insisted she loved Cosmo and wanted to marry him.

Her parents knew this marriage was a huge mistake but decided to handle it with grace. The young couple was married in a Catholic ceremony in the chapel of St. Andrew's Church that was attended by the immediate families. A lovely reception at the Bradford home followed the service.

The "happily ever after" only lasted a month. Gloria accused her new husband of abuse and filed for divorce. She moved back into her parents' home and her dad took out a restraining order on Cosmo. Her parents surrounded her with love and understanding during her pregnancy and the mother-to-be continued to socialize with her girlfriends. Gloria gave birth to a healthy baby girl, Bethany, and her parents agreed to raise the darling child until their daughter completed her education.

Rachel couldn't believe they were going through this again.

After dinner, they found Robert Bradford in the library. He was sitting in a worn leather office chair, behind a massive walnut desk that had once belonged to his grandfather. He was working on year-end sales reports and making strategic plans for the new year when Rachel and Faith walked into the room.

The library/family room was a large, comfortable room with a distinctive golf décor. The custom- made walnut bookshelves behind Robert's desk were filled with an assortment of best sellers, family photos and an impressive collection of golf trophies and awards. A baby grand piano, a game table and comfortable chairs completed the décor.

As the two women walked into the room, Faith's eyes were downcast. She couldn't look at her father. She sat on the piano bench and waited for her mother to speak. Rachel sat on the edge of the tartan plaid chair across from Robert's desk and let out a sigh.

"What's up?" the unsuspecting father asked playfully. "Did Santa miss something on your wish list?"

Rachel bit her lip, gulped and said, "Robert, Faith's pregnant."

Robert felt his neck tighten and his face grew red as a flare of anger rushed through his veins.

"God damn it Rachel, two out of three of your daughters can't keep their pants on!" he shouted, slamming his fist on the desk. "We can't go through this again!"

"How long have you known about this?" he demanded, turning to Faith who was trying to make herself as small as possible.

"I just figured it out a couple of weeks ago," Faith whispered. "I waited to tell you and Mommy until after Christmas. I didn't want to spoil the holidays for anyone."

"Who is the father?" he demanded.

"Daddy, it's Adam Collins," Faith confessed in a trembling voice.

"Who?" he asked. Then it hit him.

 "The kid who was killed in the auto accident?"

"Yes," his tearful daughter replied.

Robert Bradford was stunned. Learning about the dead boy and seeing his daughter's tears immediately deflated his anger.   He rose from his desk, sat down on the bench beside his youngest daughter and cuddled her next to his chest.

"Lammy Jammies, I am so sorry this has happened to you. We love you so much and will help you through this ordeal," he said.

Faith felt safe under his strong embrace and when he called her Lammy Jammies, his favorite childhood nickname for her, she knew everything would be all right.

Robert then turned to his wife. "Rachel, do you have a plan?" he asked in desperation.

"Robert, I've called Theresa and sent out an SOS," she replied. "Faith and I are off to her house in Rochester first thing tomorrow morning. We will figure out something and do what's best for Faith."

That night the anguished parents had little sleep. They talked for hours about what to do.

There weren't a lot of options. Keeping the baby was not a good idea. They had already gone down that emotional road with Gloria and in the years since then, Rachel had experienced some serious health issues. They were hesitant to make the commitment to raise another child. They also reasoned that getting the dead boy's family involved would be a nightmare.

As dawn approached, the parents made a decision they felt would be best for Faith, her baby and the family. Faith would have the baby and give it up for adoption.

This   would   become   a   family   secret   for   decades   to   come.

CHAPTER EIGHT

Ft. Lauderdale, Florida
December 1938

Rachel and her twin sister, Theresa, grew up in Batavia, New York, enjoying a life of privilege. They attended St. Joseph's Catholic Elementary School in Batavia during the fall and spring sessions. But the winter months were spent in Ft. Lauderdale, Florida, where their parents Elizabeth and Edgar Hamilton, went to escape the brutal winters. There, the girls were tutored by Dr. Mae McMillan. After finishing with their assignments each day, the girls had fun in the sun – swimming, playing golf and sailing with their winter friends.

Carefree summers were spent at the Hamiltons' sprawling lake house on Canandaigua Lake, 60 miles southeast from Batavia, where they continued to sail and play golf. They also enjoyed family dinners at The Inn on the Lake, cruises on the Canandaigua Lady and visits to the Sonnenberg Gardens.

The two girls were identical in looks, but had slightly different personalities. Theresa was more serious – a talented musician who preferred to spend her time reading and mastering classical pieces on the piano. Rachel was more fun-loving – a competitive spirit who loved winning in golf and sailing.

The sisters were outstanding students and excelled at Ruth Knox School, a private high school for girls in Cooperstown, New York. But then it was time for them to go to college. After a life time of doing everything together, the girls made a difficult decision and chose different colleges.

Theresa went to Rollins College in Florida and earned a degree in business administration, while Rachel graduated from Duke and obtained a degree in psychology. When Theresa and Rachel completed their studies in May of 1938 their proud parents treated the young women to a ten-week European cruise as a graduation present.

By winter 1938, the twins were in Ft. Lauderdale at the Hamilton compound, pondering their futures. Theresa had fallen in love with Robert Maloney, a Rollins classmate from Chicago and they were planning a summer wedding to be held in Batavia. Rachel was undecided about her future but was helping Theresa with wedding plans.

Patricia Daum

The Society column in the Ft. Lauderdale News was filled with all the winter activities of the "colony" from Batavia. There were bridge tournaments, sailing competitions at the Lauderdale Yacht Club, and golf championships at Ft. Lauderdale Golf and Country Club. Their social calendars were also filled with engagement announcements, parties and luncheons honoring visiting guests and family members.

Julia, the twins' older sister, was a delightful hostess and spent most of the year in Florida. She and husband Robert Marshall, who had relocated from Chicago, enjoyed entertaining the constant stream of house guests from up north. This year, the week between Christmas and New Year's was especially busy. They had a full house including Robert Maloney, Theresa's fiancée, and Robert Bradford, another friend from Chicago.

The three Roberts had grown up together in Kenilworth Village, an exclusive community along Chicago's north shore and attended North Shore Country Day School. The trio had been team-mates on the high school's basketball team that won the District Championship during their senior year. They had remained close friends ever since.

Robert Bradford was going to be a groomsman for his friend's summer wedding and had traveled to Florida for the engagement party. He had no inkling that this trip would be life-changing.

His first evening in town, Julia and Robert Marshall hosted a small dinner party for family and friends at their home. Theresa and Robert Maloney, the bride and groom to be, would be there along with Julia's younger sister Rachel, who would be alone.

Robert Bradford was invited, but was dreading it. He hated these intimate dinners and the small talk with women he didn't know. But he vowed to try and be engaging for the sake of his hostess.

The evening turned out to be one of the best of his life. He met his future bride.

Rachel was lovely, smart and one of the most interesting women he had ever met. After dinner they found a quiet corner on the patio and talked for hours. As midnight approached, Rachel said. "I really need to be getting back to my parents' home. They will be worried and think an alligator has grabbed me."

"Alligators, are you serious?" Robert asked, looking around with suspicion.

"Yes, we have alligators in Florida," Rachel said starting to laugh. "They have been known to roam around the canal."

As he walked her home, two houses away, he said, "I'm only here for a couple more days. I would like to see you again. Are you free tomorrow and the next day?"

"I would love to see you again," she said. "Do you play golf? My family has a couple of tee times reserved for tomorrow morning.

"Would you like to join us?" she asked. "I'm sure Julia and Robert have an extra set of clubs you could borrow."

"Yes, I would like that," Robert said. "See you tomorrow."

The next day after a competitive round of golf, the twosome sat on the veranda overlooking the course and tallied the scores. "Rachel, you know, you beat me by two strokes," Robert said. "That's embarrassing."

"Robert, don't feel too bad. You have a great game, but in all fairness, you haven't played for a couple of months and you were using borrowed clubs," Rachel said and then turned a challenging look his way. "We will have to have a rematch your next visit."

Robert's spirits soared. There will be a next time! This experience was a first for Robert, a smart pretty girl who was a good golfer. "This relationship has definite potential," he thought.

Robert and Rachel were together again that evening at the engagement party, and he didn't leave her side. He was smitten. It was a festive affair with friends and family gathered together for this happy occasion, sharing memories and laughter. "What a fun-loving family," he thought. "So very different from my solemn strait-laced parents."

After dinner he asked, "What are you doing New Year's Eve?"

"Isn't that the name of a song?" she replied with a giggle.

"Right now, I don't have plans but I hope I can convince you to stay an extra day," she said. "The Lauderdale Yacht Club will host their first New Year's Eve celebration. I've heard it's going to be a fabulous party and all our friends will be there. I would love for you to be my date."

"I would be happy to escort you," he said.

New Year's Eve was magical. Rachel was stunning in a cobalt blue gown with a slit that exposed her ankle and high-heeled silver slippers. Her dark hair fell in soft curls around her face and Robert couldn't stop looking at her.

"You look lovely tonight," he said as he handed her a beribboned box containing a wrist corsage of yellow rose buds.

"Robert, you look very handsome tonight and the corsage is beautiful! How did you know yellow roses are my favorite flower?" she asked.

"Your sister Julia told me," he admitted.

The theme of the party was "Sailing into the New Year," and the Yacht Club had done an outstanding job with the decorations. The centerpieces featured miniature sail boats floating in a sea of magnolia leaves and white orchids. Instead of glittery cardboard top hats and tiaras, the men received a classic captain's cap embossed with the Yacht Club's logo – the women received a matching first mate's cap.

Throughout the evening guests feasted on an elaborate buffet and enjoyed dancing to music by The Ocean Reef Band.

As the clock was nearing midnight waiters in black ties began handing out flutes of champagne. The young couple took two and slipped out onto the veranda overlooking the marina. An almost-full moon and hundreds of twinkling stars luminated the night sky. They could hear the crowd in the main dining room chanting the count-down, and as the clock struck midnight, they toasted each other with champagne and welcomed a New Year – 1939. Then, Robert swept her in his arms and the two exchanged a passionate kiss.

"Rachel, this has been the most wonderful week of my life and I have fallen in love with you," he said. "This has all happened so fast, do you feel the same way?"

"It's been a magical week for me, too," she replied as she looked up into his eyes. "I knew that first night at dinner that we were supposed to be together."

"I want to spend the rest of my life with you. Will you marry me?" he asked.

"Yes," she replied without hesitation.

"Rachel, you have made me the happiest man in the universe!" he exclaimed.

"We should tell your family," he said.

"Robert, I would like to shout it out to the world tonight, but I think we should wait until your next visit," she said. "My dad is old-fashioned and will be impressed if you are the proper gentleman and speak with him before we make the announcement."

"Rachel, I don't want this magical week to end, but I have to catch the train to St. Louis in a few hours. I will return in a couple of weeks and speak to your father," he promised.

"What about your parents?" she asked.

"They are going to be harder to convince," he said. They are hard-core Episcopalian and generations of my family have been listed in the Chicago Blue Book. They are not going to be happy about me marrying a Catholic girl from upstate New York."

"But don't you worry, they will eventually come around. I've been on my own for a few years and certainly don't need their permission," he replied.

Rachel was disappointed that Robert had to leave, but she knew in her heart that he was sincere and would return soon. If she had the slightest doubts, they were dispelled when she began receiving a single yellow rose each day that he was away. "This is so romantic," she thought.

Patricia Daum

Her parents had a feeling that love was in the air, but when the roses began arriving, they knew this relationship was more serious than they had anticipated. They began asking questions. Rachel wasn't able to wait for Robert to speak with her father, so she wisely discussed the relationship with her parents. They thought she was moving way too fast.

"You have only known him for a week!" they said.

"I know," she said. "It seems improbable that I have fallen in love with him, but I know in my heart that he is the perfect match for me. I hope after you think about this, you will give us your blessings."

Elizabeth and Edgar Hamilton knew that Robert was from a wealthy well-established family in Chicago and that his parents also spent the winter in Ft. Lauderdale. Robert was a successful businessman living in St. Louis and should be able to provide for their daughter. He was childhood friends with Julia's husband and Theresa's fiancée and would fit nicely in the family circle. The only downside was his religion. They had hoped Rachel would fall in love with a fine man from a Catholic family.

In the end, however, Rachel's happiness was what really mattered to them.

Two weeks later, Robert showed up on Rachel's doorstep with a glorious bouquet of yellow roses and a heart-stopping diamond engagement ring. Her parents were enjoying evening cocktails in the courtyard when the young couple suddenly appeared.

"Robert, what a surprise! It's good to see you," they said.

"It's nice to see you, too," he replied with the widest of grins.

"Mr. and Mrs. Hamilton, Rachel and I have an announcement to make," he said as he grasped Rachel's hand. "We have fallen in love and plan to marry. Would you give us your blessing?"

Rachel's parents looked at the young couple and then glanced at each other. Edgar rose from his chair and spoke.

"Robert, you are a fine man and we want our daughter to be happy. You certainly have our blessing."

As the young couple began to exclaim their thanks, Edgar continued. "However," he said making sure he had their attention, "we need one promise from you – that our grandchildren will be raised in the Catholic faith."

Robert eagerly replied, "I love your daughter with all my heart and promise the children will be raised as Catholics,"

There were handshakes and hugs all around and Rachel proudly showed off the beautiful engagement ring. Then the couples settled in for some more serious discussion.

"What do your parents think about this marriage?" Edgar asked Robert.

"Mr. Hamilton, I must admit, they are struggling with the idea. But it's my decision and my life. I'm sure once they get to know Rachel and your family, everything will be fine," he said.

"Robert, I can sympathize with you." Rachel's father said as he turned to his wife with a knowing smile.

"Years ago, when I fell in love with Rachel's mom, my family was very upset. Elizabeth was an Irish immigrant and was working in our shoe factory. It was unheard of that I would marry one of the factory girls. But we prevailed and they learned to love her. She has been a wonderful wife and mother and she is the best thing that ever happened to me and our family," he said with an adoring look at his wife.

Rachel broke in excitedly, "Mom and Dad, we would like to set a wedding date. When do you think would be a good time?"

"Well, Rachel, you know that we are in the midst of planning Theresa's wedding this summer," her mother said. "Can you wait until then? Maybe we could have a double wedding?"

The newly engaged couple looked at each other and shook their heads. "That's too far off," Rachel said. "A long- distance romance is not in our future.

Patricia Daum

"Besides, we would prefer to have a small elegant ceremony, instead of a lavish event."

The couple got their wish and they were married two months later in a private ceremony at Rachel's family home in Ft. Lauderdale. The Society page featured a lengthy article about the all-white wedding, including a photo of the newly-weds. It showed a modern bride in a white silk jersey afternoon dress, with a white pill box hat accented with a long drape of silk and a handsome groom in a white tuxedo.

The attendants were Rachel's three sisters, Theresa, Emily and Julia, and they wore matching white dresses. Continuing with the all-white theme, the male members of the wedding party were dressed in white tuxes, shirts and ties. Rachel's father gave her in marriage, and her brother Richard was best man. Robert Marshall and Robert Maloney, Robert's childhood friends, were his groomsmen.

Following the ceremony, a wedding luncheon was held at the Orchid Conservatory of the Governor's Club Hotel. The wedding and luncheon were attended by the immediate family.

Robert's mother attended.

His   father   refused.

CHAPTER NINE

St. Louis, Chicago, Canandaigua Lake
1939-1946

Love and romance were in full bloom for the Hamilton family in 1939. Rachel and her sister Theresa were married within a few months of each other and both sets of newlyweds moved to the Midwest – Rachel in St. Louis and Theresa in Chicago. The two couples were a train ride away and visited often the first two years of their marriages.

Then came the attack on Pearl Harbor.

The war disrupted everyone's lives with strict rations on sugar, tires and gasoline. Families shopped with ration booklets and everything from meat, dairy, cooking fats and even baby food was rationed. Gasoline ration stamps were distributed according to need. Pleasure driving was out, defense travel was top priority. Travel was curtailed, even for the wealthy.

Residents across the country engaged in civil defense drills and supported war efforts with scrap drives and war bond purchases. It seemed every city near the coast was on high-alert. German U-Boats had had been spotted all along the Atlantic seaboard and attacked several American ships. Rachel and Theresa were concerned about the safety of their families in Florida, but industrial cities along the Great Lakes were not immune to possible attacks.

Theresa experienced all these changes first-hand. In Chicago there were thousands of Block Captains who volunteered to conduct Civil Defense drills and on designated nights there were mandatory black-outs in the city. Block Captains would patrol the neighborhoods to make sure no lights were shining.

"It is a frightening time," she wrote in a letter to Rachel.

There were major changes in the workforce, too. Robert Bradford had been a successful sales executive for St. Louis Car, a manufacturer of subway cars, until the company switched production and started making amphibious attack vehicles for the military. He was no longer selling subway cars to cities in the U.S. and abroad. The U.S. government was the company's only account and Robert had a new position – procurement officer.

Patricia Daum

Robert Maloney, Theresa's husband, worked for Conlon Development Company in downtown Chicago. Construction had come to a screeching halt during the war, and the company struggled. However, the owners had deep pockets and continued lining up investors, purchasing land and planning for life after the war.

While Rachel chose the path of motherhood and welcomed baby Laura in 1940 and Gloria in 1944, Theresa's life took a different path. With her business degree in hand, she began working for Northern Trust Bank in Chicago and by 1942 had advanced to trust officer. This coveted position became available when the young male executives left the bank to serve in WWII.

After the war ended, life returned to "normal" for the families, but a series of events led them back to Batavia. Rachel's father had always doted on his four daughters and with the rations and travel restrictions during the war he had missed having his family around. When his wife became ill, Edgar Hamilton began to formulate a plan to have all his daughters nearby.

Emily had spent the war years in Batavia while her fiancée was in the Marine Corps. She had always loved horses, so her dad bought Seven Springs Stables, a short trot from Batavia, where she bred and trained American Saddlehorses.

In October of 1945 she married Daniel Fischer and the two made their home in Janesville, Wisconsin, Daniel's hometown. However, she continued to be a frequent visitor to Batavia and Seven Springs Stables during the summer, when she traveled to major shows and competitions in New York State and Canada.

Julia and Robert were not an issue. They lived in Ft. Lauderdale near her parents' winter home, and Julia and her children spent many summers on Canandaigua Lake at the Hamilton's home.

Theresa and Robert were entrenched in Chicago with their careers, but promised to visit often during the summer holidays.

Rachel and Robert were going to take more convincing to make the move to Batavia. The growing family was settled in St. Louis with two young girls, and Rachel was recovering from a miscarriage. Robert was working at St. Louis Car and had returned to his sales position.

But then his father-in-law approached him with an offer that he couldn't refuse.

The Hamilton Company had managed to weather the Depression and survive the war years, but the struggles to keep the company profitable and the illness of his beloved wife, had taken a toll on Edgar Hamilton. He was planning to retire as CEO and turn the company over to his son Richard, who had some innovative ideas about expanding the business and increasing production. The company needed a top-notch salesman, and Edgar turned to Robert Bradford.

Edgar knew he could count on Robert and offered him the position of vice-president of sales and marketing – if Robert and his family would relocate to Batavia. He sweetened the generous salary with the promise of annual bonuses and the purchase of a new home for Robert and his family.

Robert was reluctant to leave bustling St. Louis, for small-town Batavia, but he respected his father-in-law and knew he ran a successful company. Robert was honored that he was offered the high-level position. He knew that Rachel would be easy to convince. She was depressed about the miscarriage and worried about her ailing mother. She would jump at the chance to move back to her home town and be near her family and childhood friends.

The couple decided to accept the job and began preparing for the move. They selected plans for a new two-story home that would be constructed on a large lot near her parents' home and across the street from Rachel's brother and his family. While the home was being constructed, Rachel and the girls spent the summer of 1946 at the Canandaigua Lake house with her parents, sisters and their families.

Robert started his new job at the Hamilton company and business was brisk. He made a point of seeing his family at the lake on weekends and giving them progress reports on the new home.

The poignant memories of that summer would remain forever. Rachel's mother was losing her battle with breast cancer and her daughters treasured the time they spent with her.

Then, another tragedy struck. In mid-June, Theresa's husband, Robert Maloney, was killed in an auto accident in Chicago. His car had been T-boned in a busy intersection by a drunken driver.

Theresa was devastated by the loss and took a leave of absence from the bank to join her family at the lake. She was surrounded with love and support and the tribe of nieces and nephews were a welcome distraction. She turned to her faith to help her through this difficult time and began attending daily mass at St. Mary's Catholic Church in the nearby town of Canandaigua.

The Fourth of July celebration was always a big event at Canandaigua Lake, with a parade, live bands and fireworks. The entire family celebrated the day with swimming, sailing and a picnic on the spacious lawn. As night fell, they enjoyed the colorful fireworks display followed by the spectacular Ring of Fire that illuminated the night. The Hamilton family joined other residents around the lake and ignited fires and flares along the shore to create the most amazing sight – the lake shore appeared to be on fire – and the fires glowed for hours.

Sadly, it would be the last time the family was together. Elizabeth Hamilton passed away on July 6, 1946.

The family was heartbroken at their loss. However, as Labor Day approached, it was time for the nieces and nephews to be returning to their homes and schools. The Bradford's were getting ready to move into their new home; and it was time for Theresa to make a decision.

CHAPTER TEN

Rochester, New York
September 1946

Theresa's family had encouraged her to move back to Batavia, but her hometown felt too small. After living in Chicago, she wanted something more. Theresa considered Rochester; it was a bigger city only 30 miles from Batavia but it had more to offer culturally.

Unfortunately, Northern Trust did not have an office there, but her father had an idea. Edgar was on the board of trustees of Canandaigua National Bank and Trust and was friends with the owners. He knew the bank had an office in Rochester; maybe they needed a trust officer. He made a call and set up an interview for her.

With her experience from the highly respected Northern Trust, she was hired. A few days later she and Rachel drove to Rochester and spent the day looking for an apartment. They finally decided on one located downtown, on a side street near the bank and within walking distance of St. Mary's Catholic Church. The apartment was on the second floor of a charming Victorian home – a spacious two-bedroom unit with a bay window.

"This is perfect," Theresa said. "I can furnish it with some of my things and put the remainder in storage. It will be a great place to live until Robert's estate is settled, and best of all, it's close enough that we can see each other frequently."

"It's lovely," Rachel said. "It reminds me of the first apartment where Robert and I lived in St. Louis."

As a trust officer Theresa handled the accounts of the bank's wealthy clients, most of them elderly widows. She was bright and businesslike in managing their accounts, but she was also kind and understanding. If they were unable to come to the bank, she made in-home visits and was diligent in making sure they were not taken advantage of by over-zealous relatives.

Her clients loved her and began referring their friends. As a result, the bank saw a significant increase in the trust department's accounts. Theresa continued to succeed and was eventually promoted to vice-president of the Trust Department.

Shortly after the promotion, Theresa found herself looking for a new place to live. In 1950 she was forced to move when a proposed new highway was set to demolish the houses on her street. She called Rachel for help and the twin sisters went house-hunting. They eventually found a charming Tudor-style home in a desirable neighborhood on East Boulevard that was perfect for Theresa.

As the years passed, Theresa never remarried. Robert Maloney had been the love of her life and when he died, she was never able to recapture that special emotion. Instead, she focused on her career and her extended family.

She developed a deep friendship with one of the bank's board of directors, but it remained platonic. The distinguished widower was charming and she enjoyed his company. He accompanied her to numerous charity events sponsored by the bank, and she reciprocated by serving as his hostess when he entertained corporate clients.

Theresa loved entertaining family and friends in her home. Rachel and Robert would visit often during the summer months, when they were competing in regional golf events, and their eldest daughter, Laura, was also a frequent visitor.

This delightful child was musically talented, and Theresa enjoyed taking her to concerts and operas in the city. She was proud of the young woman's accomplishments, and when Laura gave her senior piano recital at Beloit College, Theresa traveled to Wisconsin to be with her family and applauded enthusiastically during the standing ovation.

CHAPTER ELEVEN

Rochester, New York
December 27, 1965

Religion was an important part of Theresa's life and she faithfully attended mass at St. Mary's Catholic Church each morning before work and on the weekends. She had settled into the routine long ago when she lived near the church and continued to be a regular there after she moved.

She was on vacation the week between Christmas and New Year's and was happy to take a rest from all the holiday festivities that she had participated in the past month. The major events sponsored by the bank were held in December and she had been to them all. They were fun but exhausting.

This Monday morning, she had driven her black BMW coupe through her tree-lined neighborhood to the ancient downtown church, arriving in time for the 9:00am mass. As she walked up the steep steps, a strong gust of wind blew against her and she struggled to open the carved wood doors. The skies were gray and threatening snow, but the inside of the church looked bright and inviting, dressed in holiday greenery. Garlands of fresh pine and holly draped over the railing of the balcony, and Christmas trees with twinkling lights towered on each side of the altar.

Theresa walked quietly down the center aisle giving a smile and nod to a few familiar faces. She slipped into her customary seat, third pew on the right. On this day as she knelt, she asked the heavenly Father for guidance in dealing with a recent family crisis.

Theresa hadn't been blessed with children of her own but had been devoted to her sister Rachel's three daughters, Laura, Gloria and Faith. The twin sisters had been close their entire lives and had turned to each other in times of turmoil. Theresa was kind, wise and principled, and Rachel could always count on her to provide the voice of reason.

Theresa thought about the times when she was able to provide support and comfort to Rachel – when she had miscarried, and again when Faith was born premature and the doctors didn't think the baby would live.

Theresa remembered steering Rachel and Robert through the storm of Gloria's disastrous marriage, her divorce and the birth of her daughter. A couple of years after that, Theresa offered a shoulder to lean on when Gloria left college and decided to marry that man with the five little girls.

"Now, here we are with baby Faith having a baby," she thought. She had lived through her own struggles and knew this pregnancy was not the worst thing that could happen.

A precious new life was about to enter the world. With the family surrounding Faith with love and understanding, she knew in her heart that everything would work out for the best.

As she left the church giant snowflakes began to fall and a calmness settled over her. Theresa's prayers were answered – a plan began to take shape in her mind.

She had only been home for a little while when Rachel and Faith knocked at her door. The snow was coming down harder and she felt the wet flakes brush her cheek as she gave both of them a hug.

"I'm so glad to see you," Theresa said. "Let me take your coats and come sit down."

Theresa and Rachel gave each other a knowing smile as they noticed that they were dressed almost alike – cashmere sweater sets and wool slacks. The twins were classic beauties cut from the same cloth. They resembled their father's side of the family – tall, dark hair, dark eyes and prominent noses. And today, they sported the same hairstyle, a fashionable page boy.

"Girls, we are so blessed. My housekeeper Katy picked up some fresh scones at Savoia Bakery this morning and I have to confess, they smelled so good that I couldn't resist. I have already tasted one and they are delicious! Would you like one?" she asked.

"That would be wonderful, Theresa, thank you," Rachel replied, settling into the comfy green sofa.

Theresa disappeared into the kitchen and returned a moment later carrying a large tray filled with assorted tea cups and a blue floral plate piled high with blueberry and cherry scones. "It's such a special treat to have you visit," she chatted as she placed the tray on the antique coffee table.

"Aunt Theresa, we have a special treat for you too," Faith said and handed her a cut-glass candy jar filled with holiday ribbon candy.

"Faith, thank you! You know how much I love Oliver's candy," Theresa said.

"Now, young lady, tell me, how are you feeling?" Theresa asked as she sat in the chair next to Faith.

"I'm fine, Aunt Theresa," Faith replied as her face flushed. "I still can't believe this has happened to me."

"What are you most worried about?" Theresa asked.

"I'm so embarrassed," Faith said. "I just don't want anyone to know."

"My dear sweet girl, I promise that you are going to be OK. Don't you worry about anything. Your parents and I will decide what's best for you," Theresa said and patted Faith's arm.

As Faith sat quietly in the wingback chair, nibbling on a sweet treat, Aunt Theresa and her mother talked about her predicament and began planning her future. After discussing several options, they came up with a plan that would keep Faith's secret, enable her to finish high school and let her get on with her life.

Thankfully, the first semester had ended before Christmas vacation and school was out for two weeks. They decided that Faith would not return to school after the holidays. Their story would be that over the winter break, Faith was diagnosed with a severe case of mononucleosis and she and her mother would travel to Florida to spend the winter in Ft. Lauderdale near Rachel's two sisters.

"Mono is the perfect diagnosis," said Theresa. "One of my friends had mono and it lingered for a few months. The symptoms were fever, sore throat and fatigue and in more severe cases like hers, she had swollen lymph nodes and a swollen spleen. The only cure was bed rest, good nutrition and plenty of water."

The Florida sunshine would be just what the doctor ordered and would help with her recovery. The pregnancy would be kept hush hush, Faith would have the baby and the infant would immediately be adopted. By spring break, Faith should be well enough to return to school and graduate with her class.

"Theresa, thank you so much," Rachel said with a sigh of relief. "This is a brilliant plan. I knew we could count on you."

"You know I use to love spending the winter months in Florida," Rachel said. "It reminds me of our childhood when we traveled there with our parents to escape the harsh winter weather. Remember that tutor we had? What was her name?"

"It was Dr. Mae; Dr. Mae McMillan," Theresa replied. "I always thought she was sickeningly sweet around our parents, but she was strict with us and made sure we kept our lessons up to date."

"We will have to find someone like that for Faith," Rachel said. "Robert and I will talk tonight. For this plan to work we have some major details to iron out and we don't have much time."

As the grandfather clock chimed a dozen times, Theresa looked up. "Oh, my, this morning has slipped away from us," she said.

"Rachel and Faith, come into the kitchen. Katy has made some lunch for us," Theresa said.

As the three women sat in the cheery breakfast nook, Theresa said, "Now that we have a plan in motion for Faith, I want to hear all about your family's Christmas celebration.

"Tell me about Gloria and her family. It must have been total joy and chaos with all those little ones."

"That's the perfect way to describe the day," Rachel said. "As you can imagine, the children were wound up and excited."

"Aunt Theresa, you should have seen Daddy down on the floor crawling around with the little girls perched on his back. That was the funniest sight ever," Faith said.

"I'm so glad to hear that he has accepted this new family," Theresa said. "I remember how upset he was when Gloria married Russ."

"I was upset too. You can't imagine how horrified we were with the living conditions at the Bell Oak farmhouse. Things are so much better for them now," Rachel said. "We helped her purchase the small farm in Medina with a modern house, and Robert was instrumental in getting Russ a steady job at the Medina Utility Company."

"Theresa, you know that Robert can never remain angry for long, especially when it comes to his girls. He loves them unconditionally, and he seems pleased that Gloria is happy and content in her new role," Rachel said. "We are pleased that Bethany is happy and loves her new sisters and the baby boy is adorable."

"Oh, we can't forget to tell you Laura's happy news. She called us on Christmas Eve from Japan. She is engaged and wants to be married in our back yard in the summer," Rachel said.

"We haven't met this man, but she insists he is the perfect match."

After an enjoyable visit, Faith and her mother headed home. Heavy snow had accumulated and made driving treacherous. There was little conversation. While Faith fiddled with the car radio and then dozed off, her mother tried to concentrate on the slippery road. But in the back of her mind Rachel was making a list of everything that would need to be done to put "the plan" in motion.

CHAPTER TWELVE

Batavia, New York
December 27, 1965

Katherine O'Reilly, the Bradford's devoted housekeeper and cook, opened the back door on Monday morning and was greeted by silence. As she unwrapped her new green wool scarf and took off her heavy coat and boots in the mud room, she called out.

"Hello?"

No answer.

"Where is everyone?" she thought.

As she padded into the kitchen in her stocking feet, she saw a note on the counter in Rachel's lovely handwriting.

> *Katherine,*
> *Hope you had a wonderful visit with your sister.*
> *.We missed you.*
> *Faith and I are in Rochester visiting Theresa.*
> *Bob is working today.*
> *We will be home in time for dinner. See you then.*
> *Love, Rachel*

"That's odd," she thought. "Why would Rachel and Faith take off to Rochester on such a snowy day?" She said a silent prayer that they would arrive home safely and went upstairs to put away her Christmas gifts.

Rachel Bradford was a wonderful wife, mother and friend. But she was never cut out to be Suzy Homemaker or Betty Crocker. She had been raised in an affluent family where domestic chores had been handled by a capable and caring staff. As a young woman Katherine O'Reilly and her sister Bridget had worked as housekeepers for Rachel's parents, but she and Rachel formed a special bond the summer of 1946, when Rachel and her two young daughters lived at the Hamilton's home on Lake Canandaigua.

As the time came for the move into the new house in Batavia, Rachel knew she was going to need household help and asked Katherine if she would like to come live with the Bradfords. With Edgar Hamilton's blessings, Katherine moved into the new home along with the family and would stay with the Bradfords until they retired and moved to Florida in 1969.

The large comfortable house had four bedrooms and Katherine was given the master bedroom suite which had an attached private bath. Through the years she had furnished her room with an   assortment of her own belongings: a twin-size maple Jenny Lind bed, a tall oak bureau and an overstuffed chair and ottoman. Katherine's most treasured possession was a battered trunk placed at the foot of her bed – the trunk she had used when she had immigrated to the United States from Ireland years earlier.

Even on a gray winter day, the room was bright and cheery with its yellow walls, a colorful quilt on the bed, and crisp white curtains trimmed in Irish lace at the windows. A quaint writing desk and straight-back chair were positioned between the two windows and a small black-and-white TV sat on a metal stand.

On her bureau, Katherine had placed a statue of the Holy Mother in a pale blue robe, alongside a treasured rosary. A framed photo of Pope John XXIII hung above her bed. The Pope with the kind face and red robe had one hand raised, and she imagined that he was blessing her each evening when she said her prayers.

After putting away her gifts, Katherine combed her silver hair into a tidy bun, slipped on her white nurses' oxfords, tied a fresh apron around her ample waist and headed downstairs to the kitchen, her favorite domain. It was time to begin preparation for the evening meal – pot roast – Mr. B's favorite.

She noticed a decoration on the refrigerator door. A reindeer face on a paper plate with brown paper antlers that had been cut by tracing around someone's little hands. A note said:

Merry Christmas Grandma and Grandpa. I love you. Bethany.

"Oh, how sweet," thought Katherine. It had been years since the Bradfords had any childhood crafts to display and she knew they adored Bethany, Gloria's five-year-old daughter.

While the meat was simmering, Katherine finished a couple loads of laundry, ironed Mr. B's dress shirts, vacuumed the falling pine needles from the Christmas tree and lit a fire in the fireplace. She spent her customary afternoon break upstairs in her comfy chair with her stocking feet propped on the ottoman, eating ice cream and watching her soaps – "As the World Turns," "Guiding Light" and "General Hospital."

When Rachel and Faith arrived from Rochester in mid-afternoon, Katherine was in the kitchen peeling potatoes and carrots and had a cake baking in the oven.

"There you are," said Katherine. "I'm so glad you got home safely. I was worried. It looks like we are getting more snow."

"Yes," Rachel said as she and Faith took off their heavy coats and boots. "The roads are getting bad. We are thankful to be home."

Faith gave Katherine a quick hug and headed upstairs. "Kay Kay, I need to make a quick trip to the bathroom," she said.

"I was surprised to get your note that you and Faith had gone to Rochester. Why would you go on such a snowy day?" Katherine asked.

"Oh, Katherine, something serious has occurred and I needed Theresa's help," Rachel said as her eyes began to tear. "You won't believe what has happened."

"I've only been gone for a couple of days, what could have possibly gone wrong to make you so upset? Are you sick?" Katherine asked.

"No, it's something else," Rachel said as she sat down at the kitchen table and put her head in her hands. "We just learned yesterday that Faith is pregnant."

"Oh, that can't be! Not Faith, not our innocent little girl!" Katherine said as the knife slipped out of her hands and bounced on the wood floor.

"Yes, it's true and it's a very sad situation. Do you remember Adam Collins, the boy who was killed last summer? He is the father," Rachel said.

"Oh, Blessed Mother!" Katherine said. "What are you going to do?"

"Robert and I talked about this last night and we have decided to keep this pregnancy a secret and give the baby up for adoption. Theresa has helped us develop a plan. We are going to say that Faith has been diagnosed with a severe case of mono. She and I will go to Florida this winter and live near my sisters until she is better. We will return after spring break," Rachel said. "Robert will come visit us in Florida and make arrangements for a private adoption.

"The only people who know about this are you and me, Robert and Theresa. I know we can count on you to keep this confidential and to take care of Robert and our house while I'm away," she said.

"Of course, you can count on me! But what does Faith think about this?" Katherine asked.

"Faith is in her own teenage world and seems to be handling the situation OK. We have told her we love her and will take care of everything. The baby will be a blessing for a loving family, and when she returns home she can get on with her life. She just has to pretend she is sick while we are in Florida and not tell a soul about this – not her best friend or her sisters," Rachel said. "No one else can know."

"I am in shock about this," Katherine said as she sat down beside Rachel. "It's no secret that Faith has been my favorite all these years. I fell in love with that little girl the first day you brought her home from the hospital. When I looked into that precious face and she wrapped her little hand around my finger, she stole my heart. She was the baby that I was never able to have and she has brought such joy into my life."

"You know the feeling is mutual. Faith loves you unconditionally and I know she will want your support," Rachel said. "Let's talk about this later when I have more of the details worked out."

As Rachel stood and walked toward the library she said, "Now, I need to call my sisters in Florida and see if they can help with this plan."

PART THREE

CHAPTER THIRTEEN

Batavia, New York
January 1966

Rachel was going to need some major assistance from her sisters in Florida. She and Faith would need a place to stay, and Faith would need a doctor and a tutor. With only a few days before school resumed, could they pull this off or would the plan totally unravel?

Julia and Emily rallied and started making calls to their friends and to local real estate offices.

But it was the week between Christmas and New Year's, and many of the offices were working with a skeleton staff. The two sisters were not having any success – seasonal rentals had been reserved months in advance.

While the sisters scrambled to find a rental and locate a tutor, Rachel had contacted the Batavia High School principal and explained that Faith would not be returning to school in January because of a severe case of mono. She was taking Faith to Florida for health reasons.

The principal referred her to the guidance counselor who agreed to contact Faith's teachers and forward lesson plans to her Florida tutor each week. With two feet of snow piling up and freezing temperatures in Batavia, the winter-weary counselor silently wished she was heading to Florida, too.

On New Year's Eve, Emily called Rachel with some promising news. "Our neighbor has a darling guest house on her estate and she is willing to do a seasonal rental. Her sister usually comes to Florida for the winter, but has decided to go to Palm Springs, California, this year instead," Emily said. "It will be perfect for you and Faith. It's private and close to my house, only a chip shot away."

"The only glitch is that our neighbor's son has been visiting during the holidays and the cottage won't be available until Saturday, January 8. Will that work for you?" Emily asked.

"Yes," said Rachel. "That will be perfect. Faith and I will head out early Monday morning and take our time driving south. We will see you on Saturday."

"That's a good date for Julia and me, too," Emily said. "Our kids and holiday guests will be gone by then and we will have an easier time keeping Faith's secret."

"Oh, before I forget," Emily added. "Julia is working on finding a tutor and a doctor. She is confident we will have those professionals lined up before you arrive."

"That's wonderful news," Rachel said. "I will be forever grateful to you and Julia. This has been such a stressful situation for us and it's a relief to know that the pieces are falling into place.

"Rachel, you know you can always count on us. That's what sisters are for," Emily said. "So far, the plan is working. All of her cousins are worried about her having mono and think it's a wise idea for her to recover in Florida."

With the Florida plans finalized, Rachel and Robert heaved a sigh of relief and got ready to attend the annual New Year's Eve Gala at Wexford Country Club. Rachel was wearing an emerald-green satin sheath that matched the stunning emerald necklace Bob had gifted her at Christmas.

As she came down the stairs and entered the living room Robert was looking in the gold leaf mirror above the mantel adjusting his tie. He turned and smiled at her. "You look beautiful! Are you ready to go?" he asked, as he hugged her and wrapped a mink stole around her shoulders.

"Here, I have something special for you," he said. He handed her a white florist box – inside was a wrist corsage of yellow roses.

"Oh Robert, this is so sweet and romantic. It reminds me of our first New Year's Eve so long ago," she said. "You know, this will always be our special night," and gave him a loving kiss.

As they entered Wexford Country Club they were greeted warmly by the veteran staff, some who had known Rachel since her childhood. The club was like a second home to her. Her father had been one of the original founders of the club, and through the years she and her mother had won multiple women's golf club championships. Rachel and Robert had continued the legacy and were the defending couples' champions.

The exclusive club was decorated in understated elegance for the season. Fresh-cut trees and evergreens embellished with gold velvet bows and ribbons adorned each room. Centerpieces of gold pillar candles in oversized glass lanterns gave a soft glow to the paneled walls and guests were warmed by the blazing fire in the massive stone fireplace.

Throughout the evening, Rachel and Robert enjoyed catching up with longtime friends and dancing the night away. As he held her close, they reminisced about 1965. It had been quite a year for them. In February, they received the good news that Rachel had reached a five-year milestone of being cancer free, after having a kidney removed in 1960.

Gloria had given birth during the summer and was happy mothering a baby boy in addition to her six little girls.

Laura was stationed in Japan working for the State Department and had called from Tokyo on Christmas Eve with exciting news. She was engaged! What would her parents think about a summer wedding in the Bradford's backyard?

And then there had been Faith's stunning announcement. They were still struggling with the fact that their immature teenage daughter was dealing with some serious adult issues – the death of a boyfriend and an unplanned pregnancy.

At the stroke of midnight, they kissed and toasted each other with champagne. They knew that 1966 would be another challenging year. However, it would also be filled with happy family memories including Faith's graduation, Laura's wedding and maybe another Club Championship.

CHAPTER FOURTEEN

Batavia, New York
to Ft. Lauderdale, Florida
January 1966

On Monday, January 3, 1966, Robert Bradford helped his wife and daughter load up the car for their trek to Florida. After packing the last of their bags in the Ford Fairlane's roomy backseat, Faith and Rachel gave Robert a final hug and kiss. Then, they were off.

The convertible looked out of place under the gray sky, heavy with the threat of snow. The weather matched his somber mood.

Robert Bradford didn't like the idea of the two women traveling to Florida alone. But he had no choice. It was the busiest time of the year for the shoe industry. Hamilton Shoes was introducing a brand-new product and Robert, the vice-president of sales, was scheduled to travel throughout New England and beyond to unveil the innovative concept to all of the company's major customers.

Rachel was a good driver, but he knew that traveling 1,300 miles on busy highways was different than traipsing across the rural landscape in upstate New York to compete in golf tournaments. To ease his mind, Rachel promised to be cautious, travel only during the daylight hours and call home each evening.

Even though he was concerned, Robert was confident that Rachel could handle the trip. To help with the preparations he sent his secretary to the local AAA office to pick up a Trip Tik for the long drive. The travel information was stuffed into a Do Not Litter bag and contained a fat narrow booklet with a white spiral binding across the top that gave page-by-page, mile-by-mile, directions. The packet also included maps and booklets for each state, highlighting hotels, restaurants and local attractions in each city.

By default, Faith was the designated navigator. Combing through the travel information each day and tracking their location kept her focused on the trip. Conversations concentrated on where they would stay, where they would eat and what attractions they would visit.

As Faith poured through the travel packet, Rachel tried to concentrate on the road. As they drove south through the rural landscape and meandered through the small hamlets of New York State, Rachel found her mind wandering. She was worried about her husband and how Faith's surprise was affecting him. He was a proud man who loved his daughters and would do anything for them. But he had already endured the gossip and inuendo regarding Gloria's risky behavior. Now, his youngest daughter was pregnant and he couldn't bear to have his friends and business associates know, especially Rachel's brother who was now running the shoe company.

Roberts colleagues at the Batavia Club and his poker pals would be sympathetic about his daughter being ill. But this group of conservative businessmen would consider another teenage pregnancy to be disgraceful. Rachel was also grateful that Robert's parents weren't alive. His stern mother would never understand this situation.

Faith interrupted her thoughts. "Mom, we have finished two pages of this Trip Tik and we are almost to Williamsport, Pennsylvania. We just passed a Howard Johnsons' sign and there is one at the next exit. Can we stop there for lunch?"

"That sounds like a good idea," Rachel said.

Howard Johnson's was a major player in the travel industry during the 1960s. Tourists couldn't miss the colorful orange-and-blue billboards along the highway promoting HoJo's ice cream shops, restaurants and motels from Maine to Florida. Faith and Rachel found them to be clean, safe places to stop for meals, restroom breaks and a good night's sleep.

Rachel had decided this would be a fun mother-daughter trip. She didn't want Faith facing this trip with dread. They took their time and visited historical spots, stopping in Gettysburg, Pennsylvania; Charleston, South Carolina; and Savannah, Georgia. While each stop brought slightly warmer temperatures, the travelers encountered rain and fog every day that cast a gray veil over the roadside landscape.

Most of the trip was uneventful, except for the area around Washington, D.C. It was white- knuckle driving for Rachel as she maneuvered through the heavy traffic and avoided the semi- trucks rumbling by. She heaved a sigh of relief when they reached Richmond, Virginia. It was smooth sailing from there.

In addition to the Howard Johnson's billboards, Burma Shave signs randomly popped up along the highways. Faith laughed out loud as she read some of the jingles. "Mom, listen to this one."

This will never
Come to Pass
A back-seat
Driver
Out of Gas
Burma Shave

"I sure hope you don't think I'm a back-seat driver," she snickered.

As they drove another 50 miles, a new set of signs appeared. "Mom, here's another one. This one is hilarious!" Faith giggled.

Ben
Met Anna
Made a hit
Neglected beard
Ben-Anna split
Burma Shave

As they continued to drive through the dreary days in the Carolinas and Georgia, Rachel's thoughts often turned to her three daughters. *And how different they were.*

Laura, her first born and had always been the easy child to raise. She was the complete package, the gifted child who had excelled in everything she tried. The tall beauty with red hair had thrived in Batavia. She had been a dear older sister to Faith, and Rachel smiled remembering how she had hovered protectively over her little sister. "There was a time when I didn't think Faith would ever walk. Between Laura, Katherine and myself, she was always being held."

Laura had excelled in the public schools, and all through high school she had surrounded herself with a large circle of friends who enjoyed hanging out at the Bradford's home. After graduation Laura made an easy transition into college life at the exclusive Beloit College in Wisconsin, where she majored in piano and sang with the voice of an angel.

"She never gave us a minute of worry," Rachel remembered. "We trusted her to make the right decisions, and she did."

Laura had not returned to small town Batavia. She chose the big-city life and began her teaching career in Chicago. Then, opportunity knocked. Rachel and Robert encouraged her to accept the one-year teaching position at the American International School near Tokyo, Japan. They thought it would be a wonderful opportunity for her to learn a different culture. How remarkable that she would meet her future husband in the far-away country.

Gloria came along four years after Laura was born. She was a darling little girl with blonde curly hair. She had lots of energy and from an early age, she loved to be the center of attention. She was bright and had an incredible imagination, but she was not a good student. When Robert and Rachel tried sending her to St. Joseph's, the Catholic elementary school, she came home after the first week, stamped her little foot and declared in a loud voice, "I'm not going back!"

"Why not?" her parents asked, dismayed at the outburst.

"The nuns have too many rules and they won't let me wear my knee socks!" Gloria exclaimed.

The parents relented and she returned to public school, promising to improve her grades.

Gloria's trials and tribulations with the Catholic church continued. Rachel smiled as she remembered Gloria's first communion. The little girl looked angelic in her ruffled white dress, and organza chapel veil. Her family was so proud of her that day as she quietly walked to the altar with the other little children, holding her white-gloved hands in a prayerful position. The children took the sacrament and were instructed to return to their families walking quietly with hands folded.

But not Gloria. She was so excited that she ran back to her parents, shouting to the entire congregation, "I just ate an Oreo cookie!"

Rachel and Robert were embarrassed at the outburst, but Rachel found herself desperately to hide her laughter. On the other hand, Laura was humiliated at her little sister's antics and it would be a long time before she forgave her.

Gloria continued her unruly ways as she grew older. In high school she was the social butterfly, attending all the dances at school and the country club. But unlike her older sister, Gloria didn't always make the best decisions. Gloria was their "wild child" and was attracted to all the "bad boys." When Gloria became pregnant at the end of her senior year, she insisted on getting married. However, the hasty marriage lasted only a few weeks and she filed for divorce.

Through an attorney that Rachel's sister Theresa knew in Rochester, the family had arranged for a private adoption, but at the last moment there was a glitch in the plan. Once Gloria saw her daughter, her motherly instincts kicked in and she refused to sign the adoption papers. Rachel and Robert agreed to raise Bethany until Gloria was on her own.

"That was such a difficult time, I didn't know if we were going to live through it," Rachel recalled.

On a happier note, she thought about Faith, who arrived four years after Gloria. Faith was the youngest child and the sweetest. She was born a few weeks early, and doctors didn't think she would live. "She will always be my miracle baby," Rachel thought.

Faith was a happy child and had been spoiled throughout her life by her parents, Katherine and Laura. She was smart, but not a good student. The Bradfords made another attempt at Catholic grade school that failed. Faith missed her friends and cried to return to public school, promising to study harder.

When it came time for high school, Rachel and Robert made the decision to send Faith to a private girls' school in Pennsylvania, hoping to improve her grades and also removing her from the drama at home with Gloria. After two semesters Faith pleaded to come home – she was homesick for her parents and friends. Again, her parents relented, and this time, she thrived surrounded by a small circle of friends from flag corps and Y-Teens.

Rachel was pleased that Faith and her friends were involved with Y-Teens. The all-girl group was a social organization sponsored by the local YWCA.

They enjoyed doing arts and crafts, learned how to do make-up and were always doing fund-raisers to earn money to attend summer camp at Silver Lake. Rachel admired their advisor, Joyce Reid, an upstanding young woman who had recently graduated from college. She was a good role model and mentor for the impressionable teenage girls.

The only serious misstep that Faith had made was the previous summer, before she had her driver's license. Rachel and Robert were away on a golf outing when Faith let her friend Carol drive Rachel's car. The girl lost control of the Buick Skylark, hit a tree and totaled the car.

Faith was horrified about the accident and was sorry about the damage to her mother's car. While her father was angry that Faith had made such a poor decision, her mother was thankful that no one was hurt. On a positive note, Rachel got a new car, the Ford convertible they were driving to Florida.

To her knowledge, Faith had never had a serious boyfriend and Rachel shook her head as she tried to figure out how she had missed her daughter's involvement with Adam.

Faith stirred and interrupted her thoughts, "Mom, what are you thinking about?"

"Oh, I was just thinking about your sisters. Laura seemed so happy when we talked to her on Christmas Eve. I can't believe it has been five years since we attended her senior recital and graduation in Wisconsin. Now, we are going to be planning a summer wedding," Rachel said. "I'm looking forward to meeting this handsome young diplomat who has stolen her heart."

CHAPTER FIFTEEN

Ft. Lauderdale, Florida
January 1966

During most of the trip Rachel and Faith had stayed at Howard Johnson motels. But they made one special side trip to Charleston and stayed at the Francis Marion Hotel. While the Charleston stop had added an hour to their journey, it had been a special memory for Rachel. As a child Rachel's family had spent the winters in Ft. Lauderdale and during their long treks south, they would always stay at the historic hotel. It had been updated in recent years, but still maintained the elegance and charm she remembered.

While they were in Charleston they needed to deal with some necessities. Faith's clothes were getting snug, and heading into warmer weather, she was not going to be able to hide her baby bump under winter sweaters.

They stopped in a department store and bought a couple of maternity tops. Faith was mortified when the chatty salesgirl started asking about the baby, when it was due, and was the father excited? She also noticed the girl staring at her bare left ring finger. Faith felt her stomach churn, excused herself and rushed to get out of the store. She waited outside and leaned against the building while her mother politely spoke with the girl, paid and carried the shopping bags.

"Oh Mommy, that was so embarrassing. How am I going to deal with this and answer those questions?" Faith asked.

"I told the girl that the baby was due in April and apologized that you had to run off so quickly. I told her you weren't feeling well," her mother replied.

Rachel had been caught off-guard, too. She hadn't thought about how these innocent questions from friendly strangers would affect her unmarried daughter. This was a new experience for both of them. Gloria's first pregnancy was different. She had been married and in the process of a divorce. No secrets there.

She turned to her daughter and said, "Faith, this is going to happen again and I don't want you to get upset. Most people are just trying to be friendly.

They are excited about a baby entering the world, but they have no idea of what you are dealing with and certainly don't need to know all the details. When we get back to the hotel room, let's talk about some possible questions and scenarios that might come up in casual conversations and how you should answer them."

They decided to stick with the basics:
When is the baby due? "In April."
When is your due date? "April 10."
Where is your husband? "He is in the Air Force."
Where is he stationed? "He is stationed at Maxwell Air Force Base in Montgomery, Alabama."
When do you get to join him? "He is receiving specialized training for the next six months. We are not sure where his next assignment will be."
Where are you staying while he is in training? "I'm living with my parents until after the baby is born."
Will he get to be with you when the baby is born? "We hope so."

The next morning, they stopped in the hotel gift shop and Faith searched through the display of handcrafted jewelry. She purchased a pretty silver band with a simple scroll design and slipped it on her left ring finger. "That should take care of any curious stares," she thought.

After the Charleston detour they wound their way along Route 17, a narrow two-lane road, connecting to I-95. Faith was puzzled when her mom stopped in the tiny town of Gardens Corner and pulled into the gravel parking lot of a simple Baptist church. "Why are we stopping here?" Faith asked. "This place is not listed in the AAA book."

"Do you remember hearing the story about my mother – your grandmother – stopping along a road and praying at the scene of an accident? Well, this is where it happened," she replied.

"It's something I will never forget."

"My sisters and I were young. We were driving to Ft. Lauderdale for the winter, stuffed into the Cadillac limousine along with my parents and the nanny. "It had been a long drive down Route 17 and unlike today portions of the road were rutted and unpaved. We girls were impatient and kept asking, 'when are we going to get to Florida?' Then, we reached this very intersection and came upon a horrible accident that had just happened.

"A rusted blue pick-up truck had collided with a huge logging truck and there were men and logs scattered everywhere. Hearing the commotion, people from the church had run out to help the victims and summon an ambulance. 'Oh, how awful,' my mother said. 'Isn't there something we can do?'

"My father didn't see how we could help and wanted to drive on. But mother was stubborn and insisted he stop. She was determined to do something. So, she had all of us pile out of the car, get down on our knees beside the road and pray for the people that were injured." she said. "We never knew what happened to the victims, but your grandmother was confident that the Lord heard our prayers and those people were OK."

***

Five days and 1,000 miles into their trip, they finally crossed the Florida state line. "Yeah!" Faith exclaimed. "We are finally in Florida!"

After days of rain and fog the sun peeked out from behind the clouds and the weary travelers stopped at the Official Florida Welcome Station.

What an experience! Women dressed in cute orange uniforms, white aprons and perky paper hats served free samples of Florida orange juice. Tourists dressed in bright colored T-shirts, jeans and sandals were taking photos in front of the giant welcome sign and reaching into their wallets to purchase souvenirs. Shelves were filled with a bounty of tacky seashell crafts, carved coconut heads, garish sunglasses, and bags of oranges and grapefruit stacked high.

Faith embraced the festive atmosphere. She picked out a green key chain shaped like the state of Florida for her friend Sherri and bought some postcards to send to her sisters. "Mommy, what do you think about buying one of these pirate coconut heads for Daddy," she giggled.

"I don't think so," laughed her mother.

Faith was excited to finally be in Florida but groaned when she looked at the map and realized that Ft. Lauderdale was more than 350 miles away. "Will we ever get there?" she thought.

Patricia Daum

Daytona Beach would be their last night on the road and as Faith was searching through the AAA travel book for a place to stay, she noticed a large colorful ad for the Hawaiian Inn. The four-story crescent-shaped hotel was on the ocean, had a huge pool and boasted a four-star rating. The front portico was designed in the shape of a giant canoe. It was different from the other places they had stayed and it looked like fun. "Let's stay here," she said, describing the hotel to her mother.

"OK, it looks like a good choice for our last night on the road," Rachel said.
They reached the motel mid-afternoon and signed in. The tropical lobby had an impressive waterfall and a winding lagoon filled with colorful carp. A large woman wearing a flowered muumuu greeted them with a warm hug and a kiss on each cheek. As she slipped pink orchid leis around their necks she said. "Aloha. Welcome to the Hawaiian Inn, enjoy your stay!"

As the bellman led them through the lobby and up to their ocean-front room, they walked by a window wall that revealed an Olympic size swimming pool with a two-story water slide. The vast Atlantic Ocean stretched beyond.

"Oh Mom, the ocean looks so beautiful with all the shades of brilliant blue and turquoise. Let's go out and take a walk along the beach," Faith pleaded.

Rachel agreed and after the two had unpacked for the afternoon they went down to sample the beach. The tide was out. "It's so wide here," said Faith. "It goes on forever."

As they walked along the coastline, the wet sand oozed between their toes and the water felt warm on their pale winter feet.

Finishing their walk, they perched on stools at the Tiki Bar and ordered festive tropical drinks served in pineapples garnished with paper parasols – a frozen mai tai for Rachel, a virgin pina colada for Faith.

As the sun began to set, a fit young man in a native Hawaiian sarong approached the Tiki Bar and started the traditional evening ceremonies by blowing long powerful notes on a huge conch shell. Then, flaming torch held high, he ran along the hotel's beach front and lit the tiki torches. What an impressive sight! Rachel and Faith decided to skip the nightly luau in favor of milder fare in the Outrigger Room, but they enjoyed listening to the traditional Hawaiian music from their balcony.

After a restful night lulled to sleep by the sound of the ocean waves, they were ready for the final leg of their trip.

As they were loading the car on Saturday morning, there was an unsettling reminder of how this entire journey had begun. Faith's heart stopped as she noticed the car parked next to them. It was Adam's car – the gold Chevy Impala sports sedan with the huge tailfins!

Her mind was playing tricks. "Oh my God, it can't be Adam's car. That car had been totaled in the accident!" she thought. Frantic, she checked the license plate – the car was from Ohio. Faith blinked back the tears. She hadn't thought about Adam for weeks.

"What's wrong Faith?" her mother asked.

"Oh Mommy, that car next to us is just like Adam's and it made me think about that horrible accident." She replied as she grabbed a Kleenex and wiped away a tear.

"That was such a tragedy," her mother said. "He seemed to be a nice young man and I'm so sorry this happened to you and his family.

"Now, dry your tears and let's think of something more pleasant," she said. "I have an idea. We have about 250 miles to go before we reach Ft. Lauderdale and we finally have a sunny day. Let's put the top down on the convertible and pretend we are famous celebrities traveling incognito."

Rachel pulled some colorful scarves out of the glove compartment. "Let's tie these around our necks and wear our glamorous sunglasses with the white frames. We will look divine," she said.

With scarves blowing in the breeze the mother-daughter duo drove off into the sunshine for the last leg of their trip.

CHAPTER SIXTEEN

Ft. Lauderdale, Florida
January 1966

As she pulled the car in front of the darling guest house that her sisters had found, Rachel was relieved that the long drive was finally over.

She and Faith began to carry in their luggage and explored the cottage. It was furnished in comfortable old-Florida décor with white wicker and faded Lily Pulitzer cushions. The living room had a wall of French doors that opened to a private patio and overlooked a well-manicured lawn and a canal.

They each had their own bedroom with an adjoining bath and there was a small study furnished with a desk and book shelves that Faith could use for her school work. Faith laughed when she first saw her bedroom. The walls were painted bubble-gum pink and the twin bed sported a pink flamingo coverlet and matching sheets. Her mother's room was more traditional – pale blue walls with a seascape coverlet on the double bed.

The kitchen was small and efficient with a cute wooden table and chairs tucked in a cozy corner. The refrigerator and pantry were stocked with basic necessities.

"Aunt Emily and Aunt Julia sure did a wonderful job of finding this place," Faith said.

"Yes, they did and it looks like they thought of everything," Rachel said, admiring the vase of yellow roses her sisters had arranged on the table.

Getting the house set up was just one of the many tasks that the sisters had worked to accomplish. They knew their prayers had been answered when their neighbor's guest house became available. Then came the hectic search for an experienced tutor that they could trust.

They had been discreet in their inquiries. During the search, they stuck with the mono story, figuring the tutor could be told the truth once she was hired. They finally located a qualified woman who had home-tutored a number of students for various reasons – recovery from surgery, serious car accidents and teenage pregnancies.

After checking her references, they were comfortable she would be the perfect fit. Adele Mercer had just finished tutoring a student who had been in an auto accident and she would be available to start right away.

Faith was also going to need a doctor. With her being so young, Julia and Emily reasoned she would be more comfortable with a female doctor and they knew if this pregnancy was going to remain a secret, she needed to see a doctor in a different community.

"Let's try Hollywood, Florida," Julia said. "It's 12 miles south and on the other side of the airport. We shouldn't run into anyone we know."

She called St. Ann's Hospital in Hollywood and spoke with one of the nurses in labor and delivery. "Do you have any women obstetricians that deliver at the hospital?" she asked.

"Yes, we do," the nurse answered. "Dr. Heather Morrison is excellent and I highly recommend her. She delivered my son 10 years ago."

Julia promptly called Dr. Morrison's office and set up an appointment for Faith. With that final call, Julia and Emily had done their job; they had found a house, a tutor and a doctor. Now Rachel and Robert could handle the rest.

The first week in the guest house was a whirlwind. Mrs. Mercer, the tutor, appeared Monday morning and was only slightly surprised when she was told that Faith was pregnant. She assured Rachel and Faith that she had handled these delicate situations before and would be discreet. She would complete the required paperwork for Batavia High School and would continue with the fictional story that Faith was recovering from mono.

"Let's get started," she said to Faith. "I will be coming on Monday, Wednesday and Friday mornings. How does 9am to noon sound to you?" she asked.

"That sounds OK to me," Faith replied turning to her mother who nodded her head in agreement.

"I want to see the books you are using and review the lesson plans your teachers have sent for this week. We don't want you to get behind in your classes," Mrs. Mercer said.

Tuesday morning, Rachel drove Faith to Hollywood for her first appointment at the doctor's office, where the staff of young women greeted her warmly. In their private consultation with Dr. Morrison, Faith and her mother found the doctor to be kind and understanding. She had experience with private adoptions and gave Rachel the number of a couple of attorneys she had worked with.

Then, while Rachel leafed through outdated magazines in the waiting area, the nurse escorted Faith into the exam room. It started out simply enough. As the two chatted, the nurse checked her height, weight, blood pressure and completed a urine test. When the doctor came in, she listened to Faith's heart, the baby's heart and measured her expanding stomach.

Then she told Faith to scoot her bare bottom down to the end of the table and anchor her feet in some medieval looking metal stirrups. Faith wasn't sure what was going to happen. Embarrassed, she clumsily moved so that the doctor could do an internal exam. It was Faith's first.

Thankfully, it was over in a few minutes. As she sat back up on the exam table Dr. Morrison told her that she and the baby were doing fine. Everything was progressing normally and her due date would be around April 15.

"You need to set up an appointment for next month," she said as she left the room.

After Faith got dressed, the nurse returned bearing gifts – a bottle of prenatal vitamins, a brochure on the stages of pregnancy and a plastic urine sample bottle for Faith's next visit.

"Faith, do you have any questions?" she asked, noticing Faith's scarlet face.

"Oh my God, that exam was so embarrassing!" Faith blurted out. "Mom didn't tell me about that! Does that happen every visit?"

"No," Linda replied with an understanding smile. "You won't need another internal exam until closer to your due date."

"That's a relief," Faith said and collected the items the nurse had given her.

During each return visit the staff of young mothers greeted her warmly and Faith began confiding in Linda, her favorite nurse. Faith asked questions about the baby and the changes that were happening to her body. As she got closer to her due date, she was apprehensive about giving birth.

"What should I expect and how painful is this going to be?" she asked.

"The nurses at the hospital will coach you through labor. Just follow their instructions. When it's time for the baby to come, you will receive anesthesia and be put to sleep. When you wake up in the recovery room it will all be over," Linda said. "Faith, you are young and healthy and I know that you are going to do well."

Linda also reassured Faith that giving up the baby for adoption was the right thing to do and was a blessing. "After the baby is born, you will need to put this experience behind you and go live your life," she counseled.

Faith was thankful that she and her mother had created responses for the casual questions about her pregnancy. They cropped up often while sitting in the doctor's waiting room with other mothers-to-be. She avoided reading the magazines and articles about setting up a nursery, selecting a name and caring for a newborn. Someone else would be doing those things.

Her wardrobe was limited. Around the guest house she wore her dad's old dress shirts with the sleeves rolled up, and capris with elastic waists. For trips to the doctor and other outings she had the maternity tops that were purchased in Charleston, plus some cute A-line dresses – hand-me-downs from Aunt Emily and Aunt Julia.

Meanwhile, the planning for the wedding of Faith's eldest sister, Laura, was beginning. In one of her letters, Laura asked Faith to be her maid of honor.

"Oh Mommy, we can't tell Laura that I'm pregnant," Faith pleaded. "She might think badly of me and not want me to be in her wedding."

"You don't need to worry about that," her mother said. "Laura loves you unconditionally, and there is no reason for you to feel guilty about being pregnant. You are not a bad girl, only bad girls use birth control," she said to reassure her daughter. "But we will keep this a secret."

The wedding wouldn't be until July – three months after the baby was born. But there was a slight problem. Laura was living in Japan and wanted the pink silk bridesmaid dress to be made there. Faith needed to send her measurements. Ever resourceful, her mother made a trip to the bridal department at Bloomingdale's and picked out a similar style bridesmaid dress in a size 10, a size larger than Faith's normal size eight.

The sales associate pulled out the tape measure. The two women carefully measured the size 10 dress and Rachel promptly sent the measurements to Laura. Rachel knew of a skilled seamstress in Batavia that could make any last-minute alterations. She knew from experience that it was easier to take in than   let   out.

CHAPTER SEVENTEEN

Ft. Lauderdale, Florida
January 1966

Adele Mercer was Faith's tutor and she showed up promptly three mornings each week. The tall, full-figured woman with short, curly brown hair was always smartly dressed and had a warm smile and personality. She was a former high school English teacher, now working for a private company that offered in-home tutoring. She enjoyed the one-on-one relationships with her students and took pride in their accomplishments.

Faith and Adele settled into a comfortable routine and followed the lesson plans coming from Batavia High School. There were books to read and book reports for English Literature; reading assignments and tests for American History; special projects for Art History and daily exercises in Typing.

Her tutor quickly learned that Faith was not an enthusiastic student, but with encouragement would finish each assignment. She sensed the teenager was homesick for her friends and feeling somewhat trapped in the guest house. After a couple of weeks, she could see that her student was overloaded with reading and reports. Adele decided to get creative and inject some interest in those subjects.

"I have an idea. How about us taking field trips for some of your assignments?" she suggested. "I think you need to get out and about and your secret will be safe. No one will make the family connection if you are with me."

"That sounds wonderful," Faith said. "Where should we go?"

"To start, we can visit the library and book stores to pick up some of the classic books you are supposed to read," Adele said. "We won't tell your teacher, but we can pick up some Cliff Notes to help you understand the symbolism of what the writer is 'really saying."

"I like that idea," Faith said. "Some of those books are so boring."

"In your Art History class, you are studying the Birth of Impressionism and Post Impressionism. I noticed in the paper that a local museum is featuring an exhibit of some of those painters. I think it would be interesting to visit that exhibit and you can pick up some brochures and postcards to help with a report," Adele said. "Since you are supposed to be recovering from mono, we will just tell your teacher that I visited the exhibit and picked up the information for you," she said. "That's a start. I'm sure we will come up with some other ideas, and they don't always have to involve your classes."

The plan worked. Faith looked forward to the outings and with the one-on-one tutoring, she improved her grades.

Through the years Adele had worked with a number of pregnant teenagers, but this case was different. While other families had been angry and disappointed in their daughters and put them on a major guilt trip about getting pregnant, this family was different – they had surrounded the girl in a cocoon of love and understanding. They had decided what was best for her future.

Adele also sensed that Faith was disconnected and in denial about the pregnancy. It was as if this was happening to someone else, not her. One morning Faith finally opened up. She and Adele were touring the Botanical Gardens when they saw a young mother pushing a buggy along the path. Adele noticed the baby girl was dressed in a pink pinafore and matching hat. She paused a moment and said, "What a beautiful baby," causing the adoring mother to beam.

Faith smiled and nodded at the mother. Once they had passed, she was quiet for a moment, then she turned to Adele and said, "Sometimes I wonder what this baby will look like?"

"What did the baby's father look like?" Adele asked, surprised by the sudden statement.

"Well, Adam was really cute, almost six feet tall, thin, with sandy brown hair and deep blue eyes," she said wistfully. "I wonder what he would think about this baby?"

"I'm guessing from your description that you will have an adorable baby with light hair and blue eyes," Adele replied.

"Who knows what Adam would think. The big question is what do **you** think about all of this?"

"I don't ask a lot of questions because it makes my parents sad," Faith said.

"They have taken care of everything for me and they have made the best decision for my future. I know that I am not ready to be a mother, maybe someday, but not now. I just hope that this baby will be as lucky as I have been with my family."

CHAPTER EIGHTEEN

Ft. Lauderdale, Florida
April 1966

As the weeks passed and her waistline expanded, Faith would occasionally feel the tiny life stir inside her. She sometimes wondered what would happen to the baby, but her mother reassured her that a loving family who wasn't able to have a child of their own would give the baby a wonderful home. Faith didn't need to worry about anything. She would have the baby, go back to Batavia and have a promising future.

Faith and Rachel had enjoyed their time in Florida, and having Adele as her private tutor had been a bonus. While Faith was working with Adele and sitting in the sunshine completing her lessons, Emily and Julia had kept Rachel busy playing golf and bridge and making plans for Laura's summer wedding. Her mother and aunts had been careful to conceal the pregnancy and it helped that the landlady was away. The woman had decided to join her sister in California.

It had been a blessing that the aunts lived nearby. Rachel and Faith spent many evenings at their homes playing cards and watching TV. They laughed at the antics on *Bewitched, I Dream of Jeannie* and *Gilligan's Island*. The silly shows were a welcome relief from the national news stories about the war in Vietnam and the protests that were going on throughout the country.

Back home in Batavia, Sherri and her other friends from Y-Teens were concerned about Faith's health. They sent cards and letters to keep her up to date on their activities and to let her know how much they missed her. Sherri was no longer seeing Wayne and had a new boyfriend. The girls in flag corps were learning new routines and marching at the basketball games. Y-Teens were planning their annual food drive and it was almost time to order graduation announcements.

"When are you coming home?" they asked.

"Soon, I hope," Faith replied. "I'm getting stronger everyday but the doctor says my immune system is still weak. She thinks it best that I wait to return to school until right after spring break. I'm so homesick to see everyone."

Faith's mother was feeling homesick, too. Although her sisters had kept her busy and she had been able to play golf, she missed her friends in Batavia. And of course, she missed Robert. Her husband had visited a couple of times – in February and most recently for their anniversary in March. But most of his time during those trips was spent making arrangements for a private adoption.

Robert had met with a respected attorney in Hollywood, where Faith would have her baby. The plan was for the adoptive parents to take the newborn home from the hospital and their names would be on the birth certificate.

On Easter Sunday, with Faith's aunts keeping an eye on their very pregnant niece, Rachel took the opportunity to attend Mass. Her heart was uplifted by the Easter service, full of hope and celebration.

Her spirits renewed; Rachel anticipated the week ahead. Faith was scheduled to go into the hospital on Tuesday. It would be a trying time, but it would mark a new beginning for two families.

CHAPTER NINETEEN

Hollywood, Florida
April 12, 1966

On a glorious spring day in April, two days after Easter, Faith gave birth at St. Ann's Hospital. Her labor was induced, and relatively short. She was put under "twilight sleep" for the delivery and, according to plan, she never saw the baby.

During Faith's labor and delivery, Rachel was the lone figure in the fathers' waiting lounge. As the hours ticked away, she leafed through dog-eared magazines and sipped bitter coffee from the vending machine. A nurse had stopped by earlier with an update. "Faith is doing fine. She is responding well to the medication and dilating quickly. It shouldn't be a lot longer," the nurse reported.

But Rachel couldn't stop worrying – she kept remembering Faith's difficult birth. The baby had arrived weeks early, blue and not breathing. Rachel closed her eyes and said a silent prayer that her miracle child – still only a teenager – did not experience any such ordeal.

When she opened her eyes, Dr. Morrison was approaching and sat beside her. "Mrs. Bradford, Faith did great. The labor was short and she came through the delivery without any problems. She told me labor felt like really bad menstrual cramps," the doctor said.

"We will keep Faith in recovery for a few hours and then move her to a private room on the third floor. You can visit her this afternoon during regular visiting hours."

"That's wonderful news," Rachel said. "I'm so relieved that Faith is doing well. What about the baby?"

"Faith had a healthy baby girl. She weighs a little over six pounds and has all her fingers and toes," Dr. Morrison said with a smile.

Although she would never see the baby, Rachel thought of her own three daughters and could easily picture the tiny infant. The baby was her granddaughter, but Rachel thought only of the loving family who would be overjoyed by this new addition to their lives.

Dr. Morrison told her that the hospital had already contacted the adoptive parents, and Rachel felt pleased that all the planning of the past few months had paid off.

As they parted, Rachel expressed her appreciation, "Dr. Morrison, I want to thank you and your staff for your kindness and understanding during this difficult chapter of our family's life. We will be forever grateful to you for the excellent care you have provided."

"It's been my pleasure to meet your family," Dr. Morrison said. "You have handled this unplanned pregnancy with dignity and grace and surrounded Faith with love and support. In my experience, that doesn't usually happen."

"We probably won't see you again," Rachel said. "Faith and I will be heading back home as soon as she is released from the hospital.

As the two women stood and exchanged a warm hug, Rachel said. "Thank you again."

Before she called her husband with the wonderful news, she headed toward the small Chapel that she had noticed near the waiting room. She slipped into the simple pew and thanked God for Faith's safe delivery and a healthy baby. As she sat quietly, a calmness swept over her and she felt the weight of the world lift from her shoulders.

It only lasted a moment.

The chapel door opened and a tall nun in full white habit swept in and sat beside her.

"Mrs. Bradford?"

"Yes," Rachel replied with concern. "Is everything alright?"

"I'm Sister Cecelia, the Director of Labor and Delivery. Faith and the baby are fine, but there has been a complication," she said. "The adoption has fallen through. The couple wanted a boy."

"Oh, that can't be!" Rachel said, panic rising as she spoke. "What are we going to do now? We can't take this baby home with us."

"I'm so sorry this has happened, but I want you to know that we will do everything we can to make sure the baby is taken care of," Sister Cecelia said. "The baby needs to stay in the hospital for a few days, so you will have time to figure this out. Maybe the attorney knows of another couple waiting for a baby girl."

"I hope so," Rachel said. "This is so upsetting. We thought we had everything in place."

"Mrs. Bradford, in cases like this we work with Children's Home Society and they always have a list of qualified parents who are waiting for a baby," Sister Cecelia said in a reassuring voice.

"Thank you," Rachel said trying to gather herself. "I will call the attorney right away to see if he has another family in mind. If he doesn't have someone, I will let you know."

The pay phone was located just outside the chapel door and with trembling hands, Rachel closed the cubicle door for privacy. Then, she fumbled through her pocketbook for change and the attorney's business card.

Her heart was racing, but she took a deep breath and said in a steady voice, "Hello, this is Rachel Bradford. I would like to speak with Spencer Howard. We   have   a   problem."

CHAPTER TWENTY

Hollywood, Florida
April 12-15,1966

Spencer Howard was a fixture in the South Florida legal community. He was a local boy who had grown up in Hollywood, the son of an attorney. He had been an outstanding football player in high school and was heavily recruited by the University of Miami. His star power continued to rise during the Hurricane's winning seasons and everyone knew his name.

As a result, a few years later when he graduated from the University of Miami's law school, he was highly sought after by the major law firms in Miami. He declined their offers, preferring to return to his hometown and join his father in a small practice specializing in family law.

After practicing for 20 years, Spencer still loved his job and the variety that each day brought. Through his family and childhood friends he had developed a clientele that included some of the more prominent members of the community and they trusted him to be discreet with their private affairs. Dr. Heather Morrison was a member of his circle of friends and had referred the Bradford family to him.

Earlier in the year, Robert Bradford had met with Spencer and explained the situation with his 17-year-old daughter. "Her mother and I have decided the baby should be given up for adoption and we want to find a good home for the infant. Can you help us?" Robert asked.

"Yes, you have come to the right place. I have facilitated dozens of successful adoptions," Spencer replied.

"The way it usually works is a private individual like yourself comes in and lets me know they have a daughter who will be giving a baby up for adoption. Sometimes I receive a call from a doctor's office, that they have a patient who wants a private adoption and they refer the patient to me. Other times an individual will call and ask me if I know of a baby that will be available," he said.

Patricia Daum

"While I am discreet and keep everything confidential, you must know that I play by the rules," Spencer said. "You may be aware that there was a huge scandal in the 1950s involving baby brokers in the state of Florida – unscrupulous people selling babies for profit. I want you to know that I refused to be involved in that horrible racket.

"You can be assured that the adoptive parents I work with have been carefully screened by Children's Home Society," Spencer said.

"I am relieved to hear that," Robert said. "My wife and I are so sad about this whole situation but we want what's best for our daughter and the baby."

"It's important to us that the baby go to a good home, but we also want to be guaranteed that this adoption is kept secret," he added. "We want our daughter to be able to put this whole episode behind her and get on with her life."

"Mr. Bradford, this will be a private adoption and the file will be closed. You can be confident that no one will ever know about this, unless you or your family decide to share the information," Spencer said.

"What do we need to do to begin this part of the process?" Robert asked.

"Since your daughter is a minor, I have some legal forms that I need for you and your wife to complete. There's also a form requesting some general family background information to share with the adoptive family. You can fill out and return to me," Spencer said.

"Do you have a family in mind?" Robert asked.

"Yes," Spencer replied. "There is a wonderful family I know from my country club who have been waiting for months for a healthy white baby. They have completed the CHS screening process and I feel sure they would be thrilled to adopt a precious infant with your family's background."

"Thank you so much," Robert said. "It's a pleasure to meet you and I'm so glad you are taking care of this. It's a huge burden lifted off our shoulders."

"It's my privilege to work with your family," Spencer said. "I am always delighted in seeing the joy that a baby brings to a waiting family.

After Robert Bradford's initial visit, Spencer worked with Rachel to complete the preliminary forms and paperwork for the adoption. He reassured her the baby was going to a loving home and the adoption would remain a secret. Everything was ready, the final surrender papers would be signed three days after the baby was born.

When Rachel called from the hospital the morning of April 12, he took her call right away. He was expecting to hear that Faith had delivered the baby and they could proceed with the adoption.

He wasn't prepared to learn that the couple had backed out. "What jerks!" he shouted, as he hurled their file across the room. "They never told me they only wanted a boy!"

"Spencer, what are we going to do?" Rachel asked in a panicked voice. "We had this all planned. I can't believe this family backed out!"

"Rachel, I'm so sorry this has happened. I have dealt with similar situations before and I promise you we will find another caring family for Faith's baby," he said in a calm, reassuring voice.

"Spencer, we only have three days before they release Faith and the baby from the hospital. Can you work that fast?" she asked. "Sister Cecelia said if you don't have a family lined up, they will take the baby to Children's Home Society and then find a home for her."

"Can you please help us?" she pleaded. "We can't leave Florida without knowing she has a family."

"Rachel, I know this is very upsetting to you, but please don't worry. I will take care of this and we will find a family for the baby," Spencer said. "Let me get to work and I will call you tomorrow, hopefully with good news."

After talking with the attorney, Rachel's next call was to her husband. "How is Faith?" he asked. "What about the baby?"

Rachel kept her composure and said, "Faith is doing fine. She delivered a healthy baby girl this morning." But then overcome with the stressful situation, she began to cry.

Patricia Daum

"Robert, something awful has happened!"

"What's wrong?" he asked, with fear rising in his chest. "Did something happen to Faith?"

"No, no," she said. "It's the adoption – it fell through!"

Rachel told him about the family changing their mind, and that the baby might be turned over to Children's Home Society if they couldn't find another family.

"That's dreadful!" her husband shouted. "I will call the attorney right away."

"Robert, I've already made that call," she said. "Spencer was really upset that the family backed out but told me he had another family in mind. He promised he would call me tomorrow."

"Well, that's encouraging news," Robert said. "I guess we have no choice. We will have to wait until tomorrow."

"Rachel, I love you, and I am so sorry that I'm not there to help you," he said trying to comfort her from afar. "Tell Lammy Jammies that I'm very proud of her and give her a hug for me."

It was finally time for visiting hours and Rachel was eager to see her daughter. She rushed in to hug Faith and was relieved to see her sitting up and looking rested. Rachel had stopped in the hospital gift shop to pick up a cheery bouquet of yellow and white daisies and as she sat them on the night table she asked, "How are you feeling?"

"Oh Mommy, I'm OK. It wasn't as dreadful as I had imagined," Faith replied. "The nurses and Dr. Morrison were very kind to me the entire time. They have given me some medication to dry up my milk and the nurse told me my swollen tummy will begin to return to normal in a couple of weeks. I'm sore where Dr. Morrison did the incision, but other than that I feel fine."

"I'm just happy that it's over," she said with a sigh of relief.

"Faith, I talked with your dad a little while ago and he said to tell you he was very proud of you and he can hardly wait for us to get home," she said.

"He's not the only one," Faith said. "I'm homesick to see Daddy and my friends."

"Mom, I know it makes you sad to talk about the baby, but I need to know something. I overheard the nurses whispering in the recovery room that the adoption had fallen through. They said I had a baby girl and the couple wanted a boy. Is that true? What's going to happen to the baby?" Faith asked.

Rachel bit her lip and pondered how much she should tell her daughter. "Faith, you had a healthy baby girl who will be a blessing for a special family," she said. "We were very upset when we learned that the adoptive couple backed out and I called the attorney right away. Spencer said he is working with another couple.

"Please don't worry. Your dad and I have taken care of this and the baby will go to a good home," she reassured her daughter.

"That's great news," said Faith. "Now when do I get to go home?"

"Dr. Morrison said she will release you on Friday. I'll make sure I have all of our belongings packed in the car and we will be on our way home to Batavia," her mother said.

The next morning Rachel received a call from Spencer. Her prayers were answered – he had found another loving family who would welcome a baby girl.

During her brief stay in the hospital, Faith had a few visitors. Her mother came each day, along with Aunt Emily and Aunt Julia who brought gifts – an armload of magazines including the newest issues of Seventeen, Mademoiselle and Teen Screen, featuring Faith's favorite rock group, the Beatles.

Adele also brought a gift – Faith's test scores and final grading report. Faith was excited to receive an A- on the research paper she had written and typed about Amelia Earhart. Faith had found it interesting that Earhart had taken off from nearby Miami Municipal Airport on her final fateful journey.

"Adele, thank you. This is my best report card ever. I might even make the honor roll this grading period. That will be a first," Faith said with a smile.

"Faith, it's been my pleasure to work with you during the past few months," Adele said. "You have accomplished your goals and we have prepared you for a promising future. Now it's time for you to get back to New York and have fun being a teenager again.

Good bye and good luck," Adele said as she gave Faith a parting hug. "I will never forget you."

Sister Cecelia also made a special effort to come sit with her one afternoon and they talked about Faith's plans for when she returned home – her graduation, her sister's wedding and college in the fall.

Sister Cecelia had avoided talking about the baby, but as she was leaving, she stood next to Faith's bed and said, "Faith, I truly believe that it was part of God's plan that you should have this baby. She is a blessing from above and will bring countless joy and love to her new family. He has something special planned for your life. Good luck and may God bless you."

Two days later, when Faith checked out of the hospital, she and her mother drove promptly to the attorney's office, a charming cottage with a white picket fence, located on a quiet street near downtown Hollywood. Spencer greeted them warmly and reassured them the baby was going to a wonderful family. The names of the adopting parents would be listed on the official birth certificate and the adoption sealed. Faith could go on with her life, and she didn't need to worry about her secret getting out.

The mother and daughter signed the official release papers and hurried back to the car. They sat there for a few moments and cried. It was a difficult moment for mother and daughter, but Rachel knew they had made the right decision. They had given a beautiful gift of life to a loving family.

They never spoke of the baby again.

Drying their tears, they said goodbye to Florida. Once again, they put on the colorful scarves and white sunglasses. With the convertible top down and scarves blowing in the breeze the mother-daughter duo headed North, destination Batavia, New York, and the next chapter of Faith's life.

PART FOUR

CHAPTER TWENTY- ONE

Opa Locka, Florida
April 10,1966

Easter weekend had been a fun time for the Whitmer family. Anne and Bob Whitmer were brimming with excitement as they prepared surprises for their 4-year-old son, Todd.

On Saturday night once Todd was asleep, Anne put together an overflowing Easter basket for her son. It was filled with a large chocolate bunny, foil-covered chocolate eggs and black jelly beans, Todd's favorite. A colorful kite poked out of the basket along with a package of Matchbox cars. Strands of the green Easter grass kept tumbling out as Anne hid the festive basket.

Meanwhile, Bob had carefully made a bunny footprint trail on the tile floor using a rubber stamp and flour – beginning at Todd's bedroom door, winding throughout the house and ending in a corner of his parents' bedroom under an empty bassinet. Along the trail Bob hid colorful plastic eggs filled with coins and tiny treasures.

Their efforts were rewarded on Easter morning as Todd squealed with delight, following the bunny trail and finding the glorious Easter basket. Before his parents could stop him, he stuffed a handful of black jelly beans in his mouth.

"Mom Mom, look what I got," Todd yelled as he saw his grandmother in the doorway and rushed toward her for a hug and a jelly bean kiss.

Anne's mother lived next door in the adjoining duplex and while hearing the happy commotion, she had opened the door between the two homes. As she reached down to hug her grandson she said, "You better not eat too much candy this morning – you have to be ready for our big Easter dinner."

Mom Mom had already spent days baking pies and cookies for the celebration and today the big ham roasting in the oven sent a mouth-watering aroma throughout the two homes. While Mom Mom stayed home and made her final preparations, Bob, Anne and Todd donned their new outfits and headed to the Opa Locka Methodist Church for the Easter service.

When they returned home, they welcomed their relatives – brothers, sisters, nieces and nephews – all bearing their favorite side dishes. The huge holiday buffet seemed to disappear as quickly as it was set out, everyone taking heaping seconds and thirds.

As everyone settled down after the feast, Anne and her sisters Karen and Vicky headed to the kitchen for clean-up duty.

"What's happening with the adoption?" Karen asked. "I noticed you have the bassinet setting out in your bedroom."

"When we were getting the Easter decorations out of the attic, Bob pulled the bassinet down. He decided that we shouldn't wait until the very last minute, so he repainted it and I bought a new mattress and pad plus the ruffled skirt. It was so much fun picking out something pink!" Anne explained.

"That's so sweet!" Karen said. "It will be good to have something in place when you finally get the call."

"Karen and Vicky, we felt like we had to do something," Anne said. "We have been on the waiting list at Children's Home Society for more than two years. The paperwork was filled out months ago, we had extensive background checks, and they made an initial visit to the house last year.

"Last month when I spoke with Christy, our social worker, she told me that we have been approved, but it's taking longer since we want a healthy, white baby girl. And the fact that we already have a child slows the process," Anne said.

"How much longer do you think it will be?" Vicky asked.

"Christy said to just be patient, our request is working its way to the top of the list and eventually we will get a baby. She had another client who waited three years," Anne answered with a groan.

"You are having the longest pregnancy ever! Have you ever thought about trying the private adoption route?" Vicky asked.

"We have considered that, but it's a long process, too," Anne replied.

"And sometimes problems occur with that route. A friend of ours had a mother back out at the last moment. After waiting all this time, we are just sticking with CHS," she said.

The family had no way of knowing that their precious baby girl was on her way.

CHAPTER TWENTY-TWO

Opa Locka, Florida
April 12,1966

When Dr. Morrison returned to her office after Faith's delivery, she was bombarded with questions from the excited office staff. "How is Faith? What did she have? How is the baby?"

After assuring them that Faith and the baby girl were fine, she said. "But, there's a problem – the adopting family backed out – they wanted a boy."

"That's awful!" Nurse Linda exclaimed. "What's her family going to do?"

"They are not sure. When I left the hospital, Faith's mom was calling the attorney to see if he had another family in mind. If he doesn't have someone, the next step would be to turn the baby over to Children's Home Society for placement," Dr. Morrison replied. "Her mother is against that idea and doesn't want to leave for New York until they know the baby has a home."

"Dr. Morrison, I need to have a private conversation with you," Linda said as she followed the doctor into her private office. "I know of a family who wants to adopt a baby girl and they would give Faith's baby a wonderful home. Do you think I should call the attorney?"

"It's worth a try," the doctor replied. "Here's Spencer's contact information. Call him right away."

Spencer Howard was in a difficult situation. The private adoption had been going smoothly. The birth mother was a girl from a wealthy family and neither she nor the birth father had a history of drugs or mental health issues. The adoptive family had been approved by CHS and everything was set for the couple to bring the baby home from the hospital. He couldn't believe they had backed out at the last minute.

He knew of another family who might be interested, but it would take weeks for them to go through the CHS process to be approved. And during that time, the baby would be housed in the nursery at McLamore House in Miami. He couldn't with good conscience tell the Bradford family that he had a family lined up, when everything was so uncertain. While he wasn't a particularly devout man, he closed his eyes and said a silent prayer.

A short time later, he received a call from Linda, the nurse in Dr. Morrison's office. "Mr. Howard, I just heard about the people backing out of the adoption of Faith Bradford's baby. Do you have another couple lined-up?" she asked. "If not, I have a wonderful family to recommend who desperately want a baby girl, and they have been screened and approved by Children's Home Society."

"Linda, this is great news, tell me more," Spencer said, not believing his luck.

"They are good friends of my family and live in Opa Locka. Bob Whitmer is a skilled mechanic in the airlines industry and his wife Anne, is a stay-at-home mom. They have a 4-year-old boy and are unable to have another child of their own. They have been on a waiting list at CHS for more than two years. I would be so happy for them if they could adopt Faith's baby and I know she would go to a good home," she said.

"Linda, your call is an answer to my prayer," Spencer replied. "I would be very interested in talking with this family. Please have them call me today. The baby will be released from the hospital in three days and I need to take care of this as soon as possible."

"Thank you, Mr. Howard. I will call my friend right away," Linda said, hanging up the phone and immediately dialing Anne Whitmer's number.

Anne was fixing lunch for her son, Todd, when she received the call. "Anne please sit down; I have some exciting news for you. Your baby girl has arrived," Linda said.

"What do you mean?" Anne asked. "Is this a joke?"

"No, it's true," Linda said as she explained the situation. "But you must call the attorney immediately if you are interested. Good Luck!"

The afternoon was a blur – Anne **never** called Bob at work, but today was the exception.

"Please page Bob Whitmer," she told the receptionist. "Yes, this is a family emergency!"

Her frantic husband answered the phone. "What's wrong?" he asked.

"Oh, Bob," she cried. "A perfect baby girl was born this morning. If we want her, we have to meet with an attorney in Hollywood later today."

"Whoa, sweetheart, this is good news!" he said. "I was terrified that something had happened to you or Todd. I'm so relieved! Give me a few more details."

She told him about the amazing call from Linda, the precious baby and the failed private adoption. When she finished, Bob said, "Yes, we want this baby girl!"

Anne set up an appointment with the attorney and they met with him that same afternoon after Bob finished his shift.

Spencer Howard was delighted to meet this fine hard-working couple. They already had a child and would know what to do with a newborn. CHS had cleared them, so that hurdle was cleared. But he could tell they were worried about something as they began filling out the legal documents for the adoption. Spencer asked if they had any questions.

"Well, Mr. Howard, we don't really know much about private adoptions," Bob said. "We were wondering how much your attorney's fees are. We might have to dip into our savings account."

Spencer smiled reassuringly, relieved that this was their only concern. "Mr. and Mrs. Whitmer, your savings are safe from me. I have already been paid by the birth mother's family, so all you will be responsible for is the CHS adoption fee," he said.

He noticed the Whitmers relaxed a bit as they continued signing the paperwork. When he had collected everything in a folder, he said, "I have been in contact with, your social worker, Christy Ferguson, this afternoon. We are hopeful that we can complete this process quickly so that you can bring the baby home from the hospital."

He shook hands with the beaming couple as they departed his office and then picked up the phone to share the good news with Rachel Bradford.

When he finished that conversation, he felt such great satisfaction, having helped two families. The Whitmers would be adopting a longed-for daughter and the Bradfords could return to New York, secure in the knowledge that the baby girl had found a loving home and that Faith could move on with her life.

CHAPTER TWENTY-THREE

Opa Locka, Florida
April-May 1966

Unfortunately, the adoption process didn't go as quickly as Spencer had hoped.

Even though the Whitmers had been approved and were on the Children's Home Society waiting list, there was additional paper work to be completed, plus a final home visit, before the baby could be theirs.

Instead of the Whitmers taking the baby home from the hospital, their social worker, Christy, took her to the McLamore House in Miami. It was a large facility run by CHS that held dozens of infants and children of all ages awaiting foster homes or adoption.

The day Christy arrived with the sleeping bundle, the nursery was full and the baby girl was gently placed in a white crib that she shared with another infant.

Christy tried her best to speed the process along but dealing with the government red-tape was maddening. It would take more than three weeks before baby girl Whitmer could go home.

The Whitmers were eager to have the baby join their family. But Christy advised them to take advantage of the time to get everything ready for her and if possible, to make some changes at their home to assure the final home visit would go well.

"CHS would prefer the baby have a room of its own," she confided.

"Are you kidding?" they replied. "That has never been mentioned before!"

They sprang into action. Their comfortable two-bedroom home was on one side of a duplex. Anne's mother lived on the other side. The two homes were connected by a door that was usually open and made a larger home for the family to enjoy, especially when aunts and uncles visited. Mom Mom adored her young grandson and her second bedroom had become Todd's playroom. With her blessings, it was quickly converted into a new bedroom for Todd.

97

Anne and Bob wanted Todd to be happy about this change and didn't want him to feel displaced. So, he helped them select the green paint for the walls, hung his clothes in the closet and carefully moved his treasured possessions into the new space.

Todd was excited when the furniture company delivered the bunk beds and was thrilled when his mom dazzled him with bedspreads and curtains featuring his favorite animals – dinosaurs. Everyone was glad he would have a couple of weeks to adjust to his new room.

Once Todd settled in, it was time to tackle the nursery. Time was running out before the final home visit. Bob stayed up late one night painting the walls a pale pink. Anne's friend gave her a pretty maple crib that her little girl had outgrown, and Anne found a vintage dresser with a harp mirror at the local antique store. A quilted pad on the top served as a changing table.

Anne and her mother went shopping at J.C. Penney's and picked out a pretty pink-and-white ruffled gingham crib set with matching bumper pads and curtains. Then, Bob's brother showed up with a family heirloom – a beautiful curly maple rocking chair that Bob's dad had made years ago. It had been used for each grandchild.

On Sunday April 24, Anne's friends and family surprised her with a baby shower…everything in pink. There were adorable newborn outfits, gowns, sleepers and frilly dresses. There was a baby bath tub, soft towels, stacks of new diapers and a basket filled with baby essentials including lotion, powder and Q-tips. One friend had embroidered and framed a pastel Noah's Ark picture and found a matching nursery lamp, while Anne's sisters pooled their resources and bought a fancy pink stroller. It was such a happy day and everyone was excited about the baby girl.

"Have you decided on a name?" they asked.

"Yes," Anne replied. "After lots of discussion we have decided to call her Penny, Penny Suzanne Whitmer. We were able to honor both sides of our families. As you know, Penney is my maiden name, and Suzanne was my mother-in-law's name."

"Bob said she will always be our Lucky Penny," Anne added.

The following morning as she washed and folded each cherished item and hung the tiny outfits in the closet, she knew they were ready. Big Brother Todd didn't go to the shower, but he helped his mom unpack all the presents and had a surprise of his own. He and his dad had gone shopping and Todd had picked out a present for the baby – a soft pink bunny for her to cuddle. As he placed the bunny in the crib, Anne gave him a big hug and planted a kiss on his cheek.

"What a sweet gift. Your baby sister will love it and I know you are going to be a good big brother," she said.

Anne and Bob were exhausted. They had accomplished an incredible amount of work in two weeks, now they were ready for their baby girl. On April 28, Christy and her supervisor made the final home visit. "This is one of the sweetest nurseries I have ever seen," Christy said.

"Yes, it is lovely," said Mrs. Curtis, her supervisor, soothing the Whitmers' jangled nerves.

"We have all your records in order, including the legal adoption papers from the attorney. I will file the final paperwork today and you should be able to bring the baby home sometime next week," said Mrs. Curtis.

"Can you tell us what day?" Anne asked. "Bob will need to request time off from work."

"I will give you a call just as soon as I know." Mrs. Curtis promised.

"Anne, do you have a 'coming home outfit' for the baby?" Christy asked. "I will make sure she is wearing it when you come to pick her up."

"Yes," Anne said as she handed Christy the gift box tied with a pink satin ribbon.

The wait was frustrating, but the call finally came on Wednesday, May 4.

"Baby Girl Whitmer is ready to come home," Christy announced with excitement. "You can pick her up tomorrow morning. Does 10am work for you?"

Patricia Daum

"That's wonderful news!" Anne said. "We can hardly wait."

May 5, 1966, was a bright sunny day in Miami, Florida, 84 degrees, a brilliant blue sky with wispy clouds. The Whitmer family – Bob, Anne and Todd – wearing their Easter Sunday best, climbed into their car, ready to welcome a baby girl into their family

The McLamore Children's Center on Fifteenth Street in Miami was an imposing two-story green building, a modern concrete block and stucco structure with dozens of windows. It didn't look welcoming, but as they entered the reception area they were ushered into a cheery receiving room.

"Please wait here, Christy will be with you shortly," the receptionist said.

The receiving room was painted in a pastel blue with framed artwork of smiling children playing in the ocean. Todd sat at a child-size table playing with a bright yellow Fisher Price school bus, filling the small round seats with assorted little people. Bob and Anne sat nervously in the blue plastic chairs. Bob, tapping his feet, Anne chewing on her bottom lip.

Finally, Christy appeared with a giant smile on her face. "Good morning, I'm so happy for all of you, this is an exciting day for your family," she said. "Todd would you like to come with me to pick out your baby sister?" she asked, reaching for the little boy's hand.

"Yes," he said with hesitation and glanced at his parents.

"You go ahead," Anne said. "We will be waiting right here for you."

Christy took his hand and they walked into the next room. There she was – a tiny bundle wrapped in a pink blanket lying in a bassinet. Todd learned over to get a closer look.

"What do you think of her?" Christy asked.

"She is so little," Todd said. "And she doesn't have much hair."

"Would you like to hold her?" Christy asked. "If you will sit down on this chair, I'll show you how."

"We have to be careful." She said as she placed the baby in his lap and cradled the infant's head in the crook of his arm. At that moment his baby sister opened her deep blue eyes and stared at her brother.

"Todd, I know you are going to be a wonderful big brother," Christy said.

"Now let's go in the next room and let your parents meet your baby sister, OK?"

"I will carry the baby but I need a strong big brother to carry this bag of supplies that your sister is going to need. Will you carry it for me?" Christy asked.

"Yes," Todd replied as he hopped out of the chair and grabbed the pink diaper bag.

Anne and Bob were in the next room standing next to the door, eavesdropping. Christy had repeated this same routine many times before and had told them what to expect. Social workers had learned it was beneficial to the big brother or sister to be introduced to the new baby all by themselves.

For years to come Todd would say, "I picked out my baby sister."

Finally, the parents got to see their baby daughter. When Christy handled this bundle of love to Anne and Bob, they melted. She had fair skin, a cap of blonde peach fuzz and the deepest blue eyes they had ever seen.

"She's perfect!" they exclaimed. And when she wrapped her tiny fingers around theirs, they bonded instantly.

"It's love at first sight," Bob said.

Anne would always remember this day and just how precious Penny looked in her coming home outfit. The long pink gown was made from the softest cotton and had a pink collar trimmed in white lace. The front of the gown was smocked in tiny pink rosebuds and it closed at the bottom with a pink satin ribbon. To complete the outfit, she was wearing a white lace bonnet tied with pink ribbons and a pair of tiny pink booties and a sweet pink blanket that Mom Mom had crocheted.

On the drive home, the baby was quiet, but Todd kept up a stream of constant chatter as he stood on the hump on the floor of the backseat between his two parents. "She is so little. Will she grow hair? Look at her tiny hands. Oh, she has the cutest dimples. When can I hold her?"

Penny was nestled safely in her mom's arms, eyes wide open, tiny fingers gripped tightly around Anne's fingers. Her dad was smiling broadly, trying to concentrate on the traffic, but stealing side-ways glances at the newest member of his family. She was beautiful. Now with a boy and a girl, their family was complete.

When they arrived home, Mom Mom was there to greet them and give her final approval. She had been the only family member who had been hesitant about the adoption. "You don't know what you are going to get," she said at the beginning of the process. But as she held Penny and looked into those deep blue eyes, she too fell in love. They would share a strong bond for the remainder of Mom Mom's life.

Penny had been calm and quiet during the entire trip, but started to cry – loudly. "Oh, my, it must be time for a feeding," Anne said.

"Why don't you go fix Penny's bottle and I will change her," Mom Mom offered and headed into the nursery. "She may have a wet diaper."

Anne was in the kitchen emptying the diaper bag from CHS and searching for the baby's formula when she heard her mother.

"Anne, come in here!" Mom Mom shouted. "No wonder she was crying. You have a perfect baby with the worst diaper rash I have ever seen!"

"Poor baby, we can't let her have a rash like that." Anne said as she dug through the supplies in the dresser drawer. "Thank goodness for all these gifts! Here's a tube of Desitin from the baby shower. Let's try it, she may have sensitive skin."

"Or, my guess is, they didn't change her very often in the nursery," Mom Mom said.

Mother's Day arrived and the family descended on the Whitmer home once again to welcome the new addition. Penny was content to be passed around from aunt to aunt, uncle to uncle and endured wet kisses from her young cousins. Everyone proclaimed her the prettiest baby ever.

Todd was the proud big brother and took everyone to see his new room and the baby's nursery. For some unknown reason he was fascinated with the blue water in the diaper pail and made a point to show it to everyone.

Once the diaper rash had cleared up, Penny truly was the perfect baby. She was a happy, cheerful infant and her family was thankful that she slept through the night. The only time she fussed was when she was hungry or needed to be changed.

Todd adored her and was a big help to his mother. As Penny became more mobile, he kept her entertained by pushing her around the house in her round walker. They would also play games of fetch– she would throw her pink bunny, Todd would retrieve and they would repeat the process over and over again, giggling all the time.

There were daily walks around the neighborhood with Anne pushing Penny in the pretty pink stroller and Todd pedaling his red bike alongside. When Penny was learning to walk, Todd would hold her hand and pick her up when she plopped down. "Try again," he would say as she toddled throughout the house.

Once it was time for Todd to start kindergarten, Penny's playing companion was gone, but her mom kept her occupied. They would take walks around the neighborhood and then Anne would sit in the rocking chair and read Dr. Seuss books before naptime. While her mom cleaned house or fixed dinner, Penny was easily amused and content to spend time in her mesh playpen hugging her pink bunny, playing with the See and Say, or jabbering on her toy phone.

Mid-afternoon, she would squeal with delight when her brother returned home, followed by hugs and kisses when Mom Mom got home from work. Then Daddy would arrive. He would pick up Todd and Penny, squeeze them tight and swing them around and around until they were dizzy. "Bob, please stop they are going to be sick," Anne pleaded.

Patricia Daum

It was a moment to treasure when they celebrated Penny's first birthday and Todd helped her blow out the single candle. Her parents marveled at their precious little girl and the joy she had brought to their family.They offered a silent prayer of thanks to the young woman who had given her life.

CHAPTER TWENTY- FOUR

Batavia, New York
April-May 1966

While the Whitmers were celebrating Penny's first birthday, Faith was 1,500 miles away, focused on completing her freshman year at college.

The events from the previous spring were a faded memory.

When Faith and her mother had arrived in Batavia after spending the winter in Florida, Katherine was the first to greet them. She gave Faith a hearty hug and didn't want to let her go.

"I'm so glad to see you, and I have missed you so much," she said. "The Florida sunshine has been good for you. You look wonderful with that golden tan."

"I have missed you, too, and I'm so happy to be home," Faith said. "I can hardly wait to see Daddy and my friends."

"Guess what we are having for dinner tonight? I have fixed your favorite – ham, pineapple souffle, and green beans with carrot cake for dessert," Katherine said.

"Oh, thank you Kay Kay, that sounds wonderful!" Faith said giving Katherine one more hug before turning to go upstairs.

"I'll see you later. I need to get unpacked and call Sherri. I'm anxious to get caught up on school activities and hear what's happening for graduation. I don't want to miss anything," she said. "Sherri told me it's time to order my cap and gown and graduation announcements."

Faith had not gained a lot of weight during the pregnancy and her body was returning to normal. For a couple of weeks, she wore a girdle to flatten her tummy and no one would guess that she had recently given birth.

Her friends were excited to see her and she jumped right into all the senior activities. Faith's social calendar for the month of May was filled. The flag corps held a luncheon to honor the senior girls and they marched in the Memorial Day Parade. Y-Teens scheduled a weekend retreat at Silver Lake, there was a senior picnic at Batavia Downs and the Batavia Club hosted the annual senior dinner in honor of the members' sons and daughters.

In addition to attending all the events, she attempted to keep up with her studies and began searching for a college – almost too late. Thanks to Adele, her grades had improved for the two grading periods that she had spent in Florida, but there was a problem. When she met with the high school guidance counselor, she learned that her grade point average and her scores on the ACT and SAT tests, which she had taken back in the fall, were not high enough for most four-year universities.

When her parents heard the news, they were not pleased, but reassured their daughter. "Faith, we know that you are going to do well in college, we just need to find the perfect school for you. Don't worry, we will work out something."

Rachel sent out an SOS call to her sisters and they helped out once again.

Emily's husband, Dan, was on the board of directors of a small private college in Milton, Wisconsin. He felt Milton College would be a good fit for his niece, and he encouraged her to send in her application. Faith promptly applied and by graduation day she had been accepted. Her parents were relieved and it was comforting to know that the school was only 10 miles away from Aunt Emily and Uncle Dan's home in Janesville, Wisconsin.

At last, graduation weekend arrived. On Sunday, June 5, St. Joseph's Catholic Church offered a special baccalaureate Mass for the graduates. The next day, the 1966 senior class of Batavia High School, at 183 strong, marched into the high school auditorium for the official graduation ceremony. As each graduate walked across the stage to receive their diploma, they were saluted with a chorus of cheers from their friends and family. When Faith's name was called, her family including sister Laura and Aunt Theresa stood to applaud. Rachel turned to Bob, squeezed his arm and whispered, "Thank God, she made it."

The summer of 1966 was a happy time for the Bradford family. Laura had finished her assignment in Japan and arrived in Batavia in time for Faith's graduation. After celebrating graduation, the family switched gears and were caught up in a flurry of wedding preparations for Laura's July 9th wedding. There were bridal showers, bridal luncheons, dress fittings and meetings with the florist and photographer.

Finally, the big day arrived. It was cloudy and a pleasant 80 degrees when Robert Bradford escorted his beautiful red-headed daughter across the family's flagstone patio to her waiting groom. Laura was stunning in the exquisite gown the Japanese seamstress had created for her. The long white sheath was fashioned from an elaborate silk brocade and complimented her tall, slender figure. The crowning touch was a vintage pearl-encrusted tiara and lace veil that Aunt Theresa had worn on her wedding day.

Faith was her sister's only attendant and looked lovely in a pink silk dress that fit her perfectly.

The private ceremony was attended by the immediate families, followed by a wedding reception at Wexford Country Club. The newlyweds spent their honeymoon at Canandaigua Lake and returned to Chicago, where they would make   their   home.

CHAPTER TWENTY-FIVE

Milton, Wisconsin
September 1966

When Faith arrived at Milton College in the fall of 1966, the college had 600 undergraduates and was affectionately known as the "second chance college." Students who had been turned away from other schools were welcomed. The devoted faculty members worked with them one-on-one to promote success.

Milton College was set to celebrate the school's centennial in 1967 and a major building project was under way. As Faith and her parents drove into what they had imagined was going to be a quiet little college town, they were met with the jarring sounds of jack hammers, cranes, bulldozers and dozens of workers in hard hats. Three new buildings were under construction: a library, a campus center and a women's residence hall.

During orientation in the historic Milton Hall, Faith was bewildered to learn that she and some other freshman girls would be living in private homes their first semester. They would move into the still-being-constructed women's residence after winter break. Her assigned house was on Burdick Street, a couple of blocks from the new campus center.

When she and her parents pulled up in front of the two-story frame house, her parents shared a sideward glance. "I can't believe this is where Faith will be living," Bob said.

The older home had seen better days. The paint was faded and the sagging shutters made the whole place look tired. As the Bradfords lugged Faith's belongings to the front porch, their mood was lifted when a cheerful young woman flung open the front door and greeted them with a smile.

"Hi, I'm Becky, let me help you," she said as she took a bundle in danger of falling from Faith's arms. "What's your name and where are you from?" she asked.

"Hi, Becky, my name is Faith and I'm from Batavia, New York. Are you a freshman, too?"

"No, I'm a senior and I am going to be your house counselor and friend," she said and nodded toward the stairway. "Faith, you are the early bird, so you get to choose your room. I have the blue room at the top of the stairs, but the other three are still available. While the bedrooms are small, the good news is everyone has a private room."

"Once you have unloaded everything, meet me downstairs and I will show you the rest of the house," Becky said.

The bedrooms were all sparsely furnished with a college-issued twin bed, dresser, student desk and metal chair. After checking out the rooms Faith selected the yellow bedroom at the end of the hall. It had a southern exposure with two windows, and it also had the largest closet. The vintage bathroom she would be sharing had cracked black-and-white tile floors and a claw-footed tub.

"Abercrombie and Fitch!" Rachel Bradford muttered, using her favorite curse words. "This is not what we had expected."

Her spirits were sinking again as she took a look around. The house was clean and neat, but it was more than 50 years old with creaky wood floors. As they met Becky downstairs, they noticed the furnishings were well-worn. There was a faded floral sofa and wingback chairs in the living room and a long wooden table and six chairs in the dining room.

The small kitchen had worn black-and-white linoleum flooring, white painted cabinets, faded black Formica countertops and older white appliances. A round wooden table and chairs were nestled into a cozy corner. Rachel raised her eyebrows when she opened the cabinets and noticed a set of mismatched dishes and pots and pans.

"Didn't we pay for a meal plan?" Robert questioned in a gruff voice.

Sensing their displeasure, Becky piped in. "Our meals are served at the campus hall, so we don't need to cook. Sometimes we fix a light breakfast and we usually have snacks and sodas on hand. If we need anything, Piggly Wiggly is close by."

"Mr. and Mrs. Bradford, I know this house is not what you had envisioned," Becky said, trying to reassure them. "The college purchased the house from an elderly widow, and as you can see, they have left her furnishings here on the first floor. It's worn and comfy, and we also have a bonus – a washer and dryer in the basement."

"I want you to know that I lived in this house last year, as an honors student," Becky continued. "It worked out just fine and with only four students, everyone got along. Faith and the other girls will only be here for a semester. The new residence hall will open in January and everything will be bright, shiny and new."

"Please don't worry about Faith. She is going to love it here," Becky said.

And she did.

Becky Olmstead took her role as a house counselor seriously. She was from Tomahawk, a small town in the Northwoods of Wisconsin, and grew up working in her family's general store.

Her family struggled to make ends meet and she was thrilled when she qualified for a work-study scholarship at Milton College. In previous years, she had worked in the college cafeteria and the library. She was grateful when she was chosen to receive the coveted position as a house counselor. Not only did she receive free room and board, but she also received a stipend.

After everyone had unpacked and suffered through tearful good-byes with their parents, the girls met in the living room for Becky's version of orientation. Her blonde hair was pulled back into a ponytail and she was dressed in her college uniform – faded blue jeans, a navy Milton sweatshirt and tasseled moccasins. With her infectious smile and perky nose sprinkled with freckles, she looked younger than her 22 years. However, she was serious as she looked around the room and welcomed the three freshman girls.

In addition to Faith, there was Denise Rayburn from Washington, D.C., and Marylou Larson from Elkhart, Indiana. Denise was a tall beauty with long black hair, smoky gray eyes and a quirky sense of humor. She had graduated from an all-girls Catholic high school in suburban D.C. and wasn't thrilled about being stuck in the small town of Milton, Wisconsin. Her parents had recently divorced and her mother had relocated to Chicago. Mrs. Rayburn wanted her daughter nearby and Chicago was only 100 miles from Milton.

Marylou was a shy girl with a slight build and a warm smile. Her parents owned an RV dealership in Elkhart and she had graduated from a private Christian high school. Her straight brown hair hung to her shoulders with long bangs hiding her dark brown eyes.

Becky silently wondered how she, the poor student from Tomahawk, had ended up as counselor to three girls from well-to-do families. Nevertheless, she was up to the challenge and took the freshmen girls under her wings.

Becky reviewed the house rules: Curfew was 10:00pm. No boys upstairs. No alcohol in the house. She wanted her girls to have fun, but she was a stickler for grades and would also be their tutor. Next, she took them on a tour of the campus, made a stop at the college bookstore and insisted they sign up for an activity.

In the 1960s Milton was known for its championship basketball and football teams. Faith and Denise caught the school spirit, joined the Pep Squad and cheered at all the games. Marylou chose a different path. She was musically talented and was selected for the award-winning college choir.

In October the campus was buzzing with a weekend full of Homecoming activities. The roommates attended the rowdy pep rally on Friday night that culminated with a huge bonfire and a parade that featured colorful floats from the campus organizations, the Queen's Court and the Wildcat marching band.

The girls skipped the Saturday morning installation of the new college president, but bundled up for the afternoon football game. They huddled together in the freezing temperatures as the Wildcats warmed a crowd of 1,000 cheering fans with a win and another conference title. Later, the crowd reconvened at the Homecoming Dance, rocking the night away with music by the Top Hatters.

After winter break the three roommates chose to stay with Becky in the Burdick Street house. They had formed a close friendship during the first semester and postponed their move to the new women's dormitory until fall.

In 1967 Milton College celebrated its 100th birthday and the Founder's Day event in March featured another weekend celebration. There were concerts, speeches, and the dedication ceremony of the three new buildings, along with a huge birthday cake in the Wildcat Lounge.

By April, the crocuses and daffodils were peeking out from the frozen ground and the maple trees and oak trees were beginning to bud. Under Becky's guidance, the freshman girls on Burdick Street were working on year-end projects and studying for finals.

They were also making plans for fall. The three girls were moving into the new Crandall Hall. Denise and Faith would be roommates and Marylou would be living next door with a friend from choir. Becky was graduating, but they would still see her on campus. She had been offered a job in admissions.

***

After completing her freshman year with a passing 2.3 grade point average, Faith was excited to be back in Batavia and reconnecting with her childhood friends. Her father encouraged her to get a summer job. He promised to buy her a new car before she returned to Milton, if she would work and save enough money to pay for the car's insurance.

He had an idea. One of his business associates from the Batavia Club owned several Atlantic Gas Station franchises and wanted to try a new marketing gimmick in Batavia – using teenage girls to work at the full-service station, instead of teenage boys. Faith and her friend Kathy applied for the jobs and spent their summer working at the station.

It wasn't a cream puff job. When customers pulled into the station, they were greeted by the smiling girls dressed in blue jeans, white shirts and white sailor caps. While Faith pumped gas and cleaned the windshields, Kathy looked under the hood checking the oil and water levels. The full-service station also offered a car wash, so when the girls weren't pumping gas, they were washing cars.

The marketing gimmick worked, and business picked up when they made the front page of the Batavia News. A large photo of Faith and Kathy in their cute uniforms appeared with the caption, "Look what the girls are doing now!"

By the end of the summer, Faith had saved enough money for the car insurance and her dad held up his end of the bargain. He was so proud of her that she returned to Milton College for her sophomore year in a brand-new

1967 dusk rose Mustang, along with the insurance money she had earned, plus a   special   bonus   –   a   credit   card.

CHAPTER TWENTY-SIX

Milton, Wisconsin
1967-1970

Faith thrived in the small, diverse college community and made friends with students from all over the United States and other countries, including a number of students from Asia and the Middle East.

Along with the new car came freedom and increased social activity. The girls were no longer confined to Milton. They traveled to college hangouts in the surrounding towns and showed up at beer parties and bonfires along the shores of Storr Lake. Faith continued with the Pep Squad and began dating and going to fraternity parties. College was a fun time for her and while there were no serious relationships, she shocked everyone by dating the handsome Khalid Al-Haboo, her sophomore crush from Baghdad, Iraq.

Faith traveled to Batavia to be with her family at Christmas, but she spent her remaining college summers in Wisconsin living with Aunt Emily and Uncle Dan. They owned a large farm outside of Janesville where Aunt Emily raised thoroughbred horses and was involved in the local 4-H programs.

Faith secured a job as a hostess at the Holiday Inn in Janesville. She worked in the dining room and returned each summer. On July 20, 1969, she joined the dining room guests and millions of people worldwide in watching Neil Armstrong set foot on the moon.

Laura was living in Chicago during Faith's college years and Faith visited her sister often. By the time of Faith's graduation, Laura had given birth to an adorable baby girl with red hair and named her Theresa, in honor of their Aunt Theresa.

As it came time for graduation, Faith was undecided about her future. After spending her life in small towns, she was ready to try something different. She and Denise were best friends during their college years and did everything together. Denise was returning to Washington, D.C., and convinced Faith to move there.

On May 9, 1970, Faith's proud parents attended the simple, elegant graduation ceremony at Milton's Dunn Center. As they watched Faith walk across the stage to receive her college diploma, they turned to each other with a satisfied glance. Their dreams for their daughter were coming true.

After Faith said her final good-byes, she packed up the Mustang and turned on I-90 – destination Washington, D.C., and the next chapter of her life.

Denise had found a furnished apartment for the two women near the Capitol building and Faith began a job search. With her bachelor of arts degree in hand, she was confident that she would find something. She quickly learned that although she had a degree, it wasn't from a prestigious university and her work experience was limited. After being turned down numerous times, she finally landed a position working at the front desk at a Holiday Inn near the Capitol.

Faith was excited about the opportunity, but before long she became disillusioned. Her dreams of being a young single in the dynamic D.C. area were not panning out. After trying big-city life for a year, Faith realized she missed the small-town life and she decided to move on.

But the small town would not be Batavia, New York.

During her sophomore year of college, there had been a major upheaval for her family. There was a change in management at the shoe company, and her father was forced to leave the family business. In the aftermath, her parents retired to a golf course community in Jupiter, Florida, and encouraged her to relocate there.

Patricia Daum

PART FIVE

CHAPTER TWENTY-SEVEN

Miami, Florida
1920s-1950s

While Faith was attending college and beginning her hospitality career in Washington D.C., Penny was thriving in her adopted home, surrounded by a loving family who had lived in the Miami area for generations.

Bob Whitmer, Penny's dad, had grown up in a working-class neighborhood in South Miami, the son of a boat mechanic. His father, Joe, was a rugged man who could fix anything. During his lifetime he worked long hours on the bustling Miami docks for a number of marine service centers, repairing everything from small fishing boats, to sailing vessels, to luxury charters and expensive yachts. Joe's skills were in constant demand and kept the family financially afloat even during the Great Depression.

When the United States entered World War II, Miami became a strategic military location and thousands of servicemen flooded into the city. When the U.S. Navy took control of Miami's docks, Joe was among the hundreds of civilians who were recruited to do maintenance on the huge war ships coming into port. They were grateful for the work and proud to serve the war effort.

Bob's mother, Suzanne, was a petite woman with dark curly hair that she was constantly trying to tame in the Florida humidity. Orphaned at a young age, she was raised by her grandmother who ran a boarding house and a bakery. The bakery was near Joe's family home and he was a frequent customer – stopping by each morning on his way to the docks to buy a chocolate brownie. Before long, he had fallen in love with the chatty Suzanne.

"You are the only man I know who likes chocolate brownies for breakfast," she teased. "How about a blueberry muffin instead?"

"Nope, I can't think of a better way to start my day," he answered and stuffed a heavenly morsel in his mouth. "You are the bright sunshine of my life and these are the most delicious brownies I have ever tasted."

"Joe, you are so sweet," she blushed as she tucked an unruly curl behind her ear. She began looking forward to his visits each morning, and eventually the two began dating and planning their life together.

When her grandmother passed away from a sudden heart attack, Suzanne married Joe and the newlyweds moved into the boarding house. Through the years, Joe renovated the two-story frame structure into a comfortable single-family home where they raised their four sons.

However, during World War II, housing in Miami was scare and the Whitmers seized on the opportunity posed by so many people seeking a place to live. Once again, their home became a boarding house. The family crowded into the first floor and rented rooms on the second. The rooms were constantly filled with wives of servicemen and single women who appreciated the clean rooms and an evening meal.

Even though strict rationing rules were in effect, Suzanne was able to provide a nourishing meal for everyone by combining her ration tickets with those from her renters. And everyone enjoyed her chocolate brownies.

While Joe and Suzanne's formal schooling was limited, education was important to the couple and they encouraged their sons to succeed. Bob and his brothers attended Miami Senior High School in downtown Miami, where students from all over Dade County flocked to the prestigious school. The Whitmer brothers became friends with a diverse group of classmates including the pretty Penney sisters from Miami Springs.

***

Penny's mother, Anne Penney, grew up in Miami Springs, a small city northwest of Miami. Her parents, Clark and Margaret, had grown up in Miami, and were both graduates of Miami Senior High School. Clark Penney, a slight studious man with wire-rimmed glasses had first noticed Margaret Brown, in a business class during their junior year. Clark was smitten with the pretty woman with dark auburn hair and began showing up at her locker before classes each morning. Margaret was shy and enjoyed the attention of this serious young man and before long they began dating.

Clark had always been a whiz at math and after graduation he secured a book-keeping position at Hotel Urmey, a luxury hotel in downtown Miami, and eventually became the hotel's accountant. Margaret excelled in her classes and after graduation she accepted a job in the business office of Miami Memorial Hospital.

A couple of years after graduation Margaret Brown and Clark Penney were married in an elegant ceremony in the Garden Room of the Urmey Hotel. The young couple set up housekeeping in a small apartment near downtown Miami and saved to buy a home. Eventually, they purchased a ranch-style home on a quiet street in Miami Springs, where they raised four children.

When it came time for high school Anne and her siblings continued the Penney family's tradition and rode the city bus to Miami Senior High. Anne met Bob Whitmer at MSH and they were part of a large group of friends that partied together. During their junior and senior high school years, they cheered for the football and basketball teams, bowled at the Palace Bowling Center and planned beach parties at Miami Beach.

While some of the students were preparing for college, others like the Penney sisters and Whitmer brothers took a different path. Anne followed in her mother's footsteps and excelled in secretarial skills. After graduation, she was hired by Southern Bell and stayed with them for more than 10 years.

In addition to an excellent business curriculum, Miami Senior High had a top-notch industrial arts program that offered extensive training for jobs that were needed to support the local economy – automotive, construction, welding, marine and airline mechanics. Bob focused on becoming an airline mechanic and had a job waiting for him when he graduated.

After graduation in 1947 they continued to party with their circle of friends on Friday evenings after work – sometimes bar hopping in Miami Beach, other times going to the famous Elbo Room in Ft. Lauderdale. As time went on, Bob and Anne eventually fell in love. But it took a while.

The tall, handsome Bob with the kind face and witty personality had always been fond of Anne. The petite blonde with blue eyes had been one of the cutest girls in his class and had a friendly personality to match. However, there was a problem – she was dating another fellow in their social circle. Bob was patient. When that relationship faltered, he was the good friend Anne turned to and the strong shoulder she leaned on. They began dating and months later, when he proposed over a romantic dinner, she said, "Yes."

As they began making plans for a small wedding at the Urmey Hotel, tragedy struck. Anne's father was diagnosed with a brain tumor and passed away a few months later. Anne had always been close to her mother and had continued to live at home with her parents and younger brother, Ben. Her two sisters, Karen and Vicky, who were married with families of their own, constantly teased her about being the "old maid."

Now, her mother was left without the love of her life and a teenage boy to raise. "Anne, what am I going to do?" the heart-broken mother asked. "I can't afford to stay in this house without your dad and I'm worried about Ben."

Anne and Bob discussed the impossible situation her mother was facing and Bob stepped in with an idea. "Margaret, I purchased a duplex in Opa Locka a couple of years ago, near the airport where I worked. It's been a good rental property and Anne and I were planning on moving into one side and renting out the other," he said.

"Instead of renting to strangers, we would be happy for you and Ben to move into the vacant side. You can sell the house in Miami Springs and live on the proceeds for a while. What do you think of that idea?" he asked.

The grief-stricken Margaret nodded her agreement, overcome with tears and a wave of relief.

On Saturday June 7, 1958, Bob Whitmer and Anne Penney were married by a justice of the peace in a simple ceremony at her sister Karen's home, instead of the elegant wedding and reception at the hotel.

Following the tradition of her older sisters, Anne wore her mother's wedding gown – a white silk organza tea-length dress with a long veil. She looked like a porcelain doll standing next to her handsome groom who was decked out in a new navy-blue suit. Their reception was a casual cook-out held in the backyard of her sister's home.

The newlyweds moved into the duplex in Opa Locka, followed a few weeks later by their new next-door neighbors, Margaret and Ben Penney.

CHAPTER TWENTY-EIGHT

Opa Locka, Florida
1958-1976

The housing arrangement in Opa Locka worked out well for both families. Bob was working for American Airlines at Miami International Airport while Anne continued to work at Southern Bell. Margaret returned to her secretarial roots and secured a job in admissions at the local hospital. After graduating from high school, Ben enlisted in the Air Force and stayed with his mother when he was home on leave.

Bob and Anne were both 29 when they married and they were eager to begin their family. However, Anne suffered from endometriosis and had a difficult time getting pregnant. It would be four years before she finally conceived. She gave birth to Todd, a healthy baby boy on February 14, 1962.

Their happiness was short-lived.

Anne had problems following the delivery and had an emergency hysterectomy. There would be no more babies for the Whitmer family.

The couple was devastated by this news, but grateful to have Todd. He was a carbon copy of his father, with dark eyes and a mop of black hair. A sweet little boy, he was in constant motion. During some of his antics, his parents would look at each other, shake their heads and say with a smile, "Maybe it's a blessing that we only have one child."

As time went by, Anne and Bob began wishing for a baby girl to complete their family and Todd began asking for a baby sister. A neighbor couple had adopted an adorable little girl and suggested they contact Children's Home Society. The couple decided to proceed and after waiting more than two years, they were blessed with Penny.

The Whitmers were a typical hard-working blue-collar family. Throughout the years Bob worked for various airlines in the Miami area to provide for his family. When Penny started school, Anne returned to work as a secretary at a local car dealership, and the two incomes helped the family weather some hard times brought on by strikes and lay-offs in the airline industry.

Penny thrived in her adopted home and learned at an early age that she was adopted and **wanted**. With both parents coming from large families that lived in the Miami area, she was surrounded by adoring aunts, uncles and cousins.

Bob's parents had passed away before Todd was born, so Margaret embraced the Whitmer in-laws and became the matriarch of the combined families. Everyone called her Mom Mom. The petite woman had a ready smile, a warm embrace and was the family peace-maker.

Mom Mom was a good cook and their home was the usual place for family celebrations and holidays. There were plenty of cook-outs, too, with Bob and his brothers grilling hamburgers, hot dogs and sausages. Aunt Patty baked the best brownies ever and would bring a big platter to share. She was always proud to say, "The brownies are made from scratch using great-grandmother Whitmer's recipe from her bakery."

Sundays were family day for the Whitmers. After attending morning services at the Methodist Church in Opa Locka, the family would often pile into the station wagon and head to one of the many attractions that Miami had to offer. Sometimes they would spend the afternoon at the beach.

Other times, they would head to Dressel's Dairy for a swirly ice-cream cone and Penny and Todd would ride the ponies and the kiddie train. On the way home, they would stop at Nelson's farm stand. While Ann filled her basket with fresh produce, the kids rushed to the sugar cane display and picked up six-inch sticks of sugar cane to suck on the way home.

The Crandon Park Zoo was always a favorite and visits there would often include meeting the aunts, uncles and cousins for a day-long adventure. The zoo was a virtual Noah's Ark, with more than 1,200 animals on display. On admission, each child received a yellow plastic key in the shape of an elephant. As they stood next to each animal's cage, they inserted the elephant's trunk into an audio display, hearing the sounds the animal makes and learning facts about that animal. Penny was fascinated with the key and would run gleefully from display to display to hear the animal sounds. Once when she was next to the rhino cage, hearing its high-pitched sound, she was terrified when the angry beast charged the bars.

After seeing the animals and eating a picnic lunch in the park area, the kids and their parents would cool off by riding the Iron Horse, a miniature train that took visitors on a leisurely ride around the perimeter of the zoo.

As the children reached school age, the extended family branched out, frequently spending weekends across the state at Marco Island, staying in modest mom-and-pop motels. The cousins had fun building sand castles, collecting shells and fishing from one of the uncle's boats. Evenings were spent around a camp fire enjoying a fish fry from the catches of the day and swatting away the no-see-ums and mosquitoes. The uncles always bragged about who had caught the largest fish and told tall tales of the big ones that got away.

At that time, Alligator Alley was a narrow two-lane road, that cut through the Everglades. Yes, they had to be watchful for alligators crossing the road. It was a three-hour journey from Miami to the west coast, with no gas stations or lights in sight. The Whitmers found that traveling in a family caravan was the safest way to go and they would burst out in cheers when they finally reached the narrow bridge crossing over to the tranquil world of Marco Island.

As major developments began to disturb the laid-back island, and their favorite motels were demolished, the extended Whitmer family decided to try something new – camping. Anne refused to sleep in a tent so Bob went in search of a small camping trailer that he could haul behind their Plymouth station wagon.

He visited the local dealerships, but found the new ones too expensive and some in the used camper lots looked like they would fall apart. Then one day a notice posted on the bulletin board at work caught his attention:

For Sale: Travel Trailer, 1965, 16' Crowncraft, sleeps six, two to a bunk.
Contains: ice-box, sink, 3 burner stove, 500 Maximum miles.
Torsion bar, Reese hitch, $500. Call Don Phillips, ext. 789.

This sounded like it might be perfect for his family. He called the number and spoke with Don Phillips, who worked in the personnel department. "Don, I've been looking for a trailer for me and my family to visit some of the Florida campsites. What kind of condition is it in?" Bob asked.

"Bob, the camper belonged to my parents and it is in great shape for its age. Dad is a retired airline mechanic and he and my mom spent several winters living in the camper in a Sebring camp ground. The only reason they are selling it is because they are having health issues," Don said. "The camper is in my driveway at home. If you are interested you can stop by on your way home from work and check it out."

Bob stopped by the Phillips' home that afternoon and bought it on the spot. The camper was dated, but it was well constructed and it was obvious that the older couple had treated it with loving care. Best of all, the price was right and he decided to bring it home the next day as a surprise.

Bob could hardly contain his excitement as he pulled up in front of the house. Todd and Penny were the first ones to see him, and as they rushed out the front door they shouted to their mother. "Mom, come see the surprise!"

Anne was preparing dinner and wiped her hands on her apron as she came to the front door. She was stunned. "What's this?" she asked.

"Sweetheart, it's our new camper," her husband said with a mischievous grin. "It sure beats sleeping in a tent. Wait until you see the inside."

The bottom half of the white trailer was painted pink – faded from years in the Florida sun. As Anne stepped through the pink door of the camper, she noted that it was clean, but dated. The black-and-white vinyl flooring was worn, but she was flabbergasted that everything was pink – pink stove, pink refrigerator, pink vinyl seat covers and pink valances!

Todd and Penny had scurried into the camper ahead of their parents and were jumping up and down with excitement, climbing over the seats and hopping into the overhead bunk. "This is the best surprise ever!" they exclaimed.

Penny jumped into her dad's arms and shouted, "I love it! Everything is pink, my favorite color!"

"With this color combination, I guess we won't have any trouble finding our camper in the campgrounds," Anne said as she shook her head.

Before long, other members of the Whitmer-Penny family purchased small travel trailers. The family caravan began spending holidays and weekends traveling to campgrounds in Marco Island, Sanibel Island and the Florida Keys. Family birthdays were often celebrated during these weekend trips with the birthday boy or girl receiving small gifts and cards. And there was always a special treat – a Carvel ice cream cake.

Summer vacations were often spent in Yogi Bear's Jellystone Park near Orlando. The park became a favorite destination with swimming pools, fishing holes and numerous kids' activities. However, once the kids returned to school in the fall, the camping trips were relegated to holiday weekends. The cousins were involved in various sports, and weekends were spent attending their games.

While big-brother Todd had a difficult time with his studies, he was a gifted athlete and his little sister was always on the side-lines cheering for him and his team. From the time he played on the Pop Warner and the Opa Locka Junior High football teams, Penny was the darling little cheerleading mascot, dressed in a green-and-white outfit, just like the older girls.

As soon as football season was over, preparations began for the holidays. Thanksgiving and Christmas were always fun and hectic at the Whitmer-Penny home and it wasn't uncommon for 18-20 family members to gather round for the holiday feasts.

Christmas was a joyful time at the home, the aroma coming from the kitchen was heavenly. Mom Mom spent days baking dozens of cookies and small loaves of pumpkin bread to share with friends and neighbors. Penny was her little helper, carefully pressing out sugar cookies and sprinkling them with red and green sugar crystals. "Mom Mom, do you think Daddy will like this one?" the little elf asked as she held up a star blanketed in red crystals.

The week before Christmas the family made the annual trip to Macy's to visit Santa. Penny, looking adorable in her red velvet dress, held Todd's hand as they walked through the Magical Forest. She smiled sweetly for the photo, sitting on Santa's lap with Todd standing guard right beside her.

After the photo with Santa, there was the exhaustive search for the perfect Christmas tree. Bob Whitmer had been known to stop at five lots before finding the right one. Once the tree was set up in the living room and Bob had finished putting on the lights, he would lift Penny above his head and she would place the tattered angel from her mother's childhood on the tree top.

Bob and Anne Whitmer always made sure their children had everything they needed, but the family budget didn't allow them to spoil Todd and Penny throughout the year with toys and trendy items. Everything was saved for Christmas and they would go overboard with all the gaily wrapped packages.

Somehow Santa always managed to bring the items that were at the top of children's wish lists. This splurge was well-planned – each January Anne opened a Christmas savings account at the local bank and faithfully deposited $3 each week.

When Penny started school, Anne Whitmer went back to work as a secretary for a local car dealership. With the two incomes, the family began saving for a new home. Their Opa Locka neighborhood was changing, and before Todd entered high school, they wanted to move into a better school system. They settled on a new neighborhood in Kendall, a growing suburb of North West Miami, that was home to many of Bob's co-workers.

In 1976, just a couple of months after Penny's 10th birthday, the Whitmer family packed up all their earthly possessions and moved into a brand-new, two-story, four-bedroom home with two baths.

By this time, Mom Mom had retired and became "the chief cook and bottle washer." She was thrilled that the kitchen had all the latest appliances including a dishwasher. Everyone loved the large backyard and screened-in patio that was great for the kids and the large family gatherings.

When one of Penny's school friends from Opa Locka visited the new house for the first time, the little girl remarked, "You are rich!"

CHAPTER TWENTY-NINE

Sailfish Bay, Florida
1971-1976

While Penny's family was moving into their new house in Kendall, Faith was attending a baby shower 100 miles north in Jupiter, Florida, where she was the guest of honor.

During her senior year in college her parents had retired to a golf course community in the small town of Jupiter. When her dad learned Faith was unhappy in Washington D.C., he networked a hotel job for her in nearby Sailfish Bay, a charming town of 5,000 residents along the Indian River Lagoon. She moved into the guest bedroom of her parents' home in 1971 and enjoyed the single life.

The Ashley Hotel was host to numerous civic meetings and special events and Faith, the pretty new girl in town, met the young movers and shakers of the small community. They partied at the popular Triangle Bar in Sailfish Bay and the Outrigger Restaurant in nearby Jensen Beach, often rubbing shoulders with Francis Langford and her celebrity guests.

Before long, Faith caught the eye of the handsome Dan Townsend whose prosperous family had been in the area for generations and owned a successful construction company. Dan had recently returned to his hometown and joined the family business after serving a tour of duty in Vietnam.

The serious young veteran was eager to get his life back on track and became infatuated – from afar – with the fun-loving Faith. He had met her at some of the local events, but one night at the Triangle Bar he finally got up enough nerve to ask her out.

"Faith, I have some tickets for the Beach Boys concert at the Sportatorium in Hollywood, Florida, would you like to go with me?" he asked with hesitation.

"Yes, that sounds like fun," she replied. Not realizing that she had just said yes to her future husband. The two began dating and spent many weekends together dining in the local restaurants, boating along the intracoastal waters and playing golf at her parents' country club.

Dan waited until Valentine's Day to propose. After enjoying a romantic dinner at the Outrigger, the young couple took a stroll along the dock where the crescent moon and thousands of stars reflected softly off the dark waters of the lagoon. As they reached the gazebo at the end of the dock, Dan surprised her by dropping down on one knee.

"Faith, I love you. Will you marry me and be my wife forever?" he asked. He presented her with an exquisite diamond engagement ring, a family heirloom that had once been his grandmother's.

"Yes," she replied as they embraced and shared a passionate kiss. "Dan, I love you too, and I will cherish your grandmother's ring forever."

The couple married a few months later on May 27, 1972, in a garden ceremony at her parents' home. Faith was overcome with happiness that afternoon and couldn't stop smiling as her dad walked her toward Dan. She was radiant in a white lace gown with a sweetheart neckline, and she continued with her sister Laura's tradition of wearing Aunt Theresa's pearl-encrusted tiara and vintage Irish lace veil.

As the bride and groom were taking their vows beneath the flower-draped arbor, Robert Bradford leaned toward Rachel and squeezed her hand. They felt blessed that their hopes and dreams for Faith had come true.

After a honeymoon cruise, the newlyweds set up housekeeping in a quaint three-bedroom cottage that Dan had renovated near downtown Sailfish Bay. Faith continued working at the hotel and the couple looked forward to starting a family.

Sundays were reserved for church and family, with Faith and Dan spending many Sunday afternoons with her parents. After a round of golf, the foursome would gather in the club house for dinner and drinks and relive the round, hole-by-hole. Her parents, who had won many club championships, never tired of beating the younger couple.

One afternoon, after toasting yet another victory by the parents, the conversation turned serious. Her mother calmly turned to Faith and said, "I have been diagnosed with breast cancer."

"Oh, Mommy, how dreadful!" Faith replied, and peppered her mother with questions.

"When did you find out? Do you need to have surgery? What kind of treatments?" she asked.

"I will know more next week after I meet with the surgeon and radiologist," her mother replied.

Rachel was diagnosed with an aggressive form of breast cancer that had killed her mother and grandmother. She battled the disease for two years and tried to maintain her normal routine at the club, playing golf, bridge and attending book club meetings. She turned to daily devotions and prayer to help her get through the difficult days. When she was too weak for golf, she spent her day writing inspiring letters to her friends and family.

Faith adored her mother and was overcome with sadness during her illness. "How could this happen to my sweet, loving mother?" she thought. "It's not fair."

In the final weeks of her life, Rachel's family surrounded her with love and support. Her sisters, Theresa, Emily and Julia traveled to be at her side, as well as her daughters Laura and Gloria who flew in from Chicago, Illinois, and Medina, New York, to be with her. Faith visited daily after work to give her grieving father a break.

The girls were able to spend one last Mother's Day with their beloved mother. She passed away in her sleep on Monday, May 12, 1975.

St. Jude's Catholic Church was filled with family and friends to say a final goodbye to this wonderful woman. During the funeral, her white casket sat at the front of the church covered in a spray of yellow roses. Near the closed casket, a joyful photo of Rachel was on display. She had a huge smile while receiving one of her championship trophies. Laura, with the voice of an angel, sang her mother's favorite hymn, *Amazing Grace.*

CHAPTER THIRTY

Sailfish Bay, Florida
1986

During the stress of her mother's illness Faith was dealing with fertility issues, which was remarkable considering how easy it had been 10 years earlier. She and Dan had desperately wanted a baby, but after three years and meeting with numerous specialists, it wasn't happening.

She continued to keep the first pregnancy a secret, telling no one, not even her doctors. But she silently wondered, "Is it possible that the baby I gave up all those years ago could end up being my only child?"

Then, a few weeks after her mother's death, Faith learned that she was pregnant. She took great joy in calling her family to spread the word.

"It's a miracle!" Laura said upon hearing the news. "This baby is a blessing from above. Faith, I am so happy for you and Dan, but I'm also thankful that our family has something happy to focus on after all the sadness surrounding Mother's passing."

During Faith's pregnancy there was another new addition to the family. Much to the family's amazement, Faith's father remarried six months after her mother's death. Jane was the wealthy widow of his former college roommate and she and her husband had been good friends of Rachel and Robert. It seemed natural that the two surviving spouses would connect. Jane had no children of her own and embraced the Bradford family's three daughters and their children.

Faith was happy and healthy during her pregnancy and she and Dan enjoyed setting up the nursery. Dan was certain the baby was going to be a boy, so they painted the room a light blue and used a nautical theme. He reasoned that if the baby was a little girl, she would like blue, too. Faith's dad and Jane got involved and purchased a white crib and matching dresser, while the Townsend family delivered a white hand-painted rocking chair with tiny blue anchors and the *Townsend* family name in script across the back.

Faith bought a blue-and-white checked comforter and matching valance for the window and found a blue-and-white hand-hooked rug. Dan surprised her with two framed watercolor paintings of children playing along the beach that he had purchased from Faith's favorite local artist. The nursery was ready for the newest addition to their family.

Jane was thrilled about the pending birth of a new grandchild and hosted a lavish baby shower for Faith at the country club. She invited Faith's sisters and friends, and during the afternoon it was hard to tell who was more excited, the new grandmother or the mother-to-be.

In April of 1976 Faith gave birth to a healthy baby boy. They named him Michael, "a gift from God."

Before long, Michael had two little sisters, Christina and Lisa. Faith was busy raising the three children and enjoyed being a stay-at-home mom. Life was good until shortly before the couple's 10th wedding anniversary. Dan came home from work one day and announced that he wanted a divorce. He was moving out.

Faith was stunned and heartbroken. She couldn't believe what she was hearing. After 10 years and three children he wanted a divorce? What happened to his promise that he would love her forever?

"Why?" she asked between the sobs.

"I'm not happy," he replied.

Faith was devastated and found it daunting to be a single mother with three active kids. For weeks, she was depressed and didn't know what to do. She turned to her faith and began listening to the PTL Club, the daily Christian television program hosted by evangelists Jim and Tammy Faye Bakker. In desperation, she mailed them a check for $100 to be put on their prayer list, and she prayed to God for help.

Faith's father stepped in and called in the cavalry. During this time, sister Gloria was living in the Tampa area and she was also going through a divorce. Robert Bradford was concerned about both daughters and enticed Gloria to move to the Sailfish Bay area. He called and said, "Come, take care of your sister."

When Gloria and her brood relocated to Sailfish Bay, Robert Bradford was happy to have his girls nearby and the two sisters took care of each other.

Robert also helped Faith buy another home in Sailfish Bay and she went back to work, this time for a local non-profit. The weeks were filled with work, the kids' after school activities and hanging out with Gloria and her family.

Dan Townsend was faithful with his support payments and was a devoted dad to his three children. He attended the children's ball games and activities, and the kids stayed with him on alternate weekends.

Patricia Daum

PART SIX

CHAPTER THIRTY-ONE

Kendall, Florida
1976-1986

While Faith and Dan were starting their family in Sailfish Bay, Penny was adjusting to a new neighborhood and school.

Penny had always been an active child who was willing to try out new activities. In grade school she was a Brownie, Girl Scout and member of the school safety patrol. When the Whitmer's moved to Kendall, the friendly child continued to be involved. The neighborhood was a bee-hive of activity, swarming with kids of all ages. Penny became best friends with five other girls who would become lifelong friends. They did everything together. They took ballet and tap lessons, attended charm school, played soccer and tried gymnastics.

When the girls became freshmen, the tight-knit group walked together each day to Miami Sunset High School, and as time went on, they excelled in different areas. Penny became a member of the Knights' golf team her freshman and sophomore years. She also made the cheerleading squad and was selected to be the captain her senior year. In her high school yearbook's Senior Hall of Fame, she was selected "Rowdiest."

When the popular young woman turned 16, she began working part time as a Publix cashier. While she continued cheerleading, she dropped out of other activities. Her prime motivation was to earn money for a car.

Penny was an average student and while some of her friends were college-bound, she was content to stay in Kendall and work at Publix. No one from Penny's extended family had attended college. It wasn't a priority. The women were stay-at-home moms, secretaries, receptionists or school aides, while the men were airplane and auto mechanics, plumbers and electricians. Her parents believed that once you graduated from high school, you were on your own and needed to support yourself.

High school graduation was a major milestone for the Whitmer family, a rite of passage into adulthood. Penny's parents and Todd attended the ceremony and beamed with pride as she walked across the stage to accept her diploma. The family celebrated that evening with dinner at the Kapok Tree Inn in Davie, where her parents gave her a beautiful white gold watch with a thin etched band.

Penny continued to live at home after high school graduation. She was eager to pay off her car, an older Chevy Malibu, and took a second job in an attorney's office as a secretary. She was a quick learner and when the senior secretary was out for six weeks recovering from surgery, Penny filled in for the woman. That was one time when she was thankful that her mother had encouraged her to take a typing class in high school.

While she had been content with her life and the direction it was taking, the experience opened a whole new world for Penny. She realized that she was smart enough to attend college and maybe become an attorney.

"How can I make this happen?" she thought. She needed a college degree, and then there was law school. How could she ever pay for that? She knew her parents loved her and would offer encouragement, but they were not in a financial position to help her pay for college.

Penny decided she would ask her boss, Mr. Katz, for advice. As a respected member of the local legal community, he surely would be able to guide her.

Gerald Katz had been in practice for twenty-two years. He was the third generation of his family to enter the profession and was a respected member of the legal community. His grandfather Abraham had opened his practice in north Miami in the 1920s and made his fortune specializing in real estate transactions during the land boom. Grandfather had been a savvy businessman, surviving the land bust and the Great Depression.

Mr. Katz was friendly but could be intimidating, especially when he was sitting behind the ancient desk in his corner office. One afternoon, when the office door was open, Penny peeked into the room to see if he was busy. The dignified man in his crisp white shirt and green-striped tie was thumbing through a law book, the fading sunlight casting a shadow on his balding head. As she tapped on the doorframe, Mr. Katz looked up, peering at her over his reading glasses.

"Penny, is there a problem?" he asked.

She entered the room and explained her dilemma. "Mr. Katz, I am interested in becoming a lawyer, but have no idea how to go about the process, especially since I will need financial aid. I wonder if it's even possible for me. What do you think?" she asked.

Mr. Katz leaned back in his chair and removed his glasses, giving this earnest young woman his full attention. "Penny, you are definitely smart enough to do this, but the first step is getting accepted into college," he said. "I would be honored to write a reference letter for you, but I think you should check with the career counselor at your high school. She would be the best one to help guide you."

Grateful for his confidence in her, Penny quickly acted on his advice. The next morning, she stopped by her high school and was waiting outside Mrs. Ralston's office door when she arrived.

"Penny!" the counselor exclaimed. "What brings you back to Miami Sunset High on this bright sunny morning?"

As she was ushered into the counselor's office, Penny explained. "I've decided I want to go to college, but I don't know where to begin. Can you help me?"

The counselor was a little surprised to see Penny. She remembered that Penny had been a cute cheerleader but was just an average student with little desire to continue her education. "Penny, let's take a look at your records and see what options we have," she said. "It's only been a few months since you graduated, so I should have everything right here in my file cabinet."

As she reviewed Penny's file and transcript, she noted that Penny was a B student and had scored above average on the ACT test. That was a plus! "For someone who wasn't interested in college, I'm shocked that you took the ACT," Mrs. Ralston said.

"Well, several of my friends were taking the test," Penny said. "They told me I should take the ACT just in case I changed my mind about college, and I ended up scoring higher than they did," she laughed.

"I wish your grade point average was higher, but it appears you have taken all the minimum course requirements for admission. With your ACT results we have a good chance of getting you accepted," the counselor said. "The fact that you were working during high school might be a plus for you. It shows motivation."

"There are no guarantees, but I think it's worth a shot," Mrs. Ralston said. "I think you should apply to the University of Florida in Gainesville first. I've worked with their admissions officer before."

By the end of the week, Penny had completed the college application forms, enclosing the glowing recommendations from Mr. Katz and the high school counselor. Penny waited and waited to learn if she would be accepted. Finally, the week of Thanksgiving, she received the official letter.

She had been accepted at UF.

"YES!!!" she shouted with excitement.

While she waited to hear from the university, she researched how she would pay for the tuition and room and board, and she developed a plan. If she was accepted, she would defer enrollment until fall, work at Publix and the law firm until then, saving as much as she could. Then, she would apply for student loans to make up the difference.

Penny entered UF in the fall of 1985 and majored in criminal justice, her back-up plan. She had saved enough money to cover the expenses for her freshman year, but her future college years were in financial jeopardy.

To help her out, Mr. Katz referred her to an attorney friend in Gainesville. During the school year Penny began working there full-time as an assistant to the paralegal. The hours were flexible so she was able to attend classes, but there was little time or money for social activities.

Penny developed a routine all through her college years. During the summers she lived at home and worked in the Kendall law office, saving as much money as she could. Then she would return to Gainesville in the fall, attend classes and work in the law office there.

Patricia Daum

After living in the dorm her freshman year, she and her high school girlfriends shared an apartment which was less expensive than the dorm. While Penny was frugal, she often found herself broke between pay checks, and would resort to pawning her high school class ring and her white gold watch to have enough money for food and gas. Then, she would retrieve her treasured items from the pawn shop until the next time she was penniless.

She didn't let her lack of funds drag her down. She shopped at Goodwill and treated herself to an occasional Big Mac. She had a bigger goal in mind and was motivated to succeed.

CHAPTER THIRTY-TWO

Gainesville, Florida
1988-1998

Penny had been popular in high school and dated occasionally, but she never had a steady boyfriend. And, she had been too busy in college to pay much attention to the guys in her classes. During the summers at home she and her friends had spent the weekends at the beach working on their tans, flirting with the lifeguards and hanging out with some high school friends. But no serious dates.

That all changed one night during her senior year, when her friends badgered her into going to "Nickel Beer Night" at one of the local bars. "You need to have some fun before we graduate," they said. "Even a penny-pincher like you can afford this."

Penny agreed, and that night would change her life forever.

September in Gainesville was always hot, in the high 80s with humidity to match and very little breeze. The three girls wore short shorts and tank tops to show off their summer tans and received some admiring glances as they sashayed into the college bar. As they sat down and ordered nickel beers, Penny noticed a cute guy with curly black hair and dark eyes sitting across the bar. He was wearing a pink dress shirt with a paisley tie, not your typical college guy.

She was intrigued and, in a spontaneous moment, decided to buy him a beer. She and her friends laughed as she asked the bartender to take him a nickel beer. The cute guy looked up, smiled and raised his glass in a toast. Then he casually walked over.

Penny learned his name was Jim Snyder, his father owned a local car dealership, and he was a salesman. He learned Penny was a senior at UF, a motivated student who worked for a local attorney. There was an instant attraction, but before they had finished a second beer, the air-conditioning died and the party was over.

Patricia Daum

Jim gave Penny his business card and also jotted down her phone number. He called a couple of days later and they began dating within the week. With their busy schedules, weekends were their only free days, and they spent as much time together as possible. The rabid Gator fans attended all the home football games in the Swamp, ate cheap dinners at Danny's Old Irish Pub, took walks in the park and played an occasional round of golf.

By January they were an item and when Jim was transferred to a dealership in Orlando, Penny commuted there each weekend. The young couple treasured their time together in Jim's tiny apartment, their "love nest."

In the spring of 1989, Penny became the first one in her family to graduate from college. Her parents, along with assorted aunts and uncles, drove six hours to Gainesville for the ceremony. They crowded together in the stadium and were bursting with pride as her name was announced – "Penny Suzanne Whitmer." They clapped and cheered as she strolled across the podium and basked in her five seconds of fame.

Jim was also there. He had driven from Orlando to celebrate this special occasion and to meet Penny's parents for the first time. Getting dinner reservations in Gainesville during graduation weekend was almost impossible, so Jim made reservations for dinner at the Gainesville Country Club, where his parents were members.

The Whitmer family enjoyed a delicious meal in a quiet setting away from the hustle and bustle in town. They talked about the lovely surroundings, and the gently rolling hills and the horse farms they had passed in central Florida, so very different from south Florida.

As they were enjoying the meal, Penny's father handed her a slim package. "What's this?" she asked.

"Just a special graduation present from your mother and me," he said. Inside the velvet box was a gold bracelet with a single gold charm. Engraved on the front was a cent sign, on the back, *Congratulations to Our Lucky Penny.*

"Thank you so much. This is lovely," Penny said as she slipped the bracelet on her wrist and gave both parents a hug.

Penny was a college graduate now, with a fresh-off-the-press diploma and student loans to repay. However, law school was still on the horizon.

She had maintained a B+ average through college and when it was time to take the LSAT, she scored high enough to apply to law school. After researching her options, she learned that St. Thomas College of Law was a new accredited law school in Miami, and seemed to be the best fit for her financially. She could live at home and work at Mr. Katz's law office, where she had been since high school days, only this time she would be working as a paralegal.

She applied to St. Thomas with glowing recommendations from Mr. Katz and the attorneys she worked for in Gainesville and she was accepted.

With the demanding schedule of law school and working full time as a paralegal, Penny was finding it impossible to commute to Orlando on the weekends to be with Jim. He missed her so much, that he transferred to a car dealership in Miami and moved into her family's home.

Mom Mom had passed away the year before and would not have approved of this arrangement, but her mother and father were OK with the plan. They were happy to have their daughter home again. Todd had moved out months earlier and they found their empty nest was way too quiet.

By fall, the couple was engaged.

One September weekend there was a bridal fair at the Fontainebleau Hotel in Miami Beach. Penny said to her mom, "Let's go, this could be fun."

As the mother and daughter entered the Grand Ballroom they were amazed at the huge turnout and the vast number of vendors set up to help with wedding preparations. They nibbled their way around the ballroom sampling appetizers and sweets from the caterers and bakeries. All the while, they filled their goodie bags with bridal magazines, brochures and business cards from photographers, florists, tux rentals and wedding planners.

David's Bridal Gowns occupied a large corner of the ballroom displaying dozens of lovely gowns. Penny found the perfect dress – a slim white satin number with an overlay of lace and a short train.

When they returned home, Penny popped the question.

There was no special down-on-one-knee moment. Instead, as they were driving to dinner she turned to Jim and said, "Jim, I think we should get married."

"OK, I think I'll ask my brother to be my best man," he replied.

Three months later on December 23, 1989, the couple was married in a traditional ceremony held in the chapel of the Kendall Methodist Church. Family and friends stood as Penny and her dad entered the church following a procession of five bridesmaids – her childhood friends – wearing pink dresses.

The bride was radiant in her satin and lace gown and her father tried not to shed a tear as he walked his daughter down the aisle. The traditional ceremony was followed by a modest reception in the church social hall featuring a three-tiered wedding cake and non-alcoholic punch. After cutting the cake and nibbling on finger food, the bridal party departed to a nearby night club where they partied until midnight.

There was no time for a honeymoon. It was back to work and school for the newlyweds.

After paying tuition for the first year of law school Penny received scholarships for the second and third years and graduated in 1992. She took her bar exam a few weeks later and was ecstatic when she passed the first time around.

During Penny's second year of law school, Jim accepted a position at a new car dealership in Ft. Myers. Penny continued to live with her parents and visited him on weekends. After graduating from law school, she moved to Ft. Myers and started a job in a law firm that specialized in insurance defense. State Farm was one of her firm's major clients, and as the years passed, her career would focus on representing insurance companies.

In the late 90s, the couple took a gamble on a new opportunity for Jim. A friend of his father's was opening a new dealership in Jacksonville and he needed an experienced sales manager. Jim accepted the challenge and the couple moved to nearby St. Augustine. With Penny's insurance experience she had no problem finding a job and in 1997 she began working for a small law firm near her new home. She stayed with the firm and prospered, eventually making partner.

After they were settled in St. Augustine, Penny began to feel her biological clock ticking. She and Jim decided it was time to start a family and they didn't have to wait long. On a cool breezy December day in 1998, Ashley was born – a healthy seven-pound baby girl, with a head of dark hair and deep blue eyes.

Penny's parents had almost given up on becoming grandparents and had been thrilled when Penny became pregnant. As soon as they heard the joyous news of Ashley's birth, the two retirees made the six-hour drive from Miami to St. Augustine to see their granddaughter. After peering at the baby through the nursery window, they entered their daughter's room and pronounced, "She's perfect!"

After hugging her daughter, Penny's mother handed her a gift box tied with a pink ribbon. "What's this?" Penny asked as she carefully unwrapped the box. Inside was a long pink infant gown with a pink collar trimmed in white lace. The front of the gown was smocked in tiny pink rosebuds and it closed at the bottom with a pink satin ribbon. There was also a pair of tiny pink booties and a soft pink blanket.

"Penny, this is the outfit that you wore when we brought you home. Mom Mom crocheted the booties and the blanket," her mother said with pride. "If you would like, it could also be Ashley's coming-home outfit."

"Oh, Mom, what a treasure," Penny said. "I can't believe you have kept this outfit all these years. It's perfect for Ashley to wear when we take her home."

Anne was overcome by the emotion of the moment. "Penny, the day we brought you home was one of the most wonderful days of our lives," she said through tears of joy.

"I have been forever grateful to the young woman who gave you life."

Patricia Daum

PART SEVEN

CHAPTER THIRTY-THREE

St. Augustine, Florida
Summer 2005

Penny had never thought about contacting her birth mother, but a couple of years after Ashley's birth, she became curious and wanted to learn more about her medical history.

As Penny approached her 40th birthday, she decided to begin the search. She was in a good place in her career and family and decided she could handle any situation.

Penny reviewed the original documents that her mother had given her and contacted the local Children's Home Society. In February of 2004, she completed an official on-line form and waited several weeks for the organization to process the request.

Then, she spoke with Molly, a case worker at CHS and paid a fee of $450.

"Are you in a rush?" Molly asked. "We are swamped with requests right now. Call back in six months and we may have some information."

"There is no hurry," Penny replied, and she called back six months later.

"We are very busy," Molly said. "Please call back in another six months."

Penny marked her calendar and dutifully checked back six months later.

"We are still very busy, call back in six months," Molly repeated.

Again, Penny added the prompt to her calendar. She was annoyed at the slow progress, but reasoned she would eventually receive the information. Besides, Penny was also swamped. She was working on a complicated case regarding a horrific truck crash in Gainesville that had involved multiple vehicles and two fatalities.

Six months later, in June of 2005, she called CHS again. "Penny, this is your lucky day. Your file is on my desk and I'm working on it right now," Molly said,

"I notice that your birth mother was a teenager and this was a private adoption handled by an attorney. I will follow up and try to make contact, but from my experience, these cases usually don't want to know about the child. Don't get your hopes up," Molly advised.

Penny was glad to hear that her case had finally reached the top of the stack, but she was apprehensive. "Will I regret beginning this search?" she wondered.

A week later Penny received a call from Molly, who had good news. "I just spoke with your birth mother," she said with excitement.

"She is willing to make contact with you, but the woman said she needs a couple of days to tell her family. This has been a secret for 40 years!"

CHAPTER THIRTY-FOUR

Sailfish Bay, Florida
July 5, 2005

It was late Tuesday afternoon at the Red Cross office in Sailfish Bay. Faith was trying to get caught up with her projects after the July 4th holiday weekend. Most of the staff was still on vacation and she was taking advantage of the solitude.

Faith was in the early stages of organizing, "Pennies Count," a fundraising campaign for the elementary schools. It had been a good day and she was happy to be marking off items on her to-do list. She had received confirmation that a community bank had agreed to sponsor the campaign and provide cute piggy banks for each elementary student. One of her talented co-workers had promised to sew a costume for the campaign's Lucky Penny mascot, and another co-worker was designing the clever posters and brochures.

As she was tidying her desk and preparing to head home, she heard the phone ringing. She realized the receptionist had left for the afternoon and considered letting the call go to voice mail, but she was concerned that someone might be needing help. She dutifully answered.

She had no warning that it would be a life-changing call for her.

"Hello, this is Faith Patterson, may I help you?"

"Yes," said a pleasant voice. "I'm calling from Children's Home Society in St. Augustine. Was your maiden name Bradford? Did you do business with our organization in 1966?"

Faith was stunned and felt faint as she slumped back into her chair. "Who was this person and why were they calling?" she thought.

She struggled to speak. "Yes, my maiden name was Faith Bradford. Why are you calling?"

"Ms. Patterson, we have been in contact with a young woman who was adopted in April of 1966. We have reason to believe you are her birth mother.

She is interested in learning about her birth parents' medical history, and we are hoping you could help her. If you are willing, she is also open to making contact with you," said the cheery voice.

"Oh, my God, I can't believe you are calling!" Faith said, her mind reeling. "This happened so long ago that I put it out of my mind and never thought about it. The adoption has been a family secret for almost 40 years. My husband, my children and even my sisters don't know anything about it."

"I realize this is sudden," the cheery voice continued. "I talk with birth mothers every day and each one reacts to the news in a different way. I can assure you that in your case the young woman is not interested in disrupting your family life, she is a successful business woman and just wants the medical information. Additional contact with you would be at your discretion."

Trying to absorb what she was hearing; Faith went on auto-pilot and offered some practical information. "She should know that there is a family history of breast cancer. My mother and grandmother both died from the disease and I have been treated for it as well."

Faith took a deep breath and continued, "As for making contact – I'm not sure. I am in total shock at this news and I will need to think about it for a few days. Please give me your name and number and I will get back to you."

As the reality began to sink in, Faith could feel her heart beating wildly and her face felt like it was on fire.

Molly O'Connor was the name attached to the cheery voice and her extension at CHS was 412. Faith's hand trembled as she struggled to write Molly's information on her telephone log. Her neck tightened in knots and she could hardly breathe. She felt panic set in.

As she hung up the phone, she said a silent prayer. "Heavenly Father, I need your help. Please give me the strength and wisdom to do the right thing."

Then she stood up and walked out into the hallway.

She had to talk with someone, anyone.

Patricia Daum

The office was unusually quiet, but she heard voices from the Volunteer Center. "Thank God someone is here," she thought.

Ellen, the director of the center, was sitting at her desk reviewing the new volunteer brochure with Jennifer, the marketing manager, when Faith abruptly appeared and collapsed in the nearest chair.

"I need your help," Faith squeaked.

The two women looked with concern at their friend and co-worker. "You look dreadful!" Ellen said with alarm. "Your face and neck are scarlet. Are you running a fever?"

"Or having an allergic reaction?" Jennifer offered.

"Should we call 911?" Ellen asked reaching for her phone.

"No!" Faith managed to whisper as she shook her head. "I have just received some shocking news and I think I'm having a panic attack."

"Sit still. Let me get you a drink," Jennifer said as she ran to the nearby water cooler.

Ellen dug into her purse and handed a Xanax to Faith. "Take this!" she demanded. "I am not in the habit of dispensing drugs, but this will help."

Jennifer returned moments later with a cup of water and knelt beside her distraught friend, hoping she and Ellen could ease their friends' distress.

Faith's hands were shaking as she took the drink and swallowed the pill. Between sips she began telling her two friends about the call and the secret that she had kept for 40 years.

"What am I going to do?" she asked as a dozen questions raced through her mind. "Should I agree to make contact? How will my husband Jason and my kids react to this news? What will my friends and co-workers think of me?"

Ellen quickly tried to reassure her. "First of all, this happened 40 years ago. It was a different time. You were very young and didn't have any options. You did a wonderful thing by giving this baby a good home."

Reaching out to touch Faith's arm, Ellen continued. "Just remember, you don't need to tell anyone. You can trust that Jennifer and I will keep this conversation confidential. However, if you chose to share your story, your friends and co-workers will understand and not think anything less of you."

Jennifer nodded her head in agreement.

In a remarkable twist of fate, both women had an adoption story to share.

"Faith, let me tell you the story about my family's experience and maybe it will help you make a decision," Ellen said. "When I was growing up, my teenage sister became pregnant and was sent to a home for unwed mothers. She gave her baby up for adoption and the adoption was closed. While our family knew of the adoption no one ever talked about it. She told her future husband, but her children knew nothing about their sibling.

"Years later, my sister received a call from a 'search angel' who was working on behalf of the adopted daughter. My sister learned that the daughter lived in California, thousands of miles from her home in Delaware. She had always wondered what happened to the child and agreed to be in contact. The two exchanged confidential letters through the 'search angel' and my sister was relieved to learn the girl had been adopted by a wealthy family and had a happy childhood.

"The daughter was curious about her birth parents and their medical histories, but once she realized my sister and the birth father came from modest backgrounds, she immediately ceased contact. She did not want to disrupt her family dynamics or have a 'reunion.' My sister was glad to know what happened to the child, and has no regrets, but she never told her children about this girl."

Jennifer, who had been sitting quietly next to Faith while Ellen spoke, had her own story to share. "Faith, I don't know if this will be helpful, but perhaps it will provide some perspective from an adopted child's point of view," she said.

"My parents told me at a fairly young age that I was adopted. When I was about 14, curiosity got the better of me and I located my birth mother and sent her a letter," Jennifer shared.

"She responded and after a few letters back and forth, we made arrangements to meet at a restaurant near where I lived in Ft. Lauderdale. She and her husband drove down from South Carolina to meet me on a Saturday. I hadn't told my parents anything about this, so I told them I was meeting a friend from school and I took a city bus to the restaurant.

"They were a nice couple and shared the story of how I was put up for adoption. He was a successful businessman and she had been his secretary. They fell in love while he was married and during their affair, she became pregnant. To avoid an office scandal, they concocted a story – she left the company to be with her sick grandmother who lived in the Midwest. He supported her financially throughout her pregnancy, and they gave me up for adoption.

"After 'caring for her grandmother' for several months, she returned to work as his secretary. A few years later when his son graduated from high school, my birth father divorced his first wife and married my birth mother. They showed me photos of their lovely home and a 12-year-old son, my biological brother.

"They said it was a pleasure to meet me and it put their minds at ease to know that I had been adopted by a nice family and that I'd had a good life. However, they let me know that this would be the only time they would ever see me. They would keep my birth a secret forever and hoped I would understand.

"I was glad to meet them too, but I wasn't sad to see them go. I had solved the mystery and knew it would hurt my adoptive parents if I had a relationship with this family," Jennifer said.

"Faith, you need to decide what's best for you and your family," Jennifer continued. "You may want to keep this confidential until you learn more about the adopted daughter. I would search the internet for suggestions on handling this situation. From stories I have read, some of the reunions turn out well and others are a disaster. Just beware."

The three women were silent for a moment. Jennifer and Ellen exchanged a worried look. "Had they overwhelmed their friend in their efforts to be helpful?"

Finally, Faith broke the silence.

"Thanks so much for listening and for sharing your stories," Faith said. "I have so much to think about, but now that this secret is out of the box, I'm not sure I want to keep it hidden any longer."

"You know that we are willing to support you whatever you decide," Ellen said.

"Good luck," Jennifer added.

Faith returned to her office and noticed a bookmark on her desk with the 23rd Psalm. As she read the familiar passage, it gave her strength. The Lord had been with her through a devastating divorce, her parents' deaths and surviving breast cancer. She wasn't sure what the future held, but she knew she could count on Him to guide her through this trial.

CHAPTER THIRTY-FIVE

Sailfish Bay, Florida
July 5, 2005

Faith shut her office door for privacy and made a call. Her oldest sister, Laura, had always been a voice of reason and Faith had turned to her many times after their mother's death. She felt that Laura wouldn't be judgmental and would know what to do.

Laura and her husband were vacationing on a mountain top near Hot Springs, Virginia. They were enjoying the serenity of the mountains and the breathtaking views from a rustic chalet. It had been a quiet week away from family and work responsibilities – mostly due to poor telephone signals. On this glorious Friday afternoon, Laura was on the deck reading the most recent John Grisham novel when her phone pinged. She picked up her cell phone and saw that it was her sister Faith.

"Hi sweetie, it's good to hear from you. We have had such poor reception this week, you are one of the few calls to make it through. I guess we should call this divine reception," she said. "What's going on with you?"

"Oh, Laura, I'm so glad you answered. Something dreadful has happened and I need your help." Faith wailed as the tears began to fall.

"What's wrong," Laura asked. "Has Jason or one of the kids been in an accident?"

"No, nothing like that," Faith sobbed. "Something that happened to me 40 years ago has come back to haunt me."

As she gasped for breath between the sobs, she continued. "While you were living in Japan, I had a baby and gave her up for adoption. Our parents and Mom's sisters were the only people who knew about this and I have kept this secret for 40 years."

Faith, why are you telling me this? What happened today?" Laura asked.

"This afternoon, I received a call from Children's Home Society. The child I gave up all those years ago hired them to find me. She would like some family medical history and is interested in making contact with me," Faith said.

"After the birth, Mom and Dad told me 'just forget this episode, put this behind you and go on with your life.' That's exactly what I did and never told anyone – not you, or Gloria, or Jason, not even my best friend," she cried.

"While it may seem improbable, I haven't thought about this child. This call today from Children's Home Society was out of the blue. I don't know what to do. I don't know how to respond. What should I do?" she pleaded.

Laura's heart went out to her little sister, and she knew just how to comfort her.

"Faith, I have always loved and adored you and I have a confession to share with you," Laura confided. "Years ago, when Mother was dying, she told me about your baby. She thought that someone in the family should know."

"You've known all this time?" Faith gasped.

"Yes, and I have kept your secret," Laura said. "The decision to give up the baby girl for adoption was the right thing to do."

"I'll tell you another thing that I think is the right thing to do. I think you should consider contacting this child. And here's why – our good friend Richard was adopted and he has spent years searching for his birth mother. After coming up empty-handed, he hired a 'search angel' and she finally located his birth mother. The 'angel' warned Bob about possible dangers in contacting the woman and gave him a script and very specific instructions about the initial contact, letter, and phone call," Laura said.

"Richard faithfully followed the instructions and made the contact," Laura continued. "The woman was thrilled to hear from him. 'I have prayed for you every day of my life,' the birth mother said.

"Like you, she had never told her husband or family. Her adult children were surprised, but welcomed the new family member. During the reunion one of Richard's siblings told him, 'I knew there was a great sadness in mom's life, now I understand why.'"

"Faith, your life is coming full circle," Laura said. "I don't think you should be afraid to make contact with this young woman. She could turn out to be a blessing for you. Just take it slow. I will get the script and instructions from Richard and send to you. Please know, I will be right there to help you every step of the way."

"That's a relief," Faith sighed. "I knew I could count on you. Thanks for telling me about your friend, Richard. It's so nice to hear a happy ending."

Faith knew that she was just getting started, though. "I'm going to call Gloria next and then go home and tell Jason," she said. "How do you think he is going to react?"

Laura tried to be reassuring. "He is definitely going to be shocked," she said. "But the two of you have overcome some serious hurdles during your marriage and I'm sure you can count on him to stand beside you. I'll say a prayer for you, sweet sister. Good luck and God bless."

***

Like Laura, Faith's sister Gloria also was on vacation in a remote setting. She and her husband, Steve, had rented a quaint cottage in a tiny village in western Wisconsin. The cottage didn't have air conditioning, so as the July day heated up, she sought relief under the shade of an ancient maple tree.

In that peaceful setting, Gloria did her daily devotions and prayed in earnest for each of her seven children and their families. She asked God to be with them and to give them strength and guidance in their lives. As part of her daily ritual, she also asked God to be with her sisters and their families.

On this day she sensed that her sister Faith and one of her children were in distress, so she prayed aloud and asked God to be with them.

Then Faith called.

Gloria listened to her story and blurted out, "It's God's time!"

"Faith, I know this sounds odd, but I felt the Holy Spirit today and was praying for you," she said as she rubbed the goosebumps on her arm. "I feel that you are destined to make contact with this young woman. If she wants to meet your family, we will welcome her with open arms."

CHAPTER THIRTY-SIX

Jensen Beach, Florida
July 5, 2005

Faith had calmed down a bit after talking with her co-workers and sisters. The panic attack was over, but as she got in her car and left for home the tears began to fall. How was she ever going to explain this entire situation to her husband? Was Jason going to feel betrayed that she hadn't shared this secret with him?

This had been a second marriage for both.

After the divorce from Dan, Faith was devastated and found it daunting to be a single mom with three active kids. But she prevailed. Her weeks were filled with work, the kids' after-school activities and hanging out with Gloria's family, including Gloria's new husband, Steve Jones.

Dan was faithful with his support payments and taking their kids on alternate weekends. Faith took advantage of those child-free weekends and began going out with her friends, often partying in group activities at church, the beach, backyard cookouts and movies.

Faith began attending Parents without Partners meetings at the First United Methodist Church and became acquainted with Jason Patterson. He was a life-long resident of Sailfish Bay, divorced and devoted to his 2-year-old daughter. Gradually, Faith became good friends with the tall, sturdy man with curly dark hair and a neatly trimmed moustache.

When Jason's tenth high school reunion rolled around in June of 1987, he needed a date. He asked Faith and she accepted. The two had always had fun at group events and it didn't feel awkward to attend his reunion. She had already met a lot of his friends and had a great time that evening.

During the slow dances, Jason held her close in his strong arms, and as she looked into his kind brown eyes a tiny flame ignited. That night when the DJ played, "Two Less Lonely People," by Rex Allen, two lonely people swayed to the music and began thinking of each other in a very different way.

After Jason's reunion, the two wounded souls found strength in each other and the courage to move forward into a new relationship. They began dating seriously and in September of 1987 they were married in a small family ceremony at the Methodist church.

Once again, Robert Bradford escorted his daughter down the aisle. Hoping for a new beginning and a "happily ever-after," Faith wore a white lace tea-length dress and carried a bouquet of pink roses. Gloria was her matron of honor and Bill Stetson, Jason's life-long friend, was best man.

During the ceremony, Faith experienced a moment of nostalgia. She missed seeing her mother and her Aunt Theresa in the family pew, but she felt their presence and sensed the twin sisters were wishing her happiness from heaven.

The newlyweds moved into Faith's home and were happy together. However, like so many couples they struggled with blending the two families.

After Faith's divorce from Dan, her son Michael had become the self-professed "man" of the family. The serious eight-year-old once told his mom, "I will take care of you."

Michael resented Jason taking over that role and it took the boy a while to adjust. As time went by, Jason won him over and the two became good fishing buddies and friends. Faith's daughters had an easier time adjusting and doted on Brittany, Jason's little daughter, when she visited on alternate weekends.

Four years after Jason and Faith's wedding, a family tragedy rocked their lives.

On Friday, May 17, 1991, Faith's father had just enjoyed a competitive round of golf with his best friends and shot his age – quite a feat at 80. The foursome celebrated at the country club that morning and made plans to return for dinner with their wives. After a glorious day on the golf course, he returned home for a well-deserved nap.

He never woke up.

Faith and her sisters gathered once more to say a final farewell, this time to their devoted father. He had been a stabilizing force throughout their lives and loved them unconditionally. After the service at the Presbyterian church, family and guests gathered at the country club for a reception. His golf buddies shared stories about his competitive spirit, their golfing adventures in Ireland and Scotland, and the final day of his life when he shot 80 on a tough course.

Laura's husband, Edward, spoke kindly of his father-in-law and then ended his eulogy by injecting a light-hearted moment. He said, "Everyone, please raise a toast to Robert Bradford. He was a saint and my hero. This experienced father-of-the-bride had three daughters and paid for eight weddings!"

***

By 2005 Faith and Jason had been married for 18 years and were enjoying their empty nest. They were involved in the Sailfish Bay community both professionally and at leisure. Jason was a career counselor at an agency that worked with disabled adults and he volunteered for the church's outreach programs. Faith was responsible for the Red Cross' annual fundraising campaign and was an officer in several professional organizations.

After Faith had recovered from her bout with breast cancer, the couple sold the family home in Sailfish Bay and downsized into a comfortable three-bedroom villa in a nearby golf course community.

Life was good and they felt blessed.

Then, came the call from Children Home Society.

As Faith drove down their street, she could see Jason's Ford pick-up truck in the driveway and pulled in behind it. He usually beat her home and started supper.

"Hi sweetheart," she said as she entered the kitchen and gave him a quick kiss. "The house smells divine."

"Hey babe, I finished work early today and decided to make some chicken parm. It should be ready in a few minutes," he said.

"That sounds good," she said half-heartedly. Suddenly, she felt faint. Her knees buckled and she quickly grabbed hold of the corner of the kitchen table to steady herself. She slipped into the nearest chair.

"What's the matter?" he asked. "You look like you are running a fever. Are you sick?"

"Oh, Jason, I'm not sick, it's more like 'sick-at-heart.' I've had an unbelievable day and I need to talk with you about something that happened," she said as she wiped away a tear.

"This sounds serious, what's up?" he asked with concern. He turned down the heat on the oven and went to his wife.

"I was at work this afternoon when I received a call from Children's Home Society. They wanted to know if I had done business with them in 1966," she began.

"That's crazy!" he said. "You were just graduating from high school. You weren't even working then."

"Please, just let me finish," she pleaded, closing her eyes and taking a deep breath.

"Actually, I **was** in Florida that spring and had a baby girl that I gave up for adoption. That child is now almost 40 years old and would like to make contact with me," she said.

In a New York minute, Jason's expression shifted from concern to disbelief and he pushed his chair back from the table.

"What! Are you kidding me?" he exclaimed. "This is unbelievable! In all the years we have been together, you didn't think it was important to tell me about this baby?"

Faith tried to calm him. "Jason, until today, the only people who knew about this baby were my parents and my aunts," she said.

"When I had this baby, I was very young and my parents handled everything. They told me that I had given a precious life to a loving family and that I should just forget about it and go on with my life and that's exactly what I did!" she said.

162

Jason crossed his arms over his chest and stared at her, questions racing through his mind.

"Who is the baby's father?" he demanded. "How did you keep this a secret?"

When she told him about Adam and the deadly accident, she could sense his anger subsiding. He was astonished that her family had come up with the story about "mono" and had brought her to Florida for the final months of her pregnancy.

"I can't believe this," Jason said, shaking his head. "Why in the world is the girl contacting you now, after all these years?"

"What does she want?"

"The woman at Children's Home Society said she wants family medical history, and if we are agreeable, she is willing to make contact," Faith responded.

Jason thought for a moment, then said, "I think it's OK to share medical information, especially with your family's history of breast cancer, but I'm not sure it's a good idea to go beyond that. What's the point?"

As he reached across the table, he placed his hand on hers and said, "Faith, you have kept this secret for 40 years. If you pursue this, I'm worried about what this might do to you emotionally, and then what about our families? Why would you willingly put yourself through another crisis?"

Sensing his worry and concern, she said, "Jason, this has been such a shock, I am physically and emotionally exhausted. I don't know what to do," she sighed.

"What did you tell the social worker?" he asked.

"I told her that I needed to talk with my family and that I would get back to her in a couple of days," she replied.

"Good, that will give us time to sort this out," he said.

A while later, the couple sat at the table picking at their cold dinner while Faith shared the adoption stories she had heard from her co-workers and her sisters. The couple discussed possible scenarios and knew they needed more information before making a decision. Faith drove to the nearby Barnes & Noble and bought a couple of books that might help, while Jason searched the internet for stories about adoption reunions.

They stayed up until dawn and were still trying to make a decision as the sun's early rays crept over the horizon.

The tipping point came when Faith turned to her husband and said, "Jason, I have been praying about this and I know in my heart that I can't keep this a secret any longer. I think we should try to meet this girl. If we don't follow through, it's something we will always wonder about," she said.

He was still skeptical but agreed. "OK, then let's move forward. But you have to promise me that we will go slow and if things start to get weird, we will back away. We don't want this situation to blow up in our faces."

"Thanks so much for understanding," Faith said, as Jason held her in a comforting embrace. "Last night, my sister forwarded us the information from her friend's search angel. It has step-by-step suggestions on making the initial contact that I think we should follow. There are even sample letters plus what to say during the first call."

"Sounds like a plan," Jason said.

"I'll go ahead and call the social worker this morning and tell her that we are willing to take the next step," Faith said.

Before leaving for work, she called Molly at CHS. The young woman was delighted when she learned that Faith was willing to proceed.

"I would like to send a letter to this girl," Faith said. "Can you give me her name and address?"

"I think that's a good way to start, but for your protection, the agency wants the first contacts to be forwarded through us," Molly said. "While I feel very positive about your case, I urge you to proceed with caution. While we hope for a positive outcome, sometimes things can go horribly wrong."

"I understand," Faith said. "I'll write the first letter and send it to you via e-mail. Say a little prayer for me."

CHAPTER THIRTY-SEVEN

St. Augustine, Florida
July 6, 2005

It was going to be another hot, humid day in St. Augustine. The temperature had been pushing past 90 degrees for over a week. Penny was returning to her suburban office after attending a monthly breakfast meeting of the local bar association. She couldn't believe someone had scheduled the July meeting at the outdoor veranda overlooking the beach. Forget about the professional, well-polished look she tried to convey; she could feel herself melting.

"Good morning Harriet," Penny said as she entered the law office. "I'm dying. This air-conditioning feels sooo good."

Harriet, her administrative assistant, looked up from her desk. "What happened to you?" she asked as she tried to suppress a smile. Penny's damp hair was plastered against her head, her silk blouse had slipped outside the waistband of her navy skirt and she was carrying the matching blazer over her arm.

"Can you believe they scheduled the meeting this morning outdoors? It was hot and breezy and to top it off, there was a random shower as we were scurrying to our cars," Penny steamed. "I must look a mess!"

"No worries," said the devoted assistant. "We don't have anyone scheduled until later, but we are making progress on the truck crash investigation. The reports from the Florida Highway Patrol are on your desk."

"Thanks Harriet, let me take a few minutes to put myself together and I will review those reports," Penny said.

An hour later, Penny was engrossed in the FHP reports when Harriet put through a call. A cheery voice greeted her.

"Penny, this is Molly from Children's Home Society. I just spoke with your birth mother and she is willing to make contact with you."

"Oh, my God! Are you sure?" Penny asked. "What did she say?"

"Yes, it's true." Molly said. "I have to tell you that I'm totally surprised that she agreed. This woman has kept your birth a secret for 40 years. Her husband and children had no idea you existed.

She would like to write you a letter and wanted to know where you lived. Per our policies I am not allowed to share that information. I asked her to send the letter to me and promised that I would forward to you.

"For everyone's protection, your first response will also go through me. After that, if you feel comfortable with the situation you can proceed at your own pace," Molly added. "My advice is to go slow and be cautious."

"I understand," Penny said. "That's a good idea. I've read where some of these long-lost connections have had some negative results, and I certainly want to avoid that."

"Your birth mother seems nice. She works as a development officer for a social service agency here in Florida. She is the mother of three adult children and is also a grandmother," Molly said.

"Molly, I still can't believe you found her and talked with her. This is a life changing day for me," Penny said, as her heart pounded wildly.

As she hung up the phone, Harriet popped in. "What's happened?" she asked. The devoted employee had been on this long journey with her friend and boss, and she was eager to hear the update.

"Harriet, you are not going to believe this," Penny said with excitement. "CHS has found my birth mother and Molly talked to her! The woman lives in Florida and is willing to communicate with me."

"Penny, that's wonderful news! Praise the Lord! I was beginning to think this day would never come for you," her assistant said.

Penny promptly called her husband. "Jim, guess what? I just received **the call** from CHS. They talked with my birth mother and she is willing to make contact."

"Are you kidding me?" he said. "That's great news! I think."

167

"I'm thrilled, but it's a little scary, too," she replied. "I wish we could look into a crystal ball and see how this is going to turn out."

"What did the social worker tell you?" he asked.

"Molly cautioned me about the initial contacts and suggested they go through her before too much information is exchanged," Penny replied.

"Sounds like good advice," he said.

"Jim, can you believe this woman has kept this secret from her family for almost 40 years?" Penny asked.

"No, and I can't imagine how difficult it will be for her to tell her family about   you   after   all   this   time,"   he   replied.

CHAPTER THIRTY-EIGHT

Sailfish Bay, Florida
July 6, 2005

After a sleepless night and weighing pros and cons, Faith decided to go forward with making the initial contacts and hoped to eventually meet this forgotten child from long ago.

When Faith arrived at her office, she saw Ellen and Jennifer and told them that she had agreed to contact this daughter and was not keeping this secret any longer. As the morning unfolded, she told the remainder of the close-knit staff about the situation and asked for their love and support.

The small, caring staff had worked together for a number of years and could be counted on to lend a helping hand when anyone of the group was dealing with life's challenges. Three years earlier, they had rallied around Faith and comforted her through her successful surgery and chemo treatments for breast cancer. While they were astounded at this recent announcement, they would stand beside her and offer encouragement and advice as she began this new journey.

After sharing the news with her co-workers, she began the awkward task of notifying her children. "Wonder how they were going to react, when I tell them they have a new sister?" she pondered. "Lord, give me courage."

Christina was in her Atlanta office enjoying a quiet moment and thinking about her future assignment. It had been a special day. She had received a memo earlier informing her that she had been promoted to management within the giant company. Her long hours and dedication had paid off, and she could hardly wait to call her mom and share the news.

At that moment, her cell phone rang. "Mom, I guess we are on the same wave length today," Christina said. "I was going to call you! I have some great news to share."

"This is a special day then, because I have some big news to share, too," Faith said. "You go first."

Patricia Daum

"Mom, I just received notice that I've been promoted to management!" she said. "I'm meeting with my boss in 30 minutes to learn more about my new position, and my sweet husband is taking me out to dinner tonight to celebrate."

"Oh, Christina, what exciting news! I'm so proud of you. You have worked hard and deserve this more than anyone I know," her mother said. "I can hardly wait to learn more about your new assignment."

"OK, I have shared my great news, what's up with you?" Christina asked.

"Sweetheart, I'm not sure how to tell you this, but here goes. When I was 17, I had a baby girl in Florida and gave her up for adoption. I received a call yesterday from Children's Home Society and learned this child from long ago would like to make contact. This has been a family secret for all these years. No one but your grandparents and my aunts knew about this."

"Oh, Mommy, I don't know what to say," Christina gasped.

"Now that the secret is out, I wanted you and your brother and sister to know. I'm not sure how things are going to turn out, but I have decided to proceed with contacting this young woman," Faith said.

"Who was the father?" Christina asked. "Has he been contacted, too?"

"Christina, he was a boy I dated in high school, and tragically, he was killed in a car accident months before I realized I was pregnant. His family knows nothing about this," her mom said.

"Mommy, this is so sad," she said. "What a difficult decision you had to make back then. Please know that this doesn't change my feelings for you. My head is spinning and I have a thousand questions to ask, but can we talk about this later tonight? It's time for me to meet my boss."

"I love you with all my heart. Bye, bye," Christina said.

***

Michael, her first born was the responsible little fellow who stated he was the "man of the house" during the years she was divorced. He never quite forgave his dad for moving out, and he struggled with the new family dynamics when Jason married his mom.

After high school graduation he joined the Navy, married his high school sweetheart and was now the father of two active little boys. He had recently become a civilian and was working as an airline mechanic. He adored his mother, often calling her on his drive home from work to share the daily news. They would have a lot to share today.

"Hi Mom, I'm in the parking lot of Home Depot. I need to pick up some supplies to repair and paint my deck. How's your day going? The boys have a tee ball game tonight, can you and Jason come?" he asked.

"Michael, we will try to be at the game, but first I have some big news to share," she said. "I'm glad you are in the parking lot and not driving."

"Are you feeling OK? You sound hoarse," he said, starting to worry about this "big news."

"Yes, I'm all right, but I received some surprising news yesterday and I need to tell you about a family secret that is older than you," she struggled to say.

"What the heck are you talking about?" he questioned.

"Michael, when I was 17, I had a baby girl and gave her up for adoption in Florida. This has been a secret for all these years and the only people who knew about this were your grandparents and my aunts." she said.

"Mom, are you kidding me! I am standing in the Home Depot parking lot! Why in God's green earth are you telling me this now?" he interrupted.

Faith kept going, wanting to get it all out. "Yesterday, I received a call from Children's Home Society. They located me at the girl's request. She wanted some family medical history and is interested in making contact. I have decided to proceed with this and wanted you and your sisters to know."

"I don't believe this!" Michael shouted. "You are the one who has always told us to tell the truth. Now we learn that you have kept this girl a secret for 40 years?"

"How could you give up your own flesh and blood?" he demanded. "And who was the father?"

"Michael, I know this is a shock, but please try to understand," Faith said. "I was only 17 and the baby's father was killed in an auto accident. I didn't realize I was pregnant until months after he died."

"Mom, that's a really sad story and I'm sorry about him dying, but what about his family? Do they know?" he asked. "Seems they had a right to know."

"No, we didn't tell anyone else. My sisters and my best girlfriend didn't even know," she said.

"Mom, I love you, but I am really upset that you have keep this secret from us. I don't think you should try and contact this girl. This could disrupt the entire family," he said. "What am I supposed to tell my two boys?"

"Michael, I'm not sure how this whole scenario is going to play out. The truth is, we may never meet this girl, so you don't need to tell the boys right away. When the time comes, we will find the best way to explain it to them," she said.

"Yeah, right!" he replied with sarcasm. "Mom, this may sound silly, but do you know what upsets me the most about this? I have always thought I was the oldest."

Before he had time to ask more questions Faith said, "Michael, we can talk about this later. Right now, I have one more call to make…to your sister Lisa," she said.

She heard her son's ornery laugh as he ended the call. "Good luck with that," he said.

***

Lisa was the youngest of the three Townsend children and the "happy-go-lucky" child. She had tried her hand at a variety of jobs and was currently working at a local florist shop with one of her cousins.

When Faith called, she had just walked into her tiny apartment, grabbed a can of Diet Coke from the fridge and plopped on her faded hand-me-down sofa.

"Hi, Mom, how was your day? Mine was crazy." Lisa chatted without taking a breath. "We have a big wedding this weekend. We just finished doing all the flowers for the church. You won't believe what happened – the huge arrangement for the altar was sitting on a table and the table collapsed! What a mess…flowers, greenery and water scattered everywhere!"

"That must have been quite a sight," her mom interrupted. "I've had a crazy day, too, and have something very important to tell you."

"Oh, you sound serious. Are you OK?" Lisa asked.

As Faith rocked back and forth in her office chair, she told Lisa about receiving the call from Children's Home Society and the story about giving the baby up for adoption and keeping the secret for 40 years.

"Wow, Mom, I can't believe you have kept this secret for so long. When are you going to meet this girl?" she asked, her excitement mounting.

"You know, I worked with a girl who was adopted and she found her birth mother," Lisa said. "She met the rest of her new family and they get along really well. Maybe that will happen for us!

"This is awesome news. I can hardly wait to tell my friends and get their reaction when I say, I'm getting a new sister and guess what, she is 39 years old! They will freak out!" she said.

Faith listened as her youngest daughter chattered on and was amazed at how each child had handled this announcement in a different way.

"Lisa, you may want to hold off telling your friends until after I've talked with her. I promised Jason that I would go slow with this process and it may take a while before we actually connect," Faith said.

"OK, Mom, but I can hardly wait to meet my new sister!"

173

PART EIGHT

CHAPTER THIRTY-NINE

Sailfish Bay, Florida
July 2005

After Faith notified her immediate family, it was time to draft the first letter to this newly found daughter. She struggled at first, stopping and starting several times. Finally, she cleared her mind, said a silent prayer and began. What should she say? How much information should she include?

July 12, 2005

Dear Daughter,

I was surprised and shocked when I received the call from CHS. Molly told me that you had been searching for me and wanted to learn about your medical history. We are basically a very healthy family, but breast cancer has been prevalent. My grandmother and mother both died of the disease and I am a breast cancer survivor.

My family is from upstate New York and I spent the last few months of my pregnancy in Florida, where my parents arranged your private adoption. During the delivery, I had twilight sleep and the nurses immediately whisked you away to the nursery. I never saw you.

A few days after your birth, my mother and I signed adoption papers at an attorney's office in Hollywood and he reassured us that you were going to a loving home. After signing the papers, I remember sitting in my mom's car and both of us cried. My parents told me to put this episode behind me and get on with my life, and I did.

Your birth has been a family secret for all these years. Until this week, the only people who knew about you were my parents and my aunts. Your birth father was killed in an auto accident months before I realized I was pregnant and his family knows nothing about the pregnancy.

Molly mentioned that you were open to making contact. I have prayed about this and after talking to my husband, my three adult children and my two sisters, I have decided to move forward. I welcome the opportunity to have contact with you.

Daughter, I have always held you close, locked in a secret chamber of my heart. I hope you have had a happy life with a loving family and I look forward to learning more about you. I understand from Molly that our next contact will be through her. If you wish to proceed please include your contact information and I promise to respond.

With Love,
Faith

***

It was a couple of weeks before Faith heard from Penny.

Faith's letter had arrived when Penny was in Miami visiting her parents. Her dad had been diagnosed with an aggressive form of lung cancer and the life-long smoker was not responding well to treatments. Her mother was frail and having a difficult time dealing with her husband's diagnosis, and brother Todd was of little help. He was battling a substance abuse problem – an ongoing struggle for him.

When Penny arrived at her office, she was thankful there was not a pressing court date for any of her cases. However, the in box on Penny's desk was overflowing. Nestled among the various notices and court documents was a large envelope from Children's Home Society. Penny ripped it open – inside was a note from Molly and the first correspondence from her birth mother.

Penny's hands were unsteady as she reverently opened the pale blue envelope and unfolded the matching pale blue letter with a scalloped edge.

Her name was Faith. Her handwriting was beautiful.

After the words of caution from Molly, Penny understood why Faith had not included a lot of personal information in this first letter. But she felt it was a positive step that Faith had finally told her family about this secret and was willing to communicate with her.

"Harriet, come in, I have something to show you," Penny said, waving the scalloped blue page with excitement. "It's the first letter from my birth mother. Guess what? Her name is Faith and she wants to hear from me."

"Faith? That's a pretty name," Harriet said. "Did she tell you much about herself?"

"No, but I learned that my birth father was a teenager when he was killed in an auto accident and his family was not aware of the pregnancy. Faith has kept this secret for 40 years and after the call from CHS, she finally told her family about me. "They have encouraged her to communicate with me," Penny said.

"The letter is pretty standard, but there is one sentence that I will treasure. She says:
'Daughter, I have always held you close, locked in a secret chamber of my heart. I hope you have had a happy life with a loving family and I look forward to learning more about you.'"

"That's sweet," Harriet said. "Are you going to respond?"

"Yes, but I need to work on the reply. This letter was sent more than two weeks ago. She may think I have changed my mind," Penny said.

Dear Faith,

Thanks so much for your recent letter. I very much appreciate having your medical history. Until I had my daughter, I never thought that much about it. Now, I look at life differently and want to be more vigilant about my health.

I want to thank you for being so generous as to give me up for adoption. I am sure that it was a very difficult time for you and your family and a difficult decision. My adoptive parents have always loved me as their own child and I have nothing but wonderful things to say about them. For as long as I can remember, I have known that I was adopted. I have always fit in with my adoptive family and never felt incomplete or that a part of me was missing.

I grew up in Miami and my parents still live in the same house we moved into when I was 10 years old. I have an older brother, Todd, and my grandmother lived with us most of my life. She was a dear lady and we were very close.

Both of my parents are still alive, but in failing health. Sadly, my father has just been diagnosed with lung cancer and I'm making frequent trips to Miami to be with him and my mother.

My husband Jim and I have been married for sixteen years and currently live in St. Augustine with our 6-year-old daughter, Ashley, and two aging cocker spaniels. I graduated from the University of Florida in 1989 and then graduated from St. Thomas Law School in 1992. I have been in private practice ever since.

I hope this letter has reassured you that your decision to give me up for adoption was the right one and that I have not suffered because of it. I am glad to hear that you are married with three children. I wish only the best for all of you.

As you can imagine, I do have quite a few questions, but we can get to them in time. Feel free to correspond with me by e-mail, phone, or snail mail at my office address. You will notice that all my contact information is included on my letterhead.

I look forward to hearing from you again.

Your birth daughter,

Penny   *Snyder*

CHAPTER FORTY

St. Augustine, Florida
September 2005

The active hurricane season of 2004 had kept Faith and her co-workers at the Red Cross busy, attempting to meet the needs of local residents, as well as helping other chapters across the state. The situation would get even worse in 2005, a year that would set records for the number and intensity of its storms. The most notorious of these was Katrina which had crossed South Florida as a relatively moderate Category 2 before it spun into the Gulf and grew into a monster storm that swamped New Orleans. Two more hurricanes affected Florida in September and more were yet to come.

Throughout the hurricane season, Faith and Penny had been exchanging polite e-mails and occasional phone conversations, learning more about each other and their families. When Faith forwarded Penny a recent photo of her and Jason, Penny said it was like "looking into a mirror." Husband Jim saw a strong family resemblance in the blonde hair, fair skin, sweet smile and cute dimples. The two women even sported a similar hair style, short with bangs. "You definitely look like her daughter!" he exclaimed.

Jim and Penny also realized something else: Many members of Faith's family had graduated from college. During one conversation with Faith, she said. "No one in my adoptive family ever graduated from college and only a few cousins even started college. For me to attend college and then law school says a lot, I think, for you as my biological mother. I guess genetics can be as strong an influence in a person's life as environment."

Faith's family was cautiously reaching out to this newest family member. Penny had received a gracious "Welcome to the Family" letter from her new sister Christina and a chatty e-mail from Aunt Gloria, who shared some information and stories about Penny's birth father, Adam Collins.

While Faith had kept this secret for 40 years and had struggled to tell her family, Penny had different issues. With her parents having serious health issues, she refrained from telling them. She told her mother she had obtained the medical history, but didn't tell her about contacting Faith. With everything her parents were dealing with; she didn't want to upset them.

However, she was able to share the exciting news with her brother, one of her aunts and Jim's parents. Todd and her aunt were happy for her and agreed that she should keep the news from her parents. Jim's family was excited and interested in learning more about this woman.

Penny also faced the challenge of explaining a birth mother and a new grandma to her 6-year- old. She tried to keep it simple and crafted a story that she hoped Ashley would understand.

One evening after supper she and Jim cuddled up with their daughter on the leather sofa and Penny said, "Ashley, I have a story to tell you. A long time ago when your Uncle Todd was 4 years old, your Grandma and Grandpa wanted a baby girl, but they weren't able to have one themselves. So, they adopted a baby girl. They went to the orphanage at the Children's Home Society in Miami and picked up a precious baby girl. That baby girl was me," Penny said.

Before her mother could continue, Ashley began to cry. "You were in an orphanage? You were an orphan?"

This was not the reaction Penny had expected.

"Oh, Ashley, it's so sweet that you are worried about me! But, dry your tears and let me finish the story. It has a happy ending, I promise." Penny said, as she hugged her daughter closer and stroked her hair.

"You see, there was a young woman who gave birth to me, but she wasn't able to keep me. So, she made arrangements for me to be placed in a wonderful home. I was only in the orphanage for a very short time before my parents – your Grandma and Grandpa – came to pick me up. I was placed in a home with a family who loved me very much and we have lived happily ever after!"

"That **is** a happy ending, Mommy!" Ashley said with delight.

"That happened a long time ago, but now there's a new part of the story," Penny said. "I have been in contact with this woman. Her name is Faith and she seems very nice. Daddy and I are making plans to meet her and her husband, Jason, one day soon. Would you like to go with us?"

Patricia Daum

"Yes," replied the sweet little voice. "But I'm still sad that you were an orphan."

***

Cocoa Beach, Florida
October 2, 2005

By the end of September 2005, it appeared that the tropics were in a lull and the two couples were finally able to set a date for a face-to-face meeting – October 2. When they determined that Cocoa Beach was the half-way point between both of their homes, Jim researched restaurants in the area and picked out the Florida Seafood Bar and Grill located on the Banana River. It would be a two-hour drive for each couple.

Penny, the young defense attorney who was fearless when facing high-powered firms in injury-related cases, found herself feeling anxious. "Would there be an instant connection? Would Faith be emotional? Would they like each other? What if they didn't?" she wondered.

She had tried to prepare herself by reading stories about other mother-daughter reunions, but they were of little help – every experience was different. Penny resolved to be cool and calm and keep her emotions in check. This would **not** be one of those televised reunions where the two women race toward each other, embrace and burst into tears upon their first meeting.

October 2 was a Chamber of Commerce day along the Space Coast of Florida. As the two couples drove toward the rendezvous, the weather was perfect – a sunny, breezy 79 degrees with white fluffy clouds floating across the heavenly blue skies.

As they crossed the Banana River Lagoon on the four-mile causeway between Merritt Island and Cocoa Beach, Penny felt a shiver of anticipation. Jim reached over from the driver's seat and grasped her hand. "Are you OK?" he asked.

"I think so," she replied. "I have butterflies in my stomach and I'm more nervous than I expected. You know I've read all those stories about reunions, but nothing can prepare you for actually meeting your birth mother," Penny said.

"You are going to be fine," Jim said with encouragement.

"Mommy, how did the butterflies get in your tummy?" Ashley piped in from the back seat.

"Oh, they're not real butterflies," her mom replied with a nervous laugh. "It just means I'm excited about meeting your new grandma. How about you?"

"Yes," replied the 6-year-old. "Do you think she will be nice? Do you think she will bring me a present?"

"I'm sure she will be nice, she has some other grandchildren and she is looking forward to meeting you," Penny said. "But don't expect any presents, young lady."

The Florida Seafood Bar and Grill was easy to find. It commanded a prime location on the corner of the causeway and A1A, overlooking the lagoon. The large single-story establishment was boldly painted in Florida Gator colors, bright orange with vivid blue shutters and boasted a spacious paved parking lot.

"Now I know why you selected this place," Penny said, turning to Jim with a smirk. "How appropriate that it would have Gator décor."

As soon as they got out of the car, Penny and Jim began scanning the parking lot for someone that resembled Faith in the photo she had sent. The restaurant was huge and as they wandered aimlessly through each section, they continued searching. They pointed out people to each other. "Is that her? Is that her?" Even Ashley got into the game, standing on her tiptoes to see someone, anyone who looked like the lady in the photo.

They didn't find Faith in the bar, or the upper and lower lounges, but finally saw her in the main dining room. There she was – dressed in navy capris and a crisp white cotton blouse – wearing a big smile. She looked just like her photo!

As Penny approached Faith, she took a deep breath to calm herself, smiled and said, "Hi, Faith. I'm Penny. It's nice to finally meet you," and held out her hand.

Time stood still as Faith gazed into Penny's deep blue eyes. "It's nice to see you, too," Faith said, as she clasped her daughter's hand for the first time. Her heart fluttered and her eyes misted. This was not the tiny hand of a newborn baby gripping her fingers for the first time. This was the firm handshake of a lovely, confident young woman.

Faith had been worried about this meeting for weeks and was a bundle of nerves during the drive to Cocoa Beach. Like Penny, she had tried to prepare herself for this day. She had been diligent in reading books and numerous articles and her co-workers had given her plenty of advice. But she had no idea of how she was going to feel, or how this day was going to pan out.

During the drive, Jason tried to reassure her. "You are going to be OK." he said. "I have faith that this meeting is going to work out just fine."

After casual introductions and a few uncomfortable moments of standing in the dining room, a friendly waitress rescued them and selected a table with an outstanding view of the Banana River. She took their drink orders and promptly delivered a basket of the restaurant's famous sugar dusted homemade fritters.

While waiting for their lunches and nibbling on the fritters, they chatted idly about the weather and the drive to the restaurant. Then Penny brought out a gift for Faith – a framed photo of Penny, Jim and Ashley. As Faith marveled at the photo of this new family, Ashley piped in, "Do you like it? I helped wrap it."

"Yes, I love it," Faith said. "Thank you very much. I will put the photo on my nightstand, next to all my other treasured photos."

"Ashley, I have something for you, too," Faith said as she handed the child a gift bag filled with a Little Mermaid coloring book with stickers and a packet of crayons.

"You **did** bring a present! Thank you!" Ashley said, already opening the crayons. "I will color a picture for you."

"Penny, I haven't forgotten you," Faith said as she gave her a small box. "I wanted you to have something of my mother's. This is one of her gold golf charms, a prize for winning a club championship. Golf was a big part of my parents' lives and they were proud of their achievements, so I thought this would be a good memento."

"Thank you, what a thoughtful gift," Penny said.

"Faith, I have something else to show you," Penny said as she pulled an envelope from her purse. "Do you remember this? It's the information about your family that Children's Home Society sent to me. They told me the form had been filled out before my adoption. It tells about your mother and father, your sisters, and a little bit about my birth father's family.

As Faith read through the document, she recognized her mother's handwriting. "Penny, I never saw this document. My mother must have completed this form when she met with the attorney," Faith said. "And some of this information is news to me. I didn't know that I had measles when I was 3 years old, and knowing my mother, I can't believe she admitted to anyone that she had false teeth!"

"There was another curious thing," Penny said. "When I read through the form, I noticed that your mom and dad and you and your sisters were all tall. Obviously, I didn't get that gene."

"I think our height comes from my dad's family and also Grandpa Hamilton's family," Faith said. "You probably take after Grandma Hamilton's family. They were more petite."

Conversation turned to exploring common bonds the couples might have. Did they know any of the same people? Had they ever been at the same place at the same time? They struck out on all counts, but the husbands found they shared passions for football, baseball and fishing. However, on the football front, Penny and Jim were avid Florida Gator fans, while Jason cheered for the rival Georgia Bulldogs.

While the men proceeded to exchange trash talk over the upcoming Florida-Georgia game, Penny and Faith chatted about family and jobs. When talk about work came up, Penny recalled the fund-raiser that Faith had told her about.

"Faith, I have to know, how did the Pennies Count event turn out?" Penny asked.

185

"It turned out great," she said. "We raised more than $5,000 in pennies!"

"The Lucky Penny mascot visited all the schools, and the community bank was thrilled with the positive publicity they received. Best of all, it was the type of event that every child could participate in, no matter what their economic situation," Faith said.

After lunch, the couples asked their waitress to take a family photo on the deck outside the restaurant. As she focused on the shot, the waitress said to Penny, "You look just like your mom!"

Penny was startled by the comment. They had had a pleasant lunch and a nice first meeting, but she wasn't ready to call Faith, "Mom." Penny already had a mother that she loved very much.

As they left the restaurant, the families agreed to stay in touch. The two women exchanged polite hugs, the men shook hands, and Ashley waved goodbye.

When they returned to the car and Ashley was getting buckled up in her seat she said, "I think Grandma Faith was nice."

"I think so too," her mom answered, marveling at how quickly Ashley accepted this new grandma and grandpa. "That was so sweet of her to bring you a present."

"Penny, what's your impression?" Jim asked as they drove across the causeway toward home.

"I feel much better after meeting Faith and Jason. After the initial awkwardness, I felt very comfortable with them," Penny said. "It was a good start."

CHAPTER FORTY-ONE

Sailfish Bay, Florida
October 2005-April 2006

Faith and Jason were standing by their car and waving good-bye as Penny and her family drove away. Faith leaned against Jason and as the tears began to fall, he wrapped his comforting arms around her and held her tight.

"This has been such an emotional day," she cried. "I didn't know what to expect, but seeing her was wonderful and my heart is overflowing."

"I think everything turned out as well as could be expected," Jason said. "They are a nice couple and I hope we get to see them again."

"Me, too," Faith said, wiping away her tears. "I felt an immediate connection with Penny, but I sensed a reluctance on her part."

Faith knew that she had enough love to include this child in her family circle, but she wisely decided to tread softly. It was easier for Ashley to have another grandmother, and Faith embraced that role, sending cute cards and tiny gifts to the girl on special occasions.

In the months following their Cocoa Beach lunch, the women continued to exchange occasional e-mails and kept each other up to date on their families. There were messages of concern when Hurricane Wilma hit Florida the end of October. Penny sent photos of Ashley at Halloween dressed in her Little Mermaid costume. Jim called Jason to gloat over the Florida Gator's 14-10 upset of the Georgia Bulldogs, and the men pledged to continue the friendly rivalry.

During the final months of 2005, Penny's father was critically ill and she spent Thanksgiving and Christmas with her family in Miami. There was minimal contact with the new family. She exchanged Christmas cards with Faith and sent her a festive floral arrangement.

Penny's father passed away in early 2006. With her busy work schedule and visiting her grieving mother, there was little time to get together with Faith and family. However, they still stayed in touch, and Faith sent comforting messages to the young woman.

As Penny's 40th birthday approached on April 12, Faith decided to do something special. She had never been able to celebrate this daughter's special day and decided to surprise her with 40 presents! She spent weeks picking out gifts and wrapping them in colorful paper.

Faith had fun buying dozens of items for the Florida Gator fan. She also purchased historical books about Batavia and Oakfield and ordered a box of chocolates from Oliver's, her family's favorite candy store in Batavia. She also found a book about Sailfish Bay's history. While visiting a local craft fair, a blue-glazed pottery jar with a quirky top caught her eye. As she looked closer, she realized it was a bank and it had a top shaped like a penny. Engraved on the top was "Lucky Pennies." She promptly added that to the gifts and filled it with 40 new pennies.

She still needed two more items. Maybe there was something from her youth that she could include. She remembered that her parents had boxed up their three daughters' childhood mementoes when they retired to Florida. Somewhere, there was a box with her name on it.

After searching the closets and under the beds she came up empty handed. Maybe it was in the attic. She recruited Jason to help her. He pulled down the folding ladder from the ceiling of the garage and climbed into the attic. She heard him shuffling boxes and spouting profanity as he bumped his head on the rafters. "I think I've found it!" he shouted. "It was hidden under the boxes of Christmas decorations."

He handed her the battered United Moving Van carton with her name on top. She recognized her mother's handwriting, "Faith's Treasures."

She carried the box into the guest bedroom, sat on the bed and began unpacking. It was a pleasant walk down Memory Lane. She smiled as she found her white patent go-go boots and blue sash from flag corps along with the photo of Sherri and Faith in the front yard of her childhood home wearing their new uniforms. She found her high school yearbooks, graduation announcement and program, high school diploma and a small album of senior pictures that she had exchanged with her friends.

"Gosh, we all look so young, and I haven't thought about some of these classmates for years," she thought and gently shook her head. Many of the photos had sweet messages on the back – "Keep Smiling," "Remember the fun times with Y-Teens," "Friends forever."

She was happy to find these items. Her 40th high school class reunion was scheduled for the summer and it would be fun to share these mementoes with her old friends.

Faith thumbed through the photos of Y-Teen activities and unfolded a newspaper clipping with the front-page photo of Faith and her friend Kathy the summer they worked at the filling station.

There were also cherished items from her first communion – a small white Bible, a child's rosary and two photos of Faith in a frilly white dress. In one she was standing between her proud parents and in the other she was standing beside her beloved Kay Kay.

Near the bottom of the carton was a valentine candy box – a faded pink satin heart.

"Wonder what this is?" she thought. She gasped as she opened the box. There was the prom photo of her and Adam, the faded ribbons from the once-beautiful wrist corsage, the newspaper clippings of his horrible accident, and his class ring.

Faith sat for a long time as **those hidden memories came rushing back.**

Then, she slipped the photo of the smiling young couple into a pretty frame and placed Adam's class ring into a velvet box. As Faith wrapped these final two gifts for Penny, she thought of Adam. She felt he would be happy that their daughter had something of his, and he would also be wishing Penny a happy 40th birthday.

***

St. Augustine, Florida
April 12, 2006

Penny had been dreading this milestone birthday and didn't feel like celebrating. This was the first year of her life that her father wasn't there to help her celebrate and to share a piece of Carvel ice cream cake. Jim, who loved surprising his wife, promised to keep this a low-key celebration.

He kept his promise.

There was not a big party. Instead, he sent a dozen pink roses to her office and treated Penny and Ashley to a birthday dinner at the Ritz Carlton on nearby Amelia Island. She received two gifts. Ashley and her dad had gone shopping and Ashley had picked out a pair of sparkly pink earrings for her mom. Jim had also selected something sparkly – a diamond tennis bracelet.

"These are beautiful! Thank you so much," Penny said as she promptly put on the new jewelry and gave Ashley and Jim a big kiss.

When the small family returned home, there was a large box sitting on the front porch. "Wonder who this is from?" Penny asked.

"It's from Faith," Jim said as he looked at the return label and carried the box into the living room. Penny was curious as she opened the box filled with presents and read the card on top.

Happy Birthday Penny! This box is filled with 40 years of belated birthday wishes. Jason and I look forward to celebrating many more birthdays with you. Love, Faith

"This is unexpected," Penny said as she turned to Jim. "Did you know anything about this?"

"No, I didn't," he replied. "But it's a sweet gesture, let's see what she has sent you."

"I'll help you open the presents!" Ashley offered and dug into the box.

Penny and Jim and Ashley began opening the gifts. "This is like Christmas!" Ashley shouted as she opened the Florida Gator items. Jim showed Penny the historical books from Batavia and Sailfish Bay, while they all nibbled on the chocolates and laughed at the "Lucky Pennies" jar filled with 40 pennies.

When Penny unwrapped the framed prom photo of Faith and Adam, she looked at the smiling teenagers and clutched the photo close to her heart. This was the only picture she would ever have of her birthmother and birthfather together.

She would cherish the photo and Adam's class ring forever.

She called Faith and thanked her for her thoughtfulness. This would always be a birthday to remember.

CHAPTER FORTY-TWO

Batavia, New York
June 2006

It was early June when Faith returned to Batavia for her 40th class reunion. As she drove down Main Street, she was reminded of the changes that had taken place. The charming town of her childhood was gone. An urban renewal project that began when she went away to college had destroyed the town center and replaced it with a non-descript mall. Most of the shops and businesses she had frequented as a child were gone.

Driving down East Street past her childhood home, she was glad to see that the neighborhood looked familiar. The young trees that had been planted along the street years earlier, were now tall and full, the spacious homes well-maintained and the lawns professionally manicured.

As she stopped in front of her former home, she noticed the beautiful maple tree. It was huge and provided a full canopy of shade for the yard. There must be a young family living there now, evidenced by a basketball hoop above the garage door and a pink bicycle lying in the driveway. She heard children laughing and splashing in the backyard swimming pool.

Faith noticed an elderly man trimming the hedges in the yard next door. She stopped to say hello. As she got out of the rental car and walked toward the stooped man, Mr. Law looked up and recognized her immediately. "Faith, what a pleasant surprise. It's so good to see you," he said as he gave her a welcoming hug. "What brings you to town?"

"Mr. Law, I'm here for my 40th high school reunion," she replied.

"That doesn't seem possible," he said. "It just seems like yesterday when you and Sherri graduated. I haven't seen her for a while, not since her parents moved."

"Actually, I'm having lunch with Sherri this afternoon, and I'm running a little late," Faith said. "Wish I could visit with you longer. But I have to ask, are you still making the ice rinks for the neighborhood kids? That was always so much fun, and I remember Mrs. Law's delicious hot chocolate."

"No, I gave that up a few years ago after I had knee surgery," he said. "My wife is going to be sad that she didn't get to see you, but please tell Sherri that we said hello."

"I will do that," Faith said as she waved good-bye.

Faith had a similar routine each time she visited her hometown. After driving past her childhood home, she would stop by the Wexford Country Club and admire the championship plaques won by generations of her family. Then she would visit Batavia cemetery to place flowers on the graves of her grandparents, Aunt Theresa and Kay Kay.

She always visited with her best friend Sherri and they would get together with their group from Y-Teens. They always had a fun time reconnecting and reminiscing.

This visit with Sherri would be different, and Faith was **anxious** about telling her oldest and dearest friend about Penny. "How would she react to learning about this long-held secret?"

The two women met at Alex's Place, a former one-room restaurant that had expanded over the years. The "hole in the wall" place from previous visits was now a white tablecloth restaurant with warm wood décor, an open kitchen and a dining room that seated 100 people.

"You look great!" Sherri said as they hugged and selected a table for two in a quiet corner. "It's been too long since we have seen each other."

"What's in your shopping bag?" Sherri asked. She started laughing as Faith pulled out the white patent go-go boots and blue sash.

"Remember these?" Faith asked.

"And I have more," she said, as she continued pulling items out of the bag. "Look at the senior pictures I found, and look at our hair styles! The girls all had short "bubbles" or long "flips" and the boys had "flat tops" or "Princeton" cuts."

"At least the guys had hair then," Sherri laughed as she thumbed through the photos. "Oh, I remember this one. We were so proud to get our new flag corps uniforms and your dad insisted that we stand in front of that huge maple tree."

After chatting about Faith's trip and sharing photos of their grandchildren, Faith told Sherri about Penny.

Sherri was flabbergasted and speechless.

As she gazed out the window and stared at the hanging basket of pink and white petunias, she didn't know what to feel, let alone what to say. "Faith had a baby all those years ago when she went to Florida and we all thought she was ill with 'mono?' It was Adam's baby and his family never knew? This was too much to process," she pondered.

After a few moments of awkward silence, she recovered. "Faith, I can't believe this. We have been friends forever and you didn't feel like you could tell me?" she said. "I feel betrayed."

"Sherri, I'm so sorry, but my parents felt it was best that I told no one. They were protecting me and took care of everything," Faith said. "They told me the baby was a blessing for another family and that after she was born, I should just forget about the experience and get on with my life. That's exactly what I did."

Sherri thought for a moment, then asked, "What about Adam's family? Don't you think they had the right to know?"

"I never questioned my parents about telling Adam's family. I was young and they knew best," Faith said. "Looking back, I think they had such an unpleasant experience in dealing with the family of Gloria's first husband after Bethany's birth, that they didn't want to go down that path again."

"Have you told anyone in Adam's family?" Sherri asked.

"Not yet," Faith said. "I wanted to tell you first."

"I know his mom and dad are both gone and his sister moved out of town a long time ago. I don't know where she lives," Sherri said.

"My sister Gloria knew Carol from when Gloria lived at Bell Oak Stables, and she heard that Carol is living in Texas. Hopefully someone around here will know her address. I plan on contacting her up when I return home."

"Faith, tell me about Penny. How did Jason and your kids react to the news?" Sherri asked.

As the afternoon wore on, Faith shared all the details and the two friends kept talking. The waiter cleared their plates and kept refilling water glasses. Sherri was startled when she glanced at her watch. It was 2:00pm.

"Faith, I really need to be going. It's been great seeing you this afternoon, but I'm running late for my hair appointment. I want to look good for the reunion tonight," she said. "Bill and I will pick you up at the motel at 6 o'clock."

"You know, as we have been talking this afternoon, I've been thinking. I don't think you should mention anything about Penny tonight. We are scheduled to have a luncheon with Y-Teens tomorrow. Wait until then. It's a small group of your friends and when they ask what's new with you, you can tell them about the new addition to your family," Sherri said.

"I'm sure they will all be as shocked as I am. But after 40 years, life has happened to all of us, and I think they will be understanding. A baby girl who was adopted by a loving family and has grown up to be a successful attorney is someone to be proud of," she said.

The old friends had a great time at the 40th reunion, and Faith was thankful for nametags.

The next morning, she had one more important stop to make before getting together with the Y-Teens group.

Faith met Wayne Woods in Oakfield.

The two old friends had agreed to meet at Bill's Donut Shoppe, which had been a bustling business in the Oakfield community for more than 50 years. It was the spot for the small town's community leaders and retired folks to gather and catch up on the news and gossip of the day.

As she pulled into the crowded parking lot, she noticed a black pick-up truck with *Woods Construction* painted on the side. Walking hesitantly into the shop, she scanned the gathering of locals and spotted Wayne right away. He looked the same, except his dark wavy hair was now a striking silver. He was handsome and fit and looked good in his faded Levi's and navy polo shirt.

He was standing in line at the counter placing an order, when Faith walked up to him and touched his arm. "Hi there handsome," she said and the two embraced.

"It's so good to see you," Faith said. "Thanks for agreeing to meet with me."

After they paid for their orders, the twosome grabbed a small table in the corner.

"I was really surprised to get your call yesterday afternoon," Wayne said. "How long has it been since we've seen each other?"

"Probably 40 years," Faith responded. "That was such a sad time when Adam died, and then you and Sherri broke up. We just lost touch."

Wayne's eyes misted as he recalled that tragedy. "You know Faith, I've never quite got over that horrible accident. After all these years, there are still some sleepless nights when I wake up and see Adam lying beside the road.

"When my kids became teenagers and got their drivers' licenses, I was terrified to think that something like that could happen to them. I'm sure they thought I was nuts when I hounded them to wear their seat belts and cautioned them about speeding every time they left the house," Wayne said, staring blankly into his coffee mug. "Somehow they lived through those teenage years and are now married with kids of their own."

Returning his gaze to Faith, he asked, "What about you?"

"Wayne, I also worried about those teenage years with my three kids and thankfully, we only had to deal with a few fender-benders. They are married now and I have a couple of grandsons," Faith said.

"Well, the years have been kind to you," he said. "You look good."

"Thanks, so do you," Faith said.

"So, what's so important that you couldn't tell me over the phone?" he asked.

"Wayne, it has to do with Adam and I wanted to tell you in person," Faith said.

"A few months after Adam died, I discovered I was pregnant with his child. I spent the winter in Florida and had a baby girl that I gave up for adoption. My parents and my aunts were the only ones who knew. This young woman has recently contacted me and I have met her. It's a secret that I have kept for 40 years, and now that's it out, I wanted you to know," Faith said.

"Are you serious?" Wayne exclaimed.

"Faith, I was like a second son to Adam's family and I was at their house all the time. I even worked for Crowncraft for a stretch after I graduated from high school. They were so sad after Adam's death. If they had known about this baby, it might have brought his family some happiness," Wayne said. "I can't believe that you never told his family!"

"Wayne, I was young and I never questioned my parents about telling Adam's family. They knew best," Faith said. "They told me that giving the baby up for adoption was a blessing for another family and to get on with my life. That's exactly what I did," Faith explained once again.

"I am so sorry to upset you, but I didn't want you to hear about this from someone else. I told Sherri the secret yesterday and I'll be sharing this story with some of my girlfriends from Y-Teens this afternoon," Faith said.

"Does his sister Carol know anything about this? You know she moved to Texas?" he said. "I have her address and telephone number if you need it."

"Thanks so much. That's a big help," Faith said. "Carol doesn't know anything about this. I was aware she moved out of town, but I didn't have her address. I plan on contacting her when I return home."

"That's good, I think Carol should know about this girl," he said. "She is her own flesh and blood."

"Tell me about this girl. What is she like?" Wayne asked.

"Penny is an attorney and lives near St. Augustine, Florida. Here's a photo that was taken a few months ago when my husband and I met her for the first time. Here's Penny, her husband Jim and their little girl Ashley," Faith said.

"Nice looking family," Wayne said as he held the photo. "She looks a lot like you, but I can see that she has Adam's blue eyes."

"I do have a favor to ask." Faith said. "I brought some flowers that I would like to place on Adam's grave. Will you take me there?"

"Sure, I can do that," Wayne said. "The cemetery is just a couple of blocks away."

The Oakfield cemetery was small and well-groomed, surrounded by mature oak trees that provided a welcoming shade on this warm summer day. "Adam's grave is over this way, next to his mom and dad," Wayne said as he led Faith through rows of flat stones.

"Here it is," he said and stopped in front of Adam's simple marker.

Adam Crandall Collins
Beloved Son
1948-1965

Faith had purchased a bouquet of green-tipped white carnations and reverently placed them in the metal urn that was attached to the stone. She bowed her head and said a silent prayer to this young man who would be linked to her forever.

***

After the emotional rendezvous with Wayne, it was time to switch gears and meet with Sherri and the group from Y-Teens.

Sherri had invited the women to her home for a casual luncheon and Faith was glad to see her old friends. As they sat on the patio and shared family photos of vacations, weddings and grandchildren, Faith listened intently to the other women chatting about their lives.

She realized that Sherri had been correct – they all had experienced some through the years. They talked about divorces, serious illnesses and children with drug problems. While most of the women lived in the area and were up to date on each other's lives, they were curious about Faith. It had been ten years since they had seen her.

As she told her story – again – there was silence.

One of the women finally spoke, "I can't believe that you kept this secret for 40 years," she said. "The months you were gone must have been so difficult for you. None of us ever suspected that while you were in Florida you were having a baby."

Another friend piped in with encouraging words, "How wonderful that this young woman was placed in a loving family and has grown up to be a success." The group of shocked friends, trying to comprehend the story they had just heard, nodded their heads in agreement.

Sherri, always the gracious hostess, broke the uncomfortable tension by announcing, "I have a surprise!" At that moment, Joyce Reid, their former Y-Teens counselor, walked onto the patio.

Faith was grateful for the diversion, as the attention was now on Joyce. The woman was greeted with cheers and hugs, and her sunny smile lit up the party. She was fit and trim – her smartly styled dark hair streaked with silver. "We haven't seen you in years," said Kathy. "What have you been doing since you moved away?"

"I'm proud to tell you that I have continued to work for the YWCA all these years, and I'm now the executive director of the YWCA in Syracuse," she said. "I'm in town this week helping my parents move to a retirement community and you won't believe what I found."

With that, she brought out an overflowing scrapbook featuring their Y-Teen activities from the 1960s. As they leafed through the pages, the women laughed and giggled at the photos, recalling paper drives, bake sales and carefree days at the YWCA camp on Silver Lake.

At the end of the afternoon when all the girls had said their good-byes, Joyce had a private moment with Faith. "I just want you to know how proud I am of you and the way you have handled this delicate situation. I wish only the best for you as you move forward in your relationship with this daughter," she said.   "Good   Luck."

PART NINE

CHAPTER FORTY-THREE

Tyler, Texas
June 27, 2006

On this bright morning, Carol was sitting at the kitchen table sipping a glass of sweetened ice-tea. As she looked out the window, she prayed for rain. The month of June had been hot and arid without a drop. The lush lawn had become scruffy and brown, and her summer flowers had shriveled on their stems.

In an effort to bolster her mood, she was listening to the oldies station on the radio and browsing through a mail-order catalogue. A set of black-and-white mugs in the shape of Holstein cows caught her attention, and she placed the order. They would be a cute addition to her collection of cow memorabilia, a pleasant reminder of the dairy farms in the Oakfield area.

The phone rang.

"Carol? This is Faith Bradford. I'm not sure if you remember me; I'm Gloria's younger sister," she said.

There was dead silence. It took a moment for the name to register.

"Hi Faith," Carol finally responded. "My goodness, this is totally unexpected. How long has it been?"

"Carol, it seems impossible, but it's been more than 40 years," Faith replied. "I thought about you when I was in Batavia a couple of weeks ago for my 40th high school reunion. While I was there, I saw Wayne Woods. He told me you had moved to Texas and gave me your address and phone number.

"I hope that's OK?" Faith said. "He told me to say hello."

"Yes, that's fine," Carol said. "We all worked together at my dad's company until it sold. Then my husband, Kevin, and I moved to Texas. He and Wayne have remained friends ever since and now we stay in contact through Christmas cards."

"How did you and Kevin, the cutest couple from Oakfield High School, end up in Texas?" Faith asked.

"Well, it's a long story, but I'll give you the short version," Carol replied.

"After my dad died and the new owners took over Crowncraft, Kevin and I lost our jobs. Kevin's brother, John, was working down here in Tyler, Texas, and encouraged us to move. John worked for Clayton Homes, a company that makes manufactured homes, and on his recommendation, Kevin was hired. Kevin did such a great job that before long they made him a supervisor.

"After growing up in small town Oakfield, we couldn't bear to live in the city, so we chose to live in this rural area called Shady Grove, just north of Tyler. We bought a new three-bedroom house, manufactured by Clayton Homes, of course, that sits on an acre lot, and we have settled into the community. We joined the Methodist Church and I found a job as a teacher's aide at a nearby elementary school," she said. "We like it down here. We miss our two kids and the grandkids in Oakfield, but we don't miss the brutal winters."

"What about you? Did I hear you are living in Florida?" Carol asked.

"Yes, I moved to Florida soon after graduating from college and Gloria and her family live nearby. We have raised our children here and see each other often." Faith replied.

"Faith, I'm curious. Why are you calling?" Carol asked. "Did something happen during your trip to Batavia? Is Wayne OK?"

Faith took a deep breath and dove right in. She told Carol about the unexpected call from Children's Home Society a year earlier and the Bradford's family secret.

"Why are you telling me about having a baby and giving it up for adoption?" Carol asked. "That's none of my business."

Faith hesitated. "Carol, the baby was Adam's," she whispered.

Before Carol could respond, Faith rambled on, eager to unload this burden. She told Carol about discovering she was pregnant months after Adam's death, then going to Florida to have the baby and giving the baby up for adoption.

Carol could feel the blood draining from her head and felt faint. After an uncomfortable silence, she was finally able to speak. "Faith, I'm having a difficult time processing this information and right now I feel numb," she said as her breath caught in her chest.

"I'm not sure how to react. I am shocked that we never knew this child existed." she said tearfully. "I am so sad that my parents are not alive to learn this news, especially my dad. He grieved for Adam his entire life. Knowing Adam's little girl was out there might have brought him some joy."

Trying desperately to keep her composure, Carol said, "It is wonderful to learn that a part of my brother is still living. Tell me about his daughter. What is her name? What is she like?"

Faith told her about Penny and her family and offered to send Carol a photo of the first meeting in October. "Carol, I know that Penny would like to contact you. She is interested in getting your family's medical history and she would like to learn more about Adam. Would it be OK for me to give Penny your contact information?" Faith asked.

"Yes," said Carol as she tried to swallow a sip of ice tea. "That would be nice."

"Carol, I apologize for upsetting you today," Faith said. "This has been a secret for 40 years and now that it has been revealed, I wanted you to hear it from me, not through the Batavia-Oakfield grapevine."

"Faith, I appreciate you calling," Carol said. "I look forward to hearing from Penny. Good-bye."

Carol's hand was shaking when she hung up the phone. As she tried to stand, she put a death grip on the handles of her walker. She was recovering from a hip replacement and was unsteady as she shuffled the dozen steps to the living room. She collapsed in the pillow-soft recliner.

Overcome with emotion she sobbed – grieving for the memory of her brother and her parents who would never know their granddaughter.

When Kevin returned home from work that afternoon, he found Carol in the recliner, with a tear-stained face. "What's wrong Sweetheart?" he asked, kneeling beside her. "Are you in pain? Do you need some medication?"

"No, it's not physical pain," she said as she reached for his hand. "I am heartbroken. I received some devastating news today about Adam."

"Carol, he's been gone for 40 years, what could have happened that would make you so upset?" Kevin asked with a frown.

She proceeded to tell him about Faith's unexpected call. As Kevin stood and listened to the story, the barrel-chested man paced the room. He was stunned and upset – Adam was a father and his baby had been adopted?

"Carol, I can't believe that Faith's family never told your parents. You know that if your parents had been aware of this pregnancy, they would have fought long and hard to have custody of that baby girl," he said.

"I know," Carol said grabbing another tissue between sniffles. "I have been thinking and praying about this all afternoon and staring at my family photos of Mom and Dad and Adam and me. We were such a happy close-knit family, now they are all gone.

"This has made me so sad, but I know that we can't change the past. We can't be bitter about what has happened. The only thing that we can do is move forward. I think that we should embrace Adam's daughter and let her know that the Collins family is here for her and that we love her," Carol said.

The next week, Carol received a letter from Penny. It was similar to the first one Penny had sent to Faith, requesting medical information and giving Carol some background about the loving family who adopted her.

In the following months the two women exchanged letters, photos and phone calls. During the contacts, Penny learned more about Adam, his family, the Crowncraft business and the family's strong work ethic. Due to Carol's ongoing health issues and the distance between Florida and Texas, they never had a face-to-face meeting.

But Carol was proud to add this young woman to their family tree, and on Penny's 41st birthday, she sent her a family treasure – a quilt that had been made years ago by her mother, Debbie.

When Penny called to thank her for the family heirloom, Carol said, "Penny, my mom was an excellent seamstress. She made beautiful quilts for each member of the family and I know she would want you to have one of her creations. You mentioned to me one time that pink was your favorite color, that's why I sent you the "Grandma's Flower Garden" design done in shades of pink."

"Carol, thank you so much for your thoughtfulness. The quilt is lovely and I will treasure it forever." Penny said with gratitude. "I feel so lucky that you have included me in your family circle."

CHAPTER FORTY-FOUR

Sailfish Bay, Florida
July 2006

After returning home from her reunion trip and contacting Carol, Faith was eager for Penny to meet the rest of her family. Penny had been in occasional contact with her new siblings through e-mails, phone calls and photos, but there had not been a face-to-face meeting.

Finally, they were able to nail down a date that would be convenient for the entire family to be together – the weekend of July 28.[th.] More than a year after making her first contact with Faith, Penny would get to meet her step-brother, step-sisters and their families.

July in Florida is hot, hot, hot, and the family weekend was no exception. Temperatures topped 90 degrees with 90% humidity during the day, with little relief at night, as the lows hovered around 80 degrees.

Penny, Jim and Ashley arrived on Friday afternoon and stayed with Faith and Jason at their golf course villa. The couple hosted a backyard cookout with hotdogs, burgers and all the fixings for their combined families. Michael, his wife and two young boys were there, along with Lisa, Christina and her husband, and Jason's daughter Brittany.

Even though the temperatures sizzled, it was a pleasant evening for everyone and the family welcomed their new sibling. Penny and Jim were not shy and joined the group in playing corn hole, horseshoes and badminton. Ashley was delighted to meet her new cousins and they had fun playing hopscotch on the driveway and running around the back yard playing tag.

At the end of the long day, Penny and Faith were in bed by 10 o'clock, while Jim and Jason stayed up until the wee hours of the morning getting better acquainted. Jim learned that Jason was a huge NASCAR fan and of course, they had deep discussions about the upcoming season for the Florida and Georgia football teams. A special bond was formed that weekend between the two men and it would be the beginning of a lasting friendship.

Saturday, while the guys played golf, the girls went to the community pool to cool off. Then, it was time for everyone to get ready to meet the extended family – Aunt Gloria and her brood of seven children, their spouses and her grandkids.

Christina and cousin Joelle had planned the family reunion and Joelle offered her home and spacious backyard. One of the cousins worked at Bono's, a popular barbeque restaurant in Sailfish Bay, and they catered the party. Everyone enjoyed heaping plates of barbeque, corn on the cob, potato salad and coleslaw.   Coolers were stocked with plenty of beer and soft drinks and the dessert was to die for – peach cobbler topped with home-made vanilla ice cream.

When Penny and her family arrived, she was momentarily overwhelmed with the dozens of people who were related to her. "Help, I need name tags," she laughed as she mingled with the friendly crowd.

Penny's siblings were there to help with introductions and small talk. Christina's husband, JD, set up a karaoke machine on the patio and encouraged everyone to perform and sing along.   The little kids got into the act and everyone clapped and cheered when Michael's sons sang "Who Let the Dogs Out," and Ashley followed with "Girls Just Want to Have Fun."

After an emotionally exhausting weekend, Penny and her family headed back home to St. Augustine.

"So, Penny, what do you think of this huge family?" Jim asked.

"They are lots of fun," she said. "It reminds me of the good times I had when I was growing up in Miami with all my aunts and uncles and cousins.

"Jim, this may sound unusual, but even though I had never met them before, I felt like I knew them," she said.

"I felt the same way," Jim said. "I look forward to seeing them again."

"You know what's amazing to me," Penny said.   "This family has no problem adding new members to the family. They have experienced weddings, new babies, divorces, new spouses, new partners and step-children. Their hearts are   big   enough   to   include   me   and   you   and   Ashley."

CHAPTER FORTY-FIVE

Daytona Beach, Florida
April 2007

The Bradford sisters had remained close during their lives and followed their father's mantra to "take care of each other." While Faith and Gloria lived in the same small town and saw each other frequently, Laura was relegated to keeping in touch through phone calls and e-mails. In an effort to remedy that situation, once the women became "empty-nesters" they planned an annual sisters' weekend. The trio would often meet at a Florida resort, a historic location along the east coast, or a Smoky Mountain retreat.

As they began making plans for the 2007 weekend, they decided to invite Penny. Laura had not been able to attend the previous summer reunion, so this would be a great time for the two women to meet each other. The sisters thought it would be fun to get to know Penny better and share some of the Bradford family stories.

Penny gladly accepted the invitation and suggested that they meet in Daytona Beach. She and her law partner had purchased a beach-front condo, and she thought it would be the perfect place for the annual gathering. The sisters quickly agreed.

They decided on a weekend in mid-April, shortly after Penny's birthday. The weather should be great and they would avoid the huge crowds of Bike Week and the Daytona 500. It was a two- hour drive for Gloria and Faith while Laura could fly direct from D.C. into the Daytona airport. The only expense would be their food and wine.

Through the years the sisters had stayed at some lovely resorts, but Penny's condo at Ocean Villas was over the top. The eleven-story building was in an idyllic oceanfront location in Daytona Shores. The women were wide-eyed as they entered the dramatic two-story lobby with marble floors and a glittery chandelier.

The sisters oohed and aahed as Penny took them on a mini tour of the building. There was a spacious indoor club room that included a pool table, baby grand piano, comfortable seating areas and a large crescent bar. The adjoining well-equipped fitness center overlooked the infinity swimming pool, hot tub and outdoor lounging area.

"Penny, this place is gorgeous!" Laura said. "How long have you had it?"

"My law partner and I purchased it last year," Penny said. "We were searching for a seasonal rental investment plus a get-away location for our families. We looked at this place and fell in love. It was brand-new and the builder was offering some generous incentives for the early-bird buyers. After checking out some other condos, we made a decision and signed the papers. We figured with it being new, it should be a few years before we have any maintenance issues. We rent it to snowbirds on a monthly basis during the winter, and so far, it's worked out fine for us."

Penny's fourth-floor condo had an open floor plan and was full of natural light with dramatic views of the beach and ocean. Decorated in a tasteful tropical theme, it featured a spacious living room with a large leather sectional sofa, an oversized teak coffee table and a 52-inch TV.

The full-size kitchen with stainless steel appliances and granite counter tops had all the amenities.

"Ladies, the kitchen is just for resale," Penny teased, as she showed everyone around. "We can have a simple breakfast here each morning, but then eat out for the other meals. I hope you are OK with that?" she asked. "I didn't get the cooking gene."

The sisters glanced at each other and nodded in agreement. "We didn't get the cooking gene either," Laura giggled. "We were all spoiled by Kay Kay, our family's long-time housekeeper and cook extraordinaire."

With three bedrooms and three baths there was plenty of room and privacy for the visitors. Ashley had accompanied her mom for the girls' weekend and she and Penny headed for the master bedroom. Laura claimed the soft turquoise bedroom with a queen-size bed while Faith and Gloria shared the pale-yellow bedroom with matching twin beds.

Later, as they were enjoying cocktails around the pool and getting acquainted, Penny asked. "Have any of you ever been to Daytona Beach?"

Laura shook her head and said, "No, but I would like to come back some day. It's lovely here."

Gloria, piped up. "Yes, it was a long time ago. Steve and I attended the Daytona 500 in 1988.

"What about you, Faith?" Penny asked.

"I almost said no, but then I remembered something from long ago," she said. "When Mother and I were driving to Florida the winter I was pregnant with you, we stopped in Daytona Beach the last night we were on the road. We stayed in this Hawaiian hotel along the beach that had a huge portico shaped like an ancient canoe.

I remember we walked along the beach and then sat at the hotel's Tiki Bar and had drinks served in pineapples decorated with tiny paper umbrellas. At sunset there was a young man in a sarong who blew a long, loud note on this huge conch shell and then ran along the beach lighting the tiki torches near the hotel."

Penny listened intently and then began digging in her beach bag, "I picked up some of those 'What's Happening this Week' brochures in the lobby. I wonder if the hotel is still listed?"

Finding one of the booklets, she flipped through the pages. "Here we go, Hawaiian Inn on Ocean Drive. Does this look like the place?" she asked, showing the ad to Faith.

"It sure does!" Faith replied. "Is it close by?"

"About a mile away," Penny said. "Let's go have a drink at the Tiki Bar!"

As they pulled into the parking lot, Faith recognized the hotel. It had been updated and an entire new wing had been added to the structure, but it still had the impressive canoe portico and the waterfall in the lobby. Instead of the lagoon she remembered, there was now a peaceful pond with luscious tropical landscaping.

As they wound their way along the path through the resort, they discovered the Tiki Bar. They took seats at a small table overlooking the ocean and for old-time's sake ordered Mai Tais and Pina Coladas, garnished with slices of pineapple and festive paper umbrellas.

Laura offered a toast, "Here's to the Bradford girls and a fun weekend!"

As they sat enjoying the beverages, Ashley noticed another little girl tossing coins into the pond and turned to her mother. Before Penny could respond, the three grandmothers had reached into their change purses and found a handful of coins for her.

"Here, Ashley, you can toss these pennies into the pond for good luck," they said.

The group decided to stay for dinner at the Hawaiian Inn and after an enjoyable meal, they returned to the condo.

FRIDAY EVENING

Robert Bradford had loved taking photos and family movies and had documented the childhood milestones of his daughters. When he passed away from a heart attack in 1991, Laura ended up with boxes and boxes of photo albums and 8mm film. Through the years she had painstakingly edited the photos and movies and transferred them to DVDs. She packed a few for the sisters' weekend and was eager to share them with her sisters and Penny.

"Penny I want you to meet your Bradford grandparents and see where we grew up," Laura said.

Penny popped some popcorn in the microwave and the group settled in to watch the "Memories of the Bradford Sisters." Laura, Gloria, and Faith shared stories as special memories appeared on the screen.

The years sped by as they recalled the carefree summers of their youth at their grandparents' home on Canandaigua Lake. "Penny, there's your great grandparents. Grandmother Elizabeth is the petite woman with silver hair holding baby Gloria, and Grandfather Edgar is the tall man with the cigar," Laura said. "Grandfather Edgar was a large man who lived large. He owned three homes, plus Seven Springs Stables, and he was always eager to invest in a new venture. He was not religious, but our grandmother was."

They watched years of ruffled white dresses and First Communions, festive birthday parties with party hats, presents and fancy birthday cakes. There was one very special birthday when Laura turned seven and received a beautiful palomino pony, Pal-O-Mine.

"Aunt Emily raised show horses and she picked this one out especially for me. He was outstanding and we won a lot of blue ribbons together." Laura, fondly remembered. "Seven Springs Stables was the splendid horse farm you saw earlier in the family movies. I spent a lot of my childhood there."

"Ladies, we may want to take a break before doing the Christmas DVD," Laura said. Penny made some more popcorn and everyone grabbed a drink before settling in for the "Christmas Memories." Each year followed the same pattern. There was a huge Fraser fir tree touching the ceiling in the spacious living room, covered with lights, dozens of ornaments and presents piled high around the tree.

Then, on Christmas Eve there was the time-honored "toasting" of all the relatives at Uncle Richard's house, followed by the two families parading across the street to the Bradfords' home for the traditional dinner. Afterwards, Laura played the piano and everyone joined in singing carols and holiday favorites.

Before bedtime, their mother read "The Night Before Christmas," and then each child was allowed to choose one present to open. The girls hung their stockings on the mantel and ceremoniously left a plate of cookies for Santa along with a bundle of carrots, one for each reindeer.

Christmas morning was joyful. Everyone lined up in the upstairs hall, from the shortest to the tallest, and descended the stairs singing "Happy Birthday Jesus," at the top of their lungs. There was a mad rush to the tree to open presents, and after the chaos they enjoyed a delicious breakfast buffet.

Weather permitting, they spent the afternoon at the neighbor's house with the girls trying out their new ice skates. There were red cheeks and cold breaths as the kids struggled to get their footing. But after a couple of falls and mastering snowplows they were soon gliding around the pond and doing swizzles.

"Wait a minute, I have a question." Penny said, interrupting the flow of images. "This Florida girl wants to know how you had a skating rink next door?"

The sisters laughed, and Faith explained. "Each year Herb Law, our next-door neighbor, built an elaborate ice-skating rink in his back yard. He was a talented engineer and started building the rink on Thanksgiving weekend. It took him weeks to complete all the stages and to make it perfect. Usually by Christmas it was frozen solid and the kids in the neighborhood could skate until the spring thaw.

During the winter it would get dark very early, so he even strung up lights so that we could skate in the evening. I also remember that his wife, Norma, was really sweet. She made the best hot chocolate for us kids and added lots of marshmallows."

With that warm thought, Laura said, "Girls, I think we have traveled down Memory Lane enough for this evening. We can save some more photos for tomorrow. Goodnight everyone. It's been a lovely day."

As Penny settled into bed, her mind replayed all the images she'd seen and stories she heard. It was nice to catch a glimpse of her grandparents, great grandparents, aunts and uncles, and many of the cousins. Although she was struggling to keep all the names and faces straight, Penny figured she would piece them all together in time.

What she was having a more difficult time wrapping her mind around was the amount of wealth and privilege Faith and her sisters experienced in their youth. She wondered just how different her life might have been if she hadn't been given up for adoption.

SATURDAY

After a light breakfast at the condo, the women spent the morning checking out the nearby consignment shops and headed to Ashley's favorite place, Congo River Golf. At the miniature golf course, the women discovered they had something else in common with Penny. The three sisters had grown up playing golf and Penny had played on her high school golf team.

Patricia Daum

The elaborate putt-putt course featured holes with giant waterfalls, rocky summits and a dark cave. The final hole was on a ship and each player had to hit the ball across a roped plank into the cup. Ashley picked up her blue ball, ran across the plank and dropped it into the cup. "Hole- n-one!" she shouted proudly, and everyone cheered.

After the round of golf, it was time to feed the live alligators and then go into the Congo Mining Company where Ashley and Grandma Faith mined for treasures. Much to their delight, after sifting through a box of sand, they discovered an arrowhead and some tiny pink gemstones.

Lunch was at Crabby Joe's, a popular seafood restaurant that was within walking distance of the condo. Then, it was off to the beach.

As they sat gazing at the ocean, casual conversation turned to discussion of the family movies from the night before.

"I'm curious about my grandmother," Penny said. "Tell me about her, what was she like?"

"Mom was a lovely person with a great personality and she treated everyone she met with dignity and respect," Faith said. "She was fun-loving and very competitive, especially in golf."

Gloria piped in with her thoughts, "Mother was a saint. She was very religious and attended Mass regularly. She was always very careful with what she said. She knew that words could hurt."

"Gloria, that reminds me of our Grandmother Bradford's visit," Laura said. "Tell Penny that story."

"Oh, right!" Gloria said. "That's a good example."

"Penny, our father's mother was a very stern lady, very proper. She lived in Chicago and came to visit us one time in Batavia. I must have been about 8 years old. I had been out playing and ran into the house to welcome her. I grabbed her hand. She looked down and said, 'Grandmother doesn't like little girls with dirty hands.'

"My mother overheard this and corrected her – 'Grandmother **loves** little girls. She doesn't like dirty hands,'" Gloria said.

216

"Penny laughed, "What a great lesson!""

"It sure was," Laura chimed in.

"Penny, mother graduated from college with a psychology degree and she had a more liberal philosophy about raising children than some of her peers. We had lots of freedom in our small town where everyone knew everyone. As we became teenagers, there were **not** a lot of rules at our house. She and daddy set a good example and trusted us to follow and make the right decisions.

"I can only remember her telling me 'no' one time, and that's when I wanted to go diving with my friends in the local gravel pit," Laura said. "Another time I wanted to go motorcycle riding with my friends and Mom consented, but only after I promised to wear a helmet."

"What about my grandfather? What was he like?" Penny asked.

"He was a very proud man who had grown up in a wealthy Chicago family. He would have preferred to live in the big cities of the Midwest, but he wanted our mother to be happy and agreed to live in small-town Batavia. He was not as religious as our mother, but he kept his promise to our grandparents and we were raised in the Catholic church. While we didn't attend Catholic schools, we did receive our religious education by attending weekly CCD classes.

"He had a temper and let us know if we had displeased him, but it was short-lived and he never carried a grudge. He loved us unconditionally," Laura said.

"Dad was also very kind and caring," Gloria said. "Early in my marriage, he did something extraordinary for one of Russ's little girls. Becky was 5 and had crossed eyes. She was getting ready to begin kindergarten and Dad was concerned that her classmates would make fun of her. Dad paid for the surgery to correct the issue."

They spent the afternoon chatting away under the shade of colorful umbrellas, building sand castles and flying kites with Ashley. The women even tried boogie-boarding – some were more successful in mastering the art than others.

217

As they returned to the condo, Penny turned to Laura and said with a grin, "Aunt Laura, today was so much fun, and you were a really good sport when that large wave knocked you over."

"I don't think I will ever try that again," Laura replied with a groan.

The women decided to stay in on Saturday night and had pizza delivered from nearby Fratelli's.

Laura had one more DVD to share. "This one is from when we were older and after the inground pool was installed in our backyard." Laura said. "That was such a fun time when all of our friends would come over. They were always amazed that we had pop and ice cream to share with everyone."

They watched for a while and then Penny asked, "I'm curious, who is this woman who appears in many of the photos? Is this another aunt? She has a very pleasant expression. Her hair is pulled back and sometimes she is wearing a long white apron."

"That's our beloved Kay Kay." Faith said. "She was our live-in housekeeper and cook the entire time I was growing up. She was with the family until Mommy and Daddy retired to Florida and then she moved into a retirement community in Batavia. She was a very special member of our family and we stayed in touch with her until she passed away in 1981."

"Her real name was Katherine O'Reilly," Laura added. "She was about 10 years older than our mother, and she never married. When Faith was born, Katherine was thrilled to have a baby in the house and practically claimed her as her own. As a toddler, Faith could not say Katherine, so she called her Kay Kay and that became her name, forever.

As the years flashed by on the screen, schoolgirls turned into teenagers. There were high school proms and graduations, and then off to college with a new car for each girl. There was a baby blue Volkswagen Beetle for Laura, a sporty red Porsche for Gloria and a pink Mustang convertible for Faith.

"You got a new car as a graduation gift from high school?" Penny asked. "I'm jealous! I had to work at Publix to buy my own car. What's wrong with this picture?" she pouted playfully.

"Actually, we received the cars as a reward after completing our freshman year of college with good grades. The car was an incentive to return to school and graduate," Laura said. "Of course, one of us didn't follow the family guidelines," she said, turning to Gloria. "And that's another story."

"Aunt Gloria, I'm shocked!" Penny said. "You told me the story about marrying Russ and his five kids, living in the Bell Oak farmhouse and Russ working for my grandfather Collins, but you never told me about the red Porsche. What happened to it?"

"Well, I had to give it back – that was the deal," Gloria said. "Daddy was so angry with me for not returning to college and then marrying this man with five kids. But he could never remain angry for long. He was horrified when he saw the rusted old heap that Russ was hauling us around in. A couple of weeks after I returned the car, he showed up at the farmhouse with a used VW van with low miles – he had traded the red Porsche for the van. In spite of everything, he wanted me and my family to be safe."

After finishing the DVD's that Laura had put together, Faith, Gloria and Penny turned to the family photos that they had brought to share. As they leafed through their pictures, they discovered that they had something in common – camping.

Through the years, Gloria and Faith's families had vacationed together and camped in various parks across the state. They had many adventures including one time when Gloria's old camper literally fell apart during a thunderstorm. "That night, I wished we had one of the sturdy Crowncraft campers that your grandfather built," said Gloria.

Penny's family had also camped when she was a child. Was it possible that their paths might have crossed years ago?

"Oh, look," said Penny. "Here's a photo of my family at Yogi Bear Jellystone Park in the mid-1970s. You have one, too." The smiling families had all posed with their campers for a traditional photo in front of the 20-foot iconic bear.

"Let's see, our photos from there would have been taken about 10 years later," Faith said.

"How fun that we all have happy memories from the same place," Penny said. "At least our families had that in common."

After a day of bonding, Ashley was exhausted and it was time for her to go to bed. Penny excused herself and said good night to Faith and the two aunts. Laura retired to her guest room and decided to soak in the jacuzzi and rest her aching body. She was hurting after taking the tumble in the surf.

Gloria and Faith continued to sift through the photos spread across the oversized coffee table, remembering priceless moments with their families. Faith was also studying Penny's photos from when she was a little girl. Did Penny look like any of her siblings or cousins? Faith didn't think so. Her three kids looked more like the Townsend family with their dark hair and dark eyes.

"I think she takes after you," Gloria said, looking at a photo of Penny. "She is more petite but she has your fair complexion, strawberry blond hair and the cute dimples. Her childhood photos reminded me of you in the old family movies."

"But she does have something of her dad's," she added. "It's those incredible deep blue eyes."

"Looking at these smiling photos of her family's outings to the beach and zoo and hearing about her childhood, it makes me happy to know that she grew up with such a nice family," Faith said.

"It's amazing that her family liked camping, too?" Faith commented as she picked up another photo.

As she studied the faded photo of Penny and her brother Todd at the Jellystone camp site, she noticed something on the front of the camper. "Gloria, look at this! What do you see?" she exclaimed.

"I see two adorable children in red-white-and-blue outfits waving a flag. It must have been the Fourth of July," her sister replied.

"Yes, but look at the camper," Faith said.

Gloria peered closer. "Well, the camper is white with a wide stripe, looks like a faded pink or orange color, and the door is the same color. What's unusual about that?" Gloria replied.

"Look closer!" Insisted her sister as she pointed to the front of the camper.

"Oh, my God! Praise be to Jesus!" Gloria shouted. "This is impossible!"
Hearing the commotion, Penny ran out of the bedroom. "Is everything all right? Are you OK Aunt Gloria?" she asked. "Faith, are you crying?"

"Penny, we have just made the most amazing discovery," Faith said as she wiped away happy tears. "Look at these photos!"

Penny had seen those photos dozens of times, "What is so amazing?" she asked.

"Penny, look closely at this logo on the camper, it says Crowncraft," Faith said. "This camper was built by your grandfather, Andrew Collins."

"Are you sure? That logo looks awfully small," Penny said.

"Penny, look, I found another photo where the logo shows up better," Faith said.

As Penny held the photo of her family – Penny, Todd, Mom and Dad all smiling broadly in front of their new camper – she could clearly see the Crowncraft logo, with the tiny crown above the capital C. "I can't believe this," she said sitting on the arm of the sofa. "What a small world!"

"You know, I remember the day this photo was taken. It was a really happy day. Daddy came home from work that afternoon, pulling this pink-and-white camper behind the station wagon," Penny said. "What a surprise! Todd and I ran out to meet him and scampered inside. Everything was pink – the little stove, the refrigerator, the seat covers, the comforters and the valances. I was so excited because pink was my very favorite color," Penny said.

"I must have been about 6 or 7 years old then and we kept the camper until I was entering high school. I have lots of happy memories from our camping days and Mom used to say that we never had any trouble finding our camper in the campgrounds. It was one of a kind," she laughed.

Patricia Daum

"This is so incredible to find out all these years later that my grandfather Collins built the camper."

SUNDAY

Sunday was a picture-perfect day in Daytona Beach, and the Bradford sisters were savoring their last few hours together before heading home. They had packed up the car and as they sat around the infinity pool gazing at the ocean, they were still talking about Penny's family owning one of the Crowncraft campers.

"What are the odds?" Laura said shaking her head.

Penny and Ashley soon appeared. "We are all packed and have checked out," Penny said. "Before we head for home, let's walk to Crabby Joe's for lunch. I know we were just there yesterday, but the food is good and it's close by."

As the family group was walking up the pier toward the restaurant, Laura noticed a heart-warming moment and nudged Gloria. There was Ashley skipping along between her mother and Grandma Faith, swinging both of their hands.

After lunch, it was time to take Laura to the airport and head for home.
"I hope you all had a good time this weekend," Penny said. "We are so fortunate the weather cooperated."

"It's been lovely," Laura said. "Penny, it's been so nice to get to know you and Ashley. You are an amazing young woman and Ashley has been a delight."

"My head is spinning from all the stories the three of you have shared this weekend. I have learned so much about the Bradford family and my heritage. I guess that's where the good golfer gene comes from," she laughed.

"We have loved visiting with you," Faith said. "Thanks so much for sharing your condo with us. It was the perfect location and you have been a great hostess."

As the group exchanged warm hugs and said their goodbyes, Aunt Gloria extended an invitation. "We hope to see you again in Sailfish Bay at the next family get-together."

"Thanks, we will try to make it," Penny said.

On the drive back to St. Augustine, Penny called her husband from the cell phone. "Well, how did it go?" Jim asked.

"It was a very nice weekend and a comfortable visit with the girls," Penny said. "We had a delightful time and I'm glad that Ashley came along. She was a good icebreaker and loved all the attention from her new grandma and aunties," Penny said.
"So, when do we see them again?" he asked.

"I'm not sure, but they have invited us for the next family get-together in Sailfish Bay this summer," she replied.

CHAPTER FORTY-SIX

Sailfish Bay, Florida
December 26, 2014

Penny's husband, Jim Snyder, loved to plan vacations and he had gone overboard to plan a celebration for the couples 25th wedding anniversary. He had booked a Western Caribbean Holiday Cruise, aboard Celebrity Cruise Lines newest ship, departing from Ft. Lauderdale on December 27.

On December 26 the couple traveled to Sailfish Bay for an overnight stay at Faith and Jason's home to celebrate a belated Christmas. Ashley did not accompany them this trip. Their daughter had celebrated her 16th birthday earlier in the month and was off to Colorado on a skiing vacation with her best friend's family.

After exchanging presents and spending the afternoon together, the two couples headed for dinner at a popular Stuart restaurant, Sailfish Grill, where a surprise was waiting.

"Would you like a table inside or outside?" the hostess asked.

"It's such a beautiful evening, let's go outside," said Faith.

When they walked out onto the covered patio, a chorus greeted the couple. "Surprise!" everyone shouted. "Happy Anniversary!"

Penny was stunned as she glanced around the joyful crowd. She noticed the beaming faces of her siblings and their families; Aunt Gloria and her huge family; Jim's brother and his wife; and the biggest surprise of all – the bridesmaids and the groomsmen from their wedding.

"What's this?" Penny said turning to Jim. "Did you plan this?"

"Yes," he answered sheepishly. "I wanted this to be a special evening to share with our friends and family. Faith and your cousin Joelle helped me with all the details."

"This is so sweet of you," said Penny planting a kiss on his cheek.

***

It had been eight years since Penny and Jim first met Faith and Jason in Cocoa Beach. During that time, the two couples had bonded and become family. They had met each other for fun weekends in Daytona Beach and had gone on cruises together. Penny and Jim had been embraced by the extended Bradford family and were regulars at the annual picnics, family weddings, showers and anniversaries.

Through the years, Penny had developed a positive relationship with her step-siblings. When she and Jim visited the family in Sailfish Bay, they always spent time with brother Michael and his family, enjoying cook-outs, attending his son's ball games, going fishing and hanging out at the beach.

Lisa, the youngest sister, had moved to Orlando and was working for a major amusement park. Occasionally, she treated Penny and her family to complimentary tickets and they enjoyed spending the day with her.

Penny had a close relationship with sister Christina. Of all the siblings, they were most alike. Christina had also graduated from University of Florida and they were both motivated career women. In another twist of fate, Christina and her husband JD were unable to have children and adopted a baby boy through Children's Home Society, using Penny as a reference.

Through the years, Jim and Jason had become good buddies and had gone on weekend outings with a group of guys, traveling to NASCAR races in Daytona Beach and Charlotte, North Carolina. Jim was active in the Jacksonville Gators Club and hosted an annual tailgate party at his home during the Florida-Georgia football games. Jason attended – showing his good humor by wearing his Bulldogs tee-shirt. Explaining their complicated family connection to others was always a comedy, so they settled on "good friends."

The relationship between Penny and Faith also blossomed, and Penny began turning to Faith for advice and support while going through life's struggles. By the time of her 25th anniversary Penny had dealt with two more devastating losses – her mother had passed away from a heart attack and her brother Todd had died of an accidental overdose. Faith's love and understanding had helped Penny to work through the sadness. To comfort her grieving daughter, Faith also gave Penny a Bible and encouraged her to return to her faith for strength.

Patricia Daum

For Faith the years since she had been reunited with Penny were filled with gratitude. "I am so thankful that she came back into my life," Faith would reflect. "It's not the normal mother-daughter relationship, but I feel blessed. She has changed my life and we are such good friends."

Along the way, they also discovered some mutual traits: they were early risers and early to bed; they were clean freaks – everything had to be neat and tidy and in its proper place; they were tech savvy – always the first to try new gadgets; they were well-grounded and focused on the present –"Don't look back, that's not the direction you are going," was a favorite motto.

***

Faith and Joelle had done a great job with all the details for the 25th anniversary celebration and thankfully, the weatherman had cooperated, with mild temperatures and a star-studded sky

The patio was decorated with tables of white tablecloths and centerpieces featuring festive clusters of silver balloons embossed with the number 25. And at each place setting there was a small silver bag filled with 25 shiny pennies.

Guests were treated to a generous buffet of Bahamian chowder, fresh salad, jumbo shrimp cocktails, fish tacos and grilled mahi-mahi. The crowning touch was a two-tier anniversary cake with a silver number 25 topper.

Fairy lights hanging from the tent gave a romantic glow to the patio, and a local band played Penny and Jim's favorite songs from the 80s and 90s, with everyone joining in the celebration. During a special anniversary dance, the happy couple held each other tight, Penny's head resting on Jim's shoulder. JD sang their favorite song, "Could I have this dance for the rest of my life?" an Anne Murray classic.

A silent tear rolled down her cheek. "What's wrong sweetheart," Jim asked.

"I just thought of my parents," she said. "Our wedding was one of the happiest days of my life and they were such a big part of that day. I am sad they are not here tonight."

"I know," Jim replied gently wiping away her tear. "I miss them, too. But I am so thankful that we have this new family who loves us and is here to help us celebrate this special night."

As Faith looked at the happy couple on the dance floor, she turned to Jason with love in her eyes.

"My heart is filled with gratitude tonight," she said. "You know, when we married, we had a daughter from your marriage, and three children from mine, but we never had our child. I will always think of Penny as our child."

"I agree," Jason said.

"She is our Lucky Penny."

AUTHOR'S NOTES

I have a vivid memory of one Sunday afternoon in the early 1960s. I was a young teen sitting on my aunt's front porch in Glendale, Ohio, sipping a glass of her delicious iced tea. I waved and smiled to a cluster of giggling teenage girls who were walking past the house on their way into the tiny town center.

My disapproving mother saw the girls pass by and issued a warning, "Let those girls be a lesson to you – that's what happens to "bad" girls!"

I didn't understand what she meant. They didn't look "bad" to me.

Later, when I innocently asked by older cousin about the girls she whispered, "Those girls are all pregnant and they have been sent to Mary Knoll, a home for unwed mothers. Once their babies are born, they are given up for adoption.

"You don't want that to happen to you," she cautioned.

According to Ann Fessler, author of "The Girls Who Went Away," the girls I saw that Sunday were part of a group of hundreds of thousands of unwed mothers who surrendered their babies during a nearly three-decade bubble known as the "Baby Scoop Era." This era encompassed the years from the end of World War II in 1945 to the Rose vs Wade decision in 1973, that made abortion legal.

"Driven by shame, these unwed teenagers were part of a generation of women that were pressured by their families to give up their babies and put the experience behind them," Fessler said.

Fast forward to today. Like Penny, some of the children who were adopted are asking questions about their birth parents. While Penny's search was relatively uncomplicated, many of our states still make it difficult to locate original birth certificates and some adoptees have searched unsuccessfully for years for their birth parents.

Many have turned to "search angels" for help, and these dedicated "angels" have helped thousands of adoptees locate their original families.

Fessler and others have written about the life-long emotional toll that birth mothers and adoptees have endured through the years – never getting over the loss.

The "Lucky Penny" story is different.

It's about two confident, well-adjusted women – a birth mother and her adopted daughter – who meet 40 years after the birth and forge a lasting friendship.

I'm   happy   to   share   their   story   with   you.

ACKNOWLEDGEMENTS

"Lucky Penny" is a work of fiction, but parts of the story are based on actual events. The names and places have been changed, but the experiences and emotions are genuine.

As any author will tell you, it "takes a village" to complete a book and I feel an immense sense of gratitude to my "village."

This book would not have been possible without the love and support of my husband Larry. He is truly my "Lucky Penny."

I am eternally grateful to Diane Tomasik, a beloved friend, who has been my copy editor extraordinaire. Her suggestions and personal experiences as an adoptee have enhanced "Lucky Penny," immeasurably.

My heartfelt appreciation also goes to Adele, Ann, Diane, Julianne, Laurel, Linda, Lucy and Penny for sharing your adoption stories and entrusting me with your memories.

Special thanks to Pat Austin, Tim Robinson, Theresa Schineis and my friends in Novel Divas and the Saturday Girls golf group who have encouraged me along this journey.

In doing research about upstate New York, I received immense help from Laurie Nanni at the Oakfield Historical Society, the staff at Holland Land Office Museum in Batavia, and Chris Whites from the Landmark Society in Rochester.

"History of the City of Batavia," by Ruth M. McEvoy and "Batavia Revisited," by Larry Barnes, provided valuable information.

"Children and Hope, A History of the Children's Home Society in Florida," by Lawrence Mahoney introduced me to the Children's Home Society and the McLamore House in Miami.

Don Boyd's Photo Galleries @www.donboyd.net, provided a trove of historical information about the people and places in Miami and Dade County.

I am also grateful to Priscilla Sharpe, a heaven-sent search angel who has helped thousands of adoptees locate their original families. The detailed information she has provided to birth parents and adoptees to help them navigate initial contacts was invaluable.

QUESTIONS AND TOPICS FOR DISCUSSIONS

Faith's family rallied around her when she discovered she was pregnant. Her parents and aunts stepped up to help carry out the plan for Faith to deliver the baby, place it for adoption, and then for her to return to school without anyone knowing. Do you think this was a good plan? Should they have asked Faith what she wanted to do?

Faith's parents had already dealt with her older sister Gloria's unplanned pregnancy. Do you think that experience affected her parents' decisions?

When you were in school? Were you aware of any pregnant teens? How was it handled? How have times changed in dealing with unwed mothers and out-of-wedlock babies?

How fair was the decision to keep the pregnancy a secret from the family of Adam Collins? If they had been aware of the baby, how do you think they would have reacted? What plan would they have hatched?

Thinking of the old argument, "Nature vs. Nurture," which would you say most influenced Penny's life? Do you think it was nature or nurture that propelled her to go to college and become a lawyer?

Penny's parents never knew that she had contacted her birth mother. If you were the adopted parents how would you feel about your child searching for their birth parents?

Penny was almost 40 years old when she decided to pursue the search for her birth parents. Why do you think she waited so long? How would you explain her patience for checking back in six- month intervals?

Penny's adoption was closed and the Whitmer's names were on her birth certificate. If you were Faith, would you have agreed to the contact with Penny, or would you have refused?

Penny's life was influenced early on by chances of fate and decisions by others. Can you give examples of this and thoughts on how different her life would have been if fate had not intervened?

Author Profile

Patricia Daum was raised in Ohio and now lives in Florida. She has written several family histories and numerous articles for newspapers and other publications in the cities where she has lived: Dayton, Ohio; Memphis, Tennessee; Burlington, Vermont; Andover, Massachusetts and Stuart Florida.

"Lucky Penny" is her debut novel.

www.patriciadaumbooks.com

71109866R00133

Made in the USA
Columbia, SC
27 August 2019